A Mother Like You

A Mother Like You

Ruby Speechley

hera

First published in the United Kingdom in 2020 by Hera Books

This edition published in the United Kingdom in 2021 by

Hera Books
28b Cricketfield Road
London, E5 8NS
United Kingdom

A CIP catalogue record for this book is available from the British Library.

Print ISBN 978 1 80032 461 9
Ebook ISBN 978 1 912973 51 4

Look for more great books at www.herabooks.com

Printed and bound in Great Britain by Clays Ltd, Elcograf S.p.A.

For my husband, Richard with love, always

Prologue

She drags herself out of bed and stands at the side of the cot in the middle of the night for the hundredth time. The little face is crimson with rage. She picks the baby up and cradles it close, jogging gently up and down, but the hot little body stiffens, and the piercing cry grows louder and louder, ringing in her ears as though it doesn't know its own mother, punishing her for being so incompetent.

She holds the baby out in front of her and yells, 'What do you want?'

Moments later, the baby is quiet, stunned. She drops it down on the mattress in a dull shallow bounce. This time the baby's cry is high-pitched. Blinking back tears, she stares at the tremor in her hands. How could she do that? What is wrong with her?

A voice behind her shouts: 'What have you done?'

She covers her ears and screams.

Chapter One

Kate Marshall's last thought before she blacked out was of the man standing at the back of the room watching her.

A moment earlier, she'd finished her presentation to an enthusiastic cheer. The conference room at stately Sopwell House was packed with businessmen and women, eager to hear about the team-building events planned for the day. As she stepped away from the podium, hot white lights gleamed in her eyes. She pressed her fingers to her brow. Her face and neck burned. Why didn't someone open a window? Her body jolted. For a split second she thought she saw his face. Blood pumped in her ears; a pain shot through her head. She scanned the room. It wasn't possible after all this time, was it? A wave of nausea swept over her. The audience became a blur and her vision folded as she sank to the floor.

When Kate came to, her first thought was of herself aged six, tripping over Angel Gabriel's tunic during the school play. Everyone had laughed. But it wasn't the laughter that had latched in her heart like a fishhook; it had been seeing her mother quietly stand up and leave.

'I'm fine, really.' Kate blinked and spread her fingers out in front of her. She tried to focus on her short, rouge noir nails and the thin, platinum wedding band. She'd been sickening for something all week.

'Can you stand?' Sally asked, nodding to Steve to take Kate's other arm.

'I think so.' She moved a strand of hair from her lips.

'Let us through, please.' Steve waved away their colleagues who had gathered round the stage. They led her to the empty lounge area. Someone passed Sally a bottle of water.

'Are you sure you're not hurt?' Sally knelt in front of her. She unscrewed the lid and handed her the drink.

'I'm sore and a bit queasy.' She was never ill. When she sipped the water, it tasted metallic. Her hand trembled. She'd never blacked out in her life.

'It is stuffy in there,' Sally said.

'I should go back and mingle.'

'No, you won't,' Steve said. 'The whole team is out there. They know the drill.'

Kate gave a thin smile. The smell of his sharp, citrus aftershave caught in her throat and almost made her gag.

'Let's help you up to your room,' Sally said.

After Sally and Steve had gone, Kate kicked off her stilettos. The ceiling seemed to press down on her. She closed the curtains. It didn't matter what time she went to bed recently, she was always tired. She set the alarm on her mobile and stretched out on the plump bed. Her stomach began to settle at last. She closed her eyes.

–

An hour later she stood in front of the full-length mirror refreshed. She smoothed the ends of her long, blunt-edged bob. Her naturally wiry hair needed to be washed and straightened every day. Perhaps she'd try a streak of red through the fringe next week. She rubbed thick medical-smelling cream up her arms, covering the patches of eczema like welts from a smack.

When she left the room, the muted sound of a conversation drifted along the corridor. A casually dressed man was chatting to a maid. He wore white chinos and a faded denim shirt and walked with a familiar gait. It was as though someone had let go of an elastic band in her chest. It *was* him, wasn't it? For a second, she dared not move, waiting for him to turn so she could see more clearly. She started to follow. The floor creaked softly beneath the carpet. He turned the corner out of sight. She hurried after him, her laptop case bouncing against her thigh. He paused outside a bedroom door. She held her key to look like she was going into a room and stole another look at him. There he was: the hair shorter and lighter, possibly greying. The outline of his tanned face, the slight smudge of a beard. Heart pounding, she rocked back on her heels and reached out to the wall, clipping a print of Morisot's *The Cradle*. She straightened it up. When she looked over again, he had gone into the room, the door sounding a loud click as it shut behind him.

Could it really have been him? She shivered, alone in the passageway, staring at the closed door, the distant drone of traffic drifting through a tiny window behind her. Her mobile beeped, making her jump. A text from Sally.

> How are you feeling?

She was supposed to have been in a meeting with her team ten minutes ago. All she wanted to do was go and lie down again. She needed to think this through. Should she knock on his door? But if it was him, how might he react? Of all the people to bump into. What was he doing here? It could be awkward with her colleagues around. She couldn't afford to ruin her reputation, or let it get back to James. The lift doors opened.

By the time Kate strode into the conference room, the briefing for the treasure hunt event round the grounds was well underway. Skipping lunch seemed to have taken the edge off her nausea.

'You okay?' Sally whispered, pouring her a cup of peppermint tea.

Kate nodded and took a ginger biscuit. She fielded questions from the enthusiastic group then helped to hand out the question sheets, clipboards and pens to each team. The room emptied as Steve led everyone out to the terrace to begin.

'I'll catch you guys later.' She ordered a bottle of sparkling water before lounging on a sofa in a quiet corner. James had left a message on her mobile. He was in York to meet potential new clients, present their corporate event packages. She called him straight back.

'How are you feeling?' he asked. 'Steve told me what happened.'

'So-so, I'll be fine.'

'All going well?'

'Seems to be. Didn't know accountants could be such an enthusiastic bunch.' The waiter brought her water and tipped half the bottle in a glass.

'Look, I'm going to be in York longer than anticipated.' He paused. 'I need someone to help me at this pitch tomorrow because Tim's fallen sick, so I've arranged for Jasmine to come up.'

'Why didn't you tell me earlier? I could have come.' Kate sipped the water, but the metallic taste was still there. They normally made decisions about the business together. They owned everything equally and therefore they made decisions jointly.

'Because you're needed there, Kate.'

She shifted but couldn't get comfortable. This girl had only started three weeks ago.

'I thought her fresh ideas could swing it in our favour.'

'So you'll be back when?'

'Not till late tomorrow. You'll be fine; you've got a great team with you.'

She didn't need him to tell her that.

'Perhaps you should get something from the chemist?'

'Maybe, I'll see how I feel.'

'One more thing, are we free at the end of the month? I can get a good deal on flights to New York. There's a Kandinsky exhibition on at the Guggenheim. If we're clear, I can book right now?'

'I'm not sure… hold off for a day or two.' This was so unlike her, but she hadn't felt this rough in a long time. Normally she'd jump at the chance to go to New York for a long weekend. Take in a show, visit the Museum of Modern Art and add in a dash of early Christmas shopping. But it wouldn't be any fun if she was ill.

'You'll be fine by then surely?'

'Don't book anything just yet.' She rubbed her stomach. Maybe she'd picked up a bug or a touch of food poisoning?

'All right, if you're sure.'

'I'll speak to you in the morning,' she said.

The lounge was humming with chatter. Kate's team were gathered on two leather sofas round the open fire. The clients were already in the dining room still buzzing from the great day they'd had.

She caught the waiter before she sat down and ordered champagne, and a glass of orange juice for herself. She hated being the only sober one.

'Come and sit by the fire, you look cold.' Sally moved along the sofa.

'Thanks.' Kate sat down, shivering.

The waiter brought the drinks and handed her the juice.

'What's this?' Steve said. 'Kate not drinking? Perhaps the sky is about to fall in.' Everyone laughed. He mimed a prayer. Kate tried to look amused.

'Very funny, Steve, but I'm still not feeling great.' The heat from the fire was warming her, making her sleepy.

'You look pale,' Sally said quietly.

Kate gave a weak smile, grateful for her concern, but she wasn't about to confide in anyone. 'Great job today everyone,' she said, raising her glass. 'Yes, even you, Steve.'

He took a bow and headed over to the bar to chat up a redhead. And, just along from them, stood the man she saw earlier, now shaved and wearing a navy linen suit and staring right at Kate. She gave a start and her face burned like it used to when she was a teenager. Why was he here? Everyone round her stood up to go to the table, but she was fixed in a stare of recognition.

'Kate, are you feeling all right?' Sally touched her arm.

'Oh yes, sorry.' Kate blinked at her.

'Sure you're well enough?' Sally linked her arm through Kate's. The others went on ahead to the dining room.

'If I need to leave early, will you see everything goes smoothly?' She glanced back, but he'd gone.

'Of course,' Sally said.

Kate picked at her meal. She tried not to engage in deep conversations with anyone, her mind too distracted. Seeing him again had stirred up feelings she'd pushed away long ago. Her gaze wandered round the room, searching for him.

When everyone had ordered their desserts, Kate said good night and headed up to her room. As she stepped out of the lift, the fire door to the stairs swung open and banged on the wall. She rummaged in her handbag for the key.

'Lost something?'

She glanced up at the familiar voice, and in a split second the last twenty years fell away. She dared not breathe as a flicker of memories passed between them.

'Kate Watson. Who'd have thought?'

'What are you doing here?' Her voice was breathless, heart thumping as she fumbled in her bag.

'You've not changed a bit.' He grinned, scanning her up and down as if she stood there naked.

'Neither have you.' She couldn't take her eyes off him. He moved closer, breathing more heavily. His warm, woody aftershave transported her back in time, stirring her with longing. She unzipped every pocket of her handbag and pulled out the key card. His hand brushed hers as he took it, sending a spark through her body. He pushed down the handle and followed her into the room, letting the door fall shut behind them.

'Have you missed me?' He stood millimetres from her, examining her. 'You left so suddenly.'

'I didn't know where you'd moved to.' She stepped backwards, clutching her bag to her chest. He looked so much older, but it suited him.

'Don't give me that nonsense.' He grinned, moving towards her. Heat radiated from his body sending a pulse of desire right through her. She dropped down on the bed, casting her bag to one side.

He leaned over her and ran a finger up her thigh, shins pressing against her legs, gently opening them with his knee.

She took in a sharp breath, her body tingling. 'Why are you here?'

'To see you.' He rested his hands on the bed either side of her. The smell of brandy wafted from his breath.

'Why now?'

'Why not?'

He was pinning her to the bed; she couldn't move.

'Tell me, how are your dear parents?'

'Dad died six months ago.' She edged her legs away from him.

'Ah right.' He nodded. 'He was a good sort. And your mother? Still playing up, is she?'

'What do you want from me?' She pushed her fists into his chest.

He tipped his head back and laughed.

'You owe me, don't you think?' A grin spread across his face. He straightened up and adjusted himself. 'Thirty grand should do it.'

'What, are you kidding me?' She sat up. 'Where on earth am I supposed to find that kind of money?'

'I think it's fair, considering.' He plucked her business card from a pile on the dressing table. 'I'll be in touch.' He gave a sour laugh as he yanked open the door. 'I hope it's all been worth it for you, Kate, I really do.'

The shame and guilt she'd tried so hard to bury rose up and washed over her. The very thing she'd been running from had finally caught up with her. She opened her mouth to speak, but the door closed before she could reach it and when she looked out, he had gone.

Chapter Two

'It's probably a bug or something. I feel so tired all the time,' said Kate at the chemists the next morning.

Mrs Ahmed gave her usual tight smile.

'Don't tell me, I've been working too hard.' She rested her handbag on the counter.

Mrs Ahmed offered a wise nod. The pharmacy was empty except for Mr Ahmed shuffling tablets into bottles behind her. A shard of sunshine fell across a poster by the till, fading the message about the symptoms of heart disease.

'I feel nauseous too, especially if I smell food. That's weird, isn't it?'

'I'll give you something to settle your stomach.' Mrs Ahmed took a bright pink bottle off the shelf.

'I've not actually been sick, but it's like a permanent nausea in my throat, and a sort of metallic taste.'

Mrs Ahmed frowned. 'Is there a chance you could be pregnant?'

Kate wrinkled her nose. 'No. My period has started.'

'I would take a test, just to rule it out.'

'Really?'

Mrs Ahmed never sold her any medicine unless she absolutely needed it or could suggest a cheaper alternative.

'Okay, if you think so.'

Back at home, Kate opened her laptop and checked her work emails. Nothing urgent, so she closed the lid and curled up on the sofa. Five minutes, that's all she needed. Moving out of central London almost a year ago to a four-bedroom house in leafy Boxmoor, Hemel Hempstead had been a bold decision for them, but it made sense for their expanding corporate events business and their personal lives. She already felt like this was where they were going to stay long-term. Moving back to Hertfordshire had prompted her to contact her parents after more than twenty years of not speaking to them. She'd made a success of her life and hoped they'd be proud of her. Nothing much had changed. They were living in the same three-bedroom house she'd grown up in, in St Albans. Sadly, her dad had advanced Alzheimer's by then, and he died two months later. As soon as she first saw him again, she'd regretted leaving it so long. In his lucid moments he said he forgave her for not staying in touch but that made her feel even more guilty. She'd missed so much of his final years. And all because she was too ashamed to admit to making mistakes.

A few minutes after dozing off, Kate woke with a jolt to her phone pinging several times. The screen was full of rows and rows of emojis: bags of dollars, hourglass timers and sculls. All text messages, but with no words, from a number she didn't recognise. It must be him. Shit. He wasn't going to let it go. Bile rose in her throat. She ran to the toilet to be sick.

She washed her face and patted it dry. She couldn't be pregnant. It wasn't possible. These were perimenopausal symptoms, weren't they? She read somewhere they started at about forty-five. Except there was that night a few weeks ago, when they ended their dinner party with shots of Sambuca. She'd vomited at least twice in the night. And then... oh God, she'd forgotten to take extra precautions. Shit, shit, shit. She lifted the toilet seat and took the test out of the packet. Moments later she sat on the side of the bath and watched one, then two pink lines appear. She stood up and flicked the stick back and forth. It must be wrong. How could a stupid piece of plastic be accurate? She took the test again with the second stick. Seriously? This could not be happening. She sat on the laundry box staring at the two pink lines. James would be furious. She leaned back against the cold slab of tiles. A pain pierced between her legs. She doubled over. This didn't feel right. She needed to see a doctor as soon as possible.

–

That afternoon, Kate parked at Hemel Hempstead Hospital. Her mobile phone rang, making her jump. She checked the screen before she answered.

'Where are you?' James asked.

'I'm... out.' Kate picked up a bottle of water from the passenger seat. Her appointment at the clinic was in five minutes and she still needed to work out where she was going. Her GP had sent her straight over for an early pregnancy scan because she was still bleeding. She ought to be pleased. It probably meant she was miscarrying. Babies didn't feature anywhere in their life plan.

'Look, I'm already on my way back—' James said.

'I wasn't expecting you until this evening.' She regretted the tone it came out in.

'They loved our pitch and booked two events straight away, so we left early.'

Kate headed for the building across the car park.

'Are you still there?'

'Yes.' Kate took a large swig of water then wished she hadn't because it felt like it might come back up.

'I thought we could meet for a late lunch, say three o'clock?'

Kate turned back, realising she hadn't bought a parking ticket.

'Where are you?' James sounded like a sullen child.

A man stood in front of her, feeding in a pile of ten pence coins as if it were a fruit machine. James evidently thought the same.

'Sounds like you're in the pub already.'

'Very funny, I'm in a car park.' If she didn't drink enough water, they wouldn't see the scan clearly.

'I can come and meet you.'

The man grinned at Kate, waving his ticket as if he'd won the jackpot. She dug into her purse for coins.

'Look, I didn't want to worry you, but I'm at the hospital; they're doing a scan to check if the fibroids have grown. I've been bleeding. I probably didn't say.' She held the mobile between her shoulder and chin and fed the correct money into the slot. In all their ten years together, she'd never deliberately lied to him. Not about anything important. Except that. He mustn't find out about any of it.

'Will you be okay?' He sounded worried.

'It'll be fine, I promise.' She made her way across to the clinic. 'Shall we meet at *The Fishery Inn*? I'll text you when I get out of here; got to go, I'm already late.' She switched her phone off and chucked it in her handbag.

Two nurses at the reception desk were deep in conversation. Kate banged her water bottle down in front of them a little louder than she meant to. The older of the two stopped talking, looked at the bottle over her half-moon glasses, then up at Kate. The other woman clicked her nails on the desk. Kate told them her name. The older woman asked her to go and sit in the waiting bay opposite.

Although she was the only person there, Kate still hadn't been called after twenty minutes. By this time, she'd drunk so much water she thought her bladder would burst. Finally, a midwife with glasses hanging from her neck called her into a dimly lit room. Kate took off her coat and lay on the couch next to a trolley full of equipment and a computer screen. The midwife opened Kate's notes and asked her to lower her trousers and lift her top up.

'This your first?' The midwife squirted gel onto Kate's stomach.

Kate nodded. The midwife pressed a smooth, cold paddle down on her lower abdomen as she concentrated on the screen. She pursed her lips and pushed deeper, twisting to the left and right. Kate held her breath.

'You've had some spotting?'

'Quite a lot of blood and really painful cramps like a period.' Surely this meant if there had been a baby it had gone.

'Ah, here we are.' The midwife flicked her glasses off her nose and swivelled the screen towards Kate so she could see the murky image of her womb. 'Baby's fine, see the heartbeat there?'

A butterfly came to life in Kate's chest. Her mouth opened. The tiny, indistinguishable shape, the winking heartbeat at its centre, transfixed her. Her baby. *Their* baby. A frisson of excitement whipped through her. Not how she expected to feel at all. She never thought this was possible. How could this be happening to her? What was she going to do? This was a miracle she didn't deserve.

'Let me measure it for you.' The midwife pulled the screen to the front and placed her glasses on the end of her nose, tilting her head closer to the image. 'Seven weeks five days.' She ripped off a piece of paper towel and wiped the gel off Kate's stomach.

'You can get up now,' she said, standing up herself. She wrote in Kate's notes on the workbench. 'I'll send a report to your GP and community midwife. You need to contact them if you have any further problems.'

Kate manoeuvered her legs off the bed and wondered if she could stand up without wetting herself. She tucked her top back in.

'Is there any fresh blood when you wipe?' the midwife asked.

'Yes, every time.'

'Do try not to worry.'

'But why am I bleeding?'

'Any number of reasons. Some women bleed throughout the pregnancy and the baby is fine.'

Kate put her coat back on. The midwife handed her the notes and showed her out, pointing to the toilet next door.

Walking back through the waiting area, Kate's head floated in a bubble. People were talking but the sounds were muffled as though none of it was real. How was it even possible at her age? What about her career, the business, the life she'd built up from nothing? She couldn't give it all up to be a mother. Was it possible to do both? Did she want to? But what about James, what they'd agreed? Oh God, it would be impossible to tell him. She cupped her stomach and imagined the rhythm of the baby's heartbeat in time with her own.

In the car, her fingers hovered over the mobile. She knew what James's reaction would be. She might still lose the baby so was there any point in telling him?

A woman pulled up next to her in a BMW soft top. Like Kate, she wore a trouser suit and heels. When she opened one of the rear doors, Kate expected her to pull out a laptop bag, but instead she lifted a toddler into her arms. The woman looked about her own age. Perhaps it was her only child, a fortunate mistake? She wanted to open her window and ask. A doctor once told her that the cut-off age for a healthy pregnancy was thirty-two. She was past that by thirteen years. More women were having them later, but it didn't mean it was safe. Could she really go through with it? What about their perfect lives, the freedom they had? Was it possible to do it all? James would not be happy. Children had never been on the agenda and he was adamant they never would be. Was she even capable of being a good mother? She switched her mobile on bracing herself for another barrage of nasty texts, but there was nothing, thank God. She texted James to say she was on her way.

Chapter Three

James sat in their usual booth by the window overlooking the Grand Union Canal. He stood up and pulled her into his arms.

'You're cold,' he said and folded his hands over hers. The blustery weather had drawn most of the leaves off the trees leaving a slippery path up to the door. She'd narrowly avoided falling over.

'Did it all go well?'

'The fibroids have grown, but I'll be fine,' she lied, looking away as she took her coat off. 'I'd rather spare you the details.'

'I'll order a bottle of white.' James called the waiter and shifted his empty whisky glass aside.

Kate held up her hand. 'Orange juice for me.'

'Don't be silly.'

'No really, my stomach is still playing up.'

'How about a spritzer, might settle it down?'

'OK, but orange juice with soda, not wine. Tell me about York.'

'Very productive. Jasmine made a big impression. Did you know she has a twelve-year-old son? Her husband works at Lola, designing racing cars.'

'She never said.' Kate stifled a yawn.

'Doesn't look old enough, does she? Anyway, I might need to go back up there next week.'

'So soon?'

'There are lots of potential clients for us. I can arrange for you to come with me instead? I'm sure Jasmine could fill you in on her next pitch. We could stay on for the weekend if you wanted to?'

'I don't know, I'll have to see how I feel. I'd hate to go all that way and be ill.' She certainly didn't need the new girl telling her what to do. 'If she's doing a good job, let her finish it.'

James pulled one of his sour faces and went over to the bar. She gazed out of the window at the passers-by being blown along. An old lady with an umbrella was almost lifted off her feet. She hated lying to James. If she was going to have a termination she may as well have a glass of wine. But the image of the tiny heartbeat flitted through her mind. Why not just tell him?

James brought their drinks over. He pulled out two menus from under his arm.

'Are we eating?' He sat down.

'You can, I'm not very hungry.' A smear of red sauce had stuck to the back of his menu.

'Will you share some loaded nachos?'

She shook her head.

'That's not like you.'

She shrugged.

James put the menu down. He stared at her as if he could read her mind. She swallowed hard and tried not to look away.

'Seriously, what's wrong? You're not yourself.'

Kate let her hair fall over her face. She picked up a beer mat and peeled back the corner. James tilted his head, waiting for her reply.

'I didn't want to tell you—'

'Look, whatever it is.'

She examined his face; the dark-rimmed eyes made him look tired even when he wasn't.

'You look upset.' He reached across the table for her hand. 'Has something happened?'

She couldn't let him be executioner when she felt so unsure of what she wanted herself. She tore off the top layer of the beer mat and took a deep breath. 'The thing is...'

He squeezed her hand gently.

She dipped her head.

'It's Mum. She has to go to hospital.' Unexpected tears pricked her eyes.

'Why? What's wrong?'

'She's been having chest pains. They think it's her heart. She's been in for tests.'

'She kept that quiet.'

'Honestly, it's way too soon after Dad.' Kate touched her lips.

The waiter came over and asked if they were ready to order.

'Give us a minute, please.' James got up and crouched in front of Kate. He took her hands in his. 'People survive these things a lot longer these days.'

'Even in their seventies?'

'She's still strong.'

'I'm not sure; she looks so frail.'

'Hang on, this is Elizabeth we're talking about. She survived the war and scarlet fever, remember? If anyone can get through this, it's her.' He sat back down.

It was true, she didn't know anyone as resilient.

'You've been getting on so much better since your dad died.'

'Have we?' Kate folded the serviette.

'You don't think so?' James stretched his arm across the back of the chair next to him.

'I am really trying.' She nodded, as if she needed to convince herself.

'That's good then, isn't it?'

'I still can't seem to do anything right.' Kate rubbed the patches of itchy skin on her hands. 'It's like I've never been away. She's still so distant.'

James kissed her hand. 'It's been twenty-odd years, give it time. You're doing your best.' He called the waiter over. 'Now please eat something. How about the chicken and bacon salad?'

'All right, but I won't be able to eat it all.'

'Can you do a starter portion?' James asked.

The waiter nodded and scribbled on his pad.

'And I'll have the steak and ale pie.' The waiter wrote it down and went across to another table.

'So, everything went well at the event?' James asked.

'Better than we expected. They rebooked for next year.'

'That's brilliant. You've got the golden touch. I told you they'd be blown away with your treasure hunt idea.'

Kate smiled.

'I have some even better news.' He slapped the table. 'Fearsome Events is up for Best Enterprising Business at the Hemel Business Awards.'

'You're joking? Have you told the guys in the office?'

'Not yet, I wanted you to know first. And my darling,' he reached over and put his hand on top of hers, 'you are on the longlist for Business Woman of the Year.'

Kate dropped back in her chair, pressing her hand to her chest. She could hardly believe it. The news she'd hoped for.

'If anyone deserves to win, it's you.' He jabbed the table with his finger.

But Kate's smile slipped as an unexpected hollowness gripped her. So much had changed in the last few months: her dad passing away, her mother becoming ill and now she was pregnant at forty-five.

'We should celebrate. Have something stronger, it'll make you feel better.'

'No, really, not today.'

'A G&T?' He stood up.

'Sparkling water will be fine, thanks.'

'Suit yourself.'

Kate watched him saunter over to the bar. He was almost indistinguishable lined up next to the other suited drinkers, puffing their chests out, laughing at their own jokes. His confidence had attracted Kate from the moment she met him. It was twelve years ago that he'd been brought into her office in central London as a contractor to shake things up, and he certainly did that. He knew what he wanted in life and he worked hard to get it. They got on immediately and worked well together. He already had ambitions to start his own corporate event business and, not long after they started dating, he invited her on board as an equal partner. She'd been flattered, excited to join him. They'd been married ten years, both happily childless until now.

'Did you check the diary for the last weekend of the month?' he asked when he came back with the drinks.

'I promised to go over to Mum's. She wants me to finish clearing out the last of Dad's things.'

'Does it have to be done then?'

'You know what she's like once she's made her mind up.'

'We could do some early Christmas shopping, visit a couple of museums.'

'I'll speak to her about going over next weekend instead, assuming I feel better.'

'Okay, don't worry if you can't, it can wait.'

'Mum won't do any of it herself. It's just so difficult and she's bound to find some excuse to start on me.'

'Elizabeth doesn't need a reason.'

The waiter arrived with their food. James ordered another glass of wine.

'Oh, I forgot to tell you, Susie and Harry want to talk to us on Saturday about being Lily's godparents. It would be rude not to.'

James groaned. 'Babies, kids – it's not us though, is it?'

Kate stared at her salad. The edges of the lettuce were brown. She pushed her plate away. He was right, of course, babies didn't fit in with their image, their lifestyle. They'd been careful about that.

'But Susie is one of your oldest friends.'

He put his knife and fork down with a clang.

How could she persuade him? An advert for a holiday in Cyprus came up on the screen behind him. It showed a bronzed couple sitting on a beach while their children paddled in the water. Kate tried to picture them doing the same one day, but was it really them? Maybe she was kidding herself.

James scraped his plate clean with a crust of bread while his jaw worked on a mouthful of steak. When he was cross, he looked so much older. He'd be off to bed as soon as they got home.

'Aren't you going to touch that?' James pushed a fork into a fatty chunk of bacon on her plate.

'It doesn't look very fresh.'

'It tastes rank.' He took the plate with him to the till for a refund.

Kate pulled her coat on and waited for him at the door. She let her hand rest on her invisible bump, feeling oddly protective over the life growing there. Her mobile beeped and a message popped up from the same number as earlier.

> I've sent you a note with instructions on where to transfer the cash to. Make sure you follow them.

Shit, did he know her home address?

'Who's that?' James pushed the door open as a gust of wind blew an empty plastic bottle rattling down the pavement.

'No one important.'

But blood pulsed in Kate's ears. Why was he coming after her now, and what did he really want?

Chapter Four

When Kate arrived the following day, her mother already had her coat on.

'It's colder in here than outside. Don't you ever put the heating on?' Kate asked.

Elizabeth ignored her and shuffled through a pile of unopened post on the telephone table. 'This came for you yesterday.'

Kate took the tatty envelope. Her stomach dipped and rose like a bouncing ball. She'd recognise the handwriting anywhere; always in capital letters, shouting at her.

'Aren't you going to open it?' Elizabeth stamped her stick on the parquet floor.

'I'll read it later.' Kate stuffed the letter in her bag. 'Have you got everything you need?' The thread of blue veins under her mother's eyes were more prominent than usual. A faint clicking noise seemed to come from the back of her throat. They stood awkwardly facing one another. If they'd been a different mother and daughter, Susie and her mum for example, they might have hugged. Instead, Kate stepped back. As she did so, a hot pain shot through her groin. She excused herself and dashed to the downstairs toilet. Fresh blood stained the tissue. This should be good news she told herself. It's what James would want. But in her diary, she'd started crossing off each day hoping to reach the safe twelve weeks mark. She would have to call the midwife. The dull ache in her lower back was what she normally felt before a period. If this really was the start of a miscarriage, she needed to know what to expect.

In the car, Kate flicked on the radio to break the silence. '*Wooden Heart*' sung by Elvis was halfway through. She hated it but thought it preferable to an awkward conversation about why she'd stayed away.

When they arrived at the hospital, they were directed to the Specialist Heart Unit. They sat in the waiting area in front of a muddled pile of magazines. A middle-aged couple looked up, both with scarlet-rimmed eyes, their arms entwined like two trees that had grown together. Elizabeth's hands showed the slightest tremor. She tried to disguise it by stroking her gloves, but in the process, she knocked one to the floor. Kate picked it up and laid it gently on her mother's arm. She frowned at Kate and drew her arm away.

A nurse called Elizabeth's name.

'Are you sure you don't want me to come in?' Kate asked.

Her mother shook her head and followed the nurse without looking back.

Kate went outside to leave a message for the midwife. She'd probably say she should be at home resting. She'd never felt maternal before, so where did this strange pull to have a baby come from? She replied to a couple of messages from work, half hoping to be interrupted by the midwife calling her back.

The hospital cafe wasn't very busy. She bought herself a coffee and sat down. Usually she'd be the first to grab the nearest newspaper, but today she swung her bag onto her lap and took out the letter. She stared at the envelope, examining her maiden name scrawled in blue writing; the person she used to be was so far removed from the person she'd become, the name may as well belong to someone else. Yet her hands became clumsy as she ripped open the gummed seam and shuffled out a scrap of paper.

> *Thirty grand is letting you off lightly. My bank details are on the back.*

Kate stared at the words, but they jumped about on the page. She folded the letter over and over into a tiny square. Thirty thousand pounds. He'd lost his mind. He clearly assumed she was rolling in it because of their successful business, her huge diamond ring and the Armani suit. But they'd worked hard to afford their lifestyle. Why should she give him a cut?

A screaming toddler arrived at the next table. The mother gave Kate a withered smile and wheeled the push-chair back and forth while the father rushed off to find a highchair. Kate unfolded the letter again. No hint of *anything else*. This was how he was going to play it. Not giving her any information in return.

When she looked up, the toddler had been installed in a highchair and was now banging a spoon on the tray. Kate flipped over the envelope. She held the two ripped pieces of paper together to read the post office date stamp. Isle of Wight. So, he'd gone back to live where he grew up. But what had prompted all this? Maybe he hadn't lied when he said he'd been at Sopwell House just to see her. He was unlikely to give up once he got an idea in his head. She folded the note up again and dropped it back in her bag.

Her mother emerged, coat slightly askew and her cloud of white hair out of place. Kate put her arm across her tiny shoulders and steered her into a seat.

'I'll get you some tea.'

Elizabeth nodded. She propped her stick against the side of the table.

Kate joined a short queue at the counter.

At that moment, the toddler let out an ear-piercing scream. Elizabeth and Kate glanced at one another across the cafe. Kate could see the young couple apologising to Elizabeth, who gave a tight smile and shook her head as if to say 'that's the least of my worries'.

'They want me back again next week,' Elizabeth said when Kate returned with their drinks. 'It is heart failure.' She emptied three tubes of sugar into her tea and stirred.

'What can they do?'

'All down to me apparently – exercise, low salt diet, no smoking.' Elizabeth took a compact out of her bag. 'They expect me to do all that at my age.' She applied lipstick to her thinned lips, emphasising the cupid's bow with precision lines. She turned the compact mirror this way and that to see all the angles of her ruffled hair. 'If only Ray was here.' Her eyes glistened.

'I'm here.' Kate scratched her dry, flaking hands. 'I know it's not the same.'

Elizabeth sipped her tea. 'Who was the letter from?'

'No one important.'

Elizabeth looked in the mirror again and patted her hair back in place.

Kate lifted her bag on the table just as her mobile started to vibrate. She stood up and made for the door.

The midwife didn't sound too concerned.

'It's too soon for another scan,' she told Kate, 'and it doesn't sound like it was very much blood, so I suggest we hang on a bit longer. Give me a call if it gets any worse.'

Kate took a deep breath, wondering if the baby would be all right. She peered through the window at her mother who was taking the folded-up letter out of Kate's bag. If only she could bang on the window. Now she was reading it.

'There's nothing I can do until then?' Kate asked, desperate for a quick solution so she could end the call.

'Not really I'm afraid; you're still so early on. If you can make it to twelve weeks, there's a much higher chance everything will be okay. Try and rest as much as you can. If the bleeding gets any worse, call me or your GP.'

Kate thanked her and switched off the phone. She stood for a moment with her fingers to her lips. She shouldn't even be upset, but if she was going to miscarry, it could be painful and messy and hard to hide from James. She would have to tell him, wouldn't she?

Back inside, the letter lay in a strange shape on the table, a checkerboard of creases. Kate snatched it up.

'What's all this about?' Elizabeth asked.

'You shouldn't read other people's letters.' Kate avoided her eye.

'That's a lot of money they're asking for.'

Kate buried the letter deep in her bag.

'Who is it thinks you owe them all that?'

'Can we leave it?' Kate zipped her bag shut.

The toddler started screaming and drumming its feet against the back of the highchair. The mother glanced at Kate and for a split second she saw desperation in the woman's eyes. Kate held her gaze, trying her best to convey some sympathy for her situation, but the woman looked away.

'Shall we go?' Elizabeth mouthed.

Kate nodded, wondering what to do about the letter. Stupid, stupid leaving it where her mother could nose round. It wouldn't be long before she made an educated guess about who it was from and then what? Would she keep it to herself? She certainly couldn't confide in her. Two whole decades apart. So much had happened in that time that her mother didn't know about. Now there was something else she didn't want to tell James. She hated keeping it from him, but what choice did she have? She'd do anything to stop him finding out what she did.

Chapter Five

Kate stared at the message on her phone:

> Pay up, or I'll come and get it myself. I
> know where you live.

How could he know? Maybe he was bluffing, just trying to scare her. But he knew where Mum lived. She did not want to get into a conversation about it; he might think he was in with a chance of getting the money. She imagined asking James how he'd found out their home address: what would he say? Through the business, through Companies House. Of course. He'd been at Sopwell House; he must know all about them and Fearless Events. Was he watching the house? She leaned across the kitchen counter. There was no one out on the green. What if he followed James on his run by the canal? He could tell him anything. He wouldn't need to say who he was. Just a stranger filling him in about the terrible thing his wife did. He'd always been the jealous type, starting fights if another man looked her way. Was James in danger?

She only had about fifteen thousand in savings, but that was it: nowhere near the thirty he wanted. She couldn't ask James to help her out because he'd want to know what it was for. The only alternative was dipping into the business account. Profits were up, but how would she explain borrowing that amount? It was out of the question.

She pushed her phone into the back pocket of her jeans and checked out of the window again. There was a cloth doll abandoned in the middle of the green. She hoped the little girl who'd been out there playing earlier would come back for it. Of the four houses on the other side of the newly cut grass, she couldn't see any front doors open or anyone about. A moment later, James put his cold face next to hers. She gasped so loud he laughed.

'Hey, you're a bit jumpy.'

'Sorry, I didn't hear you come in. How was your run?' She kissed his ruddy cheek, trying to calm her breathing.

'Good, but it's a fresh wind.' They gazed out at the dancing trees. The bright sun was deceiving with its lack of warmth.

'See many people about?' She picked up the chopping knife and started on the onions.

'Only a couple of dog walkers.'

'Speak to anyone?' The knife was poised above half an onion. Her eyes tingled.

'No.' He frowned and rooted under her jumper, settling his hands on her stomach.

'Careful.' She flinched and pulled away.

'What's wrong?' James asked.

'Your hands are freezing and, in case you hadn't noticed, I'm holding a knife.'

'Should I be worried?' He laughed.

'Of course not.' But if pushed to the edge, wasn't she capable of almost anything? She put the knife down.

'But you're so nice and warm and that smells delicious.' He cupped her face and kissed her lips. A waft of sweat caught in her throat. Today even the smell of frying minced lamb was making her stomach churn.

'Why don't you grab a shower and I'll make coffee?' She finished chopping the onions and scraped the pile into the cinnamon-spiced meat juices. A cloud of steam ballooned up from the pan.

'What time are Susie and Harry coming?' He collected up the peelings and tipped them into the countertop compost tray.

'Five o'clock.'

He washed his hands and stripped off his top in front of her.

'James! Someone'll see you.' She pulled at the blind, but it wouldn't budge. She scanned outside. There was no one there.

'Never bothered you before, darling.' He kissed her on the cheek. 'They're getting a babysitter, are they?'

'No, I told you, they're bringing Lily with them. She's still so small.'

'So Harry won't be drinking?' He stood naked in front of her, hands on hips, flexing his abs.

'Susie will be driving. She's still breastfeeding.'

James pulled a face before going into the downstairs wet room.

'Oh and don't forget, they want to talk to us about being godparents,' she called after him. She tipped her ear, expecting his reply.

He groaned. 'Surely they'd be better off asking people who have sprogs themselves?'

Kate turned back to the frying pan. Her eyes smarted and started to water. She'd quite like to be Lily's godparent. She never imagined she of all people would think it was a good thing. But it would be nice, wouldn't it? To be some sort of parent. She dabbed her nose with the back of her hand. The silliest things were making her cry this week. She didn't answer and he didn't call out again.

—

Susie and Harry arrived an hour late. When Kate opened the door, Susie bustled in carrying a large holdall and a bottle of wine. Harry followed with Lily in the baby car seat.

'I tried to call on your mobile, but it said it was switched off.' Susie took off her boots. 'It's turned into winter out there.'

'Sorry, I didn't think.' Kate hadn't wanted to leave her phone lying round and risk James seeing any of the threatening messages. Lily was crying so much her face had turned dark pink. James stood at the end of the hallway, buffing a wine glass with a tea towel. He squinted at the noise and retreated into the kitchen.

'She's hungry again,' Harry said. 'Or does she need changing?'

'Do you want to take her up to our bedroom?' Kate kissed them on both cheeks and helped Susie off with her coat. Milk had leaked through her blouse.

In the master bedroom, Harry unstrapped Lily and picked her up, but she wouldn't stop crying. Kate pulled the blind down on the grey day and switched on a dim lamp. She felt surprisingly tearful watching the two of them fretting over Lily. Susie settled herself in the armchair. She undid her blouse and hitched up her camisole. Harry handed Lily over and kissed Susie's forehead. As soon as Lily latched on, they all sighed and burst into silent laughter. Kate wiped tears from her eyes and hoped neither of them noticed.

Harry followed Kate downstairs and hung his coat in the hall before joining her and James in the kitchen.

'I don't know how you manage it,' James said. He took off his reading glasses and folded the copy of *The Times*. The two men shook hands.

'That's about as bad as it gets; she's an absolute angel most of the time,' Harry said.

James poured a large glass of red wine to match his own and thrust it towards Harry. Kate took a tumbler out of the cupboard and poured herself lemonade with ice.

'Are you not drinking again?' James said.

'Maybe she's pregnant,' Harry said. Both men laughed.

Oh, very funny. Turning away, she sipped her drink, the ice rattling. She poured a glass of orange and dropped in two chunks of ice. On the stairs she paused a moment to calm herself.

'You're a lifesaver.' Susie took the glass and drank half of the juice.

Kate switched the lamp off and raised the blind a few inches. An orange sun had appeared behind a row of distant houses giving the room a soft glow, diffusing the black lines of the East Asian-style furniture. She sat on the carpet next to Susie's chair. Lily had already swapped sides.

'I hope we're not holding up dinner,' Susie said.

'Not at all, don't worry.'

'I fed her before we left, and normally she'd sleep for two hours or so, but maybe she didn't have enough. I think this is a top-up, so we won't be long. See, she's almost asleep.'

Kate sat up on her heels. Lily's eyes half closed, and her mouth stopped sucking for a moment or two before starting again. A pang reverberated through Kate's chest like a broken guitar string.

Lily's tiny hand gripped Susie's thumb.

'Did you…' Kate sat back down and flipped up the hem of her skirt, examining the zigzag stitching, '…did you always want kids?'

Susie laughed. She glanced down at Lily who was now fast asleep with her lips slightly parted. 'I was a lot like you not so long ago,' Susie offered Lily to her, 'before you and I met.'

Kate sat up, trying not to look alarmed.

'Do you mind?' Susie asked.

She could hardly refuse. She swallowed hard, arms out.

'Don't look so worried. You just need to support her head.'

Lily settled into her arms. She was surprised by her lightness. The faint smell of milk and baby powder was strangely intoxicating.

'I couldn't bear the thought of having children, losing my figure, not just for nine months, but afterwards. We've all seen it, your body changes permanently and before you know it your other half is looking at all the younger, slimmer versions of you. I should know, I was that younger, slimmer singleton once, having a fling with a married man whose wife had not long given birth. Sickens me now, of course, but then I didn't think about anyone else, maybe because I didn't have to.' Susie buttoned up her blouse. 'But mostly, I was petrified of the responsibility. Looking after another person day in day out for years and years seemed overwhelming, and it is, if you think about it like that. I try not to. A day at a time is my policy.' She laughed. 'I'm lucky though, my mum comes and helps out with Lily during the week. I don't know how I'd cope without her.'

Kate didn't know how to respond.

'I'm the eldest so Mum and I have that special bond.'

Kate concentrated on Lily's face, trying not to wish her mother was the tiniest bit like Susie's.

'She's chuffed to bits we named Lily after her mother. I think she'll burst with pride at the christening. Which reminds me – you two will be godparents, won't you?'

Kate nodded. 'You might want to speak to James.'

'Moaning about it, is he?'

'Afraid so.'

Susie tutted.

'So was Harry the same – not wanting kids?'

'Oh no, Harry always wanted children. We nearly didn't stay together because of it.' She reached over and finished her orange juice.

'So, he persuaded you?' Kate was surprised at how comfortable she felt holding Lily. Her brown hair was so delicate and soft, the miniature features perfect.

'Quite the opposite. He never made a fuss about it. He left me to change my mind by myself. Shame I left it so late though; we won't be able to have any more. As it is Lily will be sweet sixteen when I hit sixty.'

'But you'll be a young sixty,' Kate reassured her.

'I hope so. James is lucky to have found you. His last girlfriend, Bella, left him because he wouldn't have kids.'

'Really?'

'They were about to get engaged but they hadn't talked about whether to have children before. Bella assumed that he would. They realised they wanted very different things. She gave him an ultimatum. I think she expected him to love her enough to change his mind, but he told her he didn't want kids, so she left. She was devastated for months after.'

'I had no idea.' Kate's head started to pound. No wonder kids were one of the first things James asked her about when they started going out. Why hadn't he told her about this? He'd presumably loved this girl enough to want to marry her. If he'd stayed with her and had children, where would she be now? Still on her own, drifting from one relationship to the next. She pictured their intimate wedding ceremony at the Old Marylebone Town Hall in the exquisite Soho room. An informal affair with only twenty guests then the biggest lavish party afterwards in the De Vere Grand Connaught Rooms, followed by a three-week honeymoon in the Maldives. She'd loved how involved James had been with the planning, suggesting the venue and the honeymoon destination, helping her choose the guest list. But now she wondered if this was what he'd originally planned with his ex, if she'd stepped into someone else's shoes without realising.

Except she was a better fit because she didn't want children. Up until now.

'He was a lot younger then, of course. Too young, maybe. Bella said she couldn't imagine going through life not being a mother. It killed her having to choose.'

'Were they together long?'

'About five years. No disrespect to you, but I thought he'd found the one.'

Did James ever think about her? Perhaps it was too painful for him to talk about.

'Having children is such a big deal for some women, isn't it? But if you don't want them, people are quick to judge you and cannot fathom why it's not a priority over your career, or they assume there's something wrong with you, especially when you get to our age.'

'Tell me about it, especially when we go abroad. People assume we're having time away from the children. Their faces are a picture when we say we don't have kids. For some that's it, they've got nothing else to say to us.'

'What is it with people? I must say I do understand that maternal need better now I'm a mum, but I certainly didn't back then. Could not imagine wanting to care for a baby twenty-four seven. Even now sometimes in the middle of the night when I can't get back to sleep and I'm utterly exhausted, I wish to God I'd never felt broody. Then I see Lily like this, and I think I'll explode with happiness.' Susie reached out to take Lily. Kate handed back the warm little bundle. She'd enjoyed holding her, watching her sleep more than she ever thought possible. So peaceful and trusting.

'Listen to me rambling on like I know it all.'

'Don't be silly, thanks for telling me. Actually, I wanted to ask you something else, in confidence?'

'Of course, go ahead.'

Kate pushed the bedroom door shut.

'Do you think it's possible that James might change his mind one day?'

'You mean about having children?'

'Well you did, didn't you?'

'Are you saying you've changed?' Susie smiled, holding Lily closer.

'It would be nice to have the choice.'

Susie stood by the window. 'Kate, if anyone can change James's mind, it's you.'

'I wish he would consider it.' She put a hand across her tiny bump. The urge to have this baby and to protect it was surprisingly strong.

'We all get that last hormonal surge: Mother Nature coaxing us one last time,' Susie said in a softer voice.

'Can you keep a secret?' Kate smiled.

'Oh my God, what are you saying? You're not, are you?' Susie whispered. Kate nodded.

'It *is* good news, isn't it?'

'I think so, but I'm not sure James will agree. It was quite a shock for me,' Kate said. Susie punched the air and cheered, careful to keep her voice low, then she reached out and hugged Kate warmly.

'How many weeks are you?'

'Eight.'

'When are you going to tell him?'

'I honestly don't know.'

'He'll have to change his mind, because it's already happening.' She strapped Lily back into the car seat and covered her with a light blanket.

'But what if he doesn't? I don't want to be a single mother.'

'Trust me, he's not going to leave you.' Susie patted her arm.

In the kitchen, James and Harry were sitting at the table, laughing. A bottle of claret stood between them.

'Sounds like we've missed all the fun,' Susie said.

'I was just saying,' Harry tried to catch his breath from laughing, 'that James should grow his own vegetables.'

'How much have you had?' Susie picked up the bottle.

Kate opened the oven to check the dinner.

'Well…' Harry already sounded drunk, '…a drop or three.'

Kate passed Susie a glass.

'Harry thinks growing veg will help me relax,' James said, pouring wine for Susie. 'Says I work too hard.'

'A tiny drop,' Susie said and showed James with her finger and thumb. 'Someone's got to drive us home later.' She pulled the glass away leaving a red ring on the table.

'Is gardening as exciting as dirty nappies and sleep deprivation?' James asked.

'You might surprise yourself.' She winked at Kate.

'Poor Harry, as far as I can see he's half the man he was two months ago. Next thing he'll have a pipe and slippers.' James laughed but no one else joined in.

'Leave it out.' Harry ran his fingers through his curly hair, but it flopped back over his forehead.

'He's on his second glass of wine and he's already half-cut.' James waved a dismissive hand at him.

'Watching your own vegetables grow is… very fulfilling,' Harry said.

'Like kids, is it?'

'Very similar yes; you should try it sometime.'

'Not a chance. Think about all the time and money you'll invest over the coming years, then your little darling will hit teenage-hood and bam, suddenly she won't want to have anything to do with you.' James puffed his chest out.

Kate pretended not to hear.

'You're so cynical, James,' Susie said.

'Is that what you were like?' Harry asked him.

'Pretty much,' James said. 'I left home at sixteen, couldn't wait.'

'Well I'm best friends with my parents,' Harry said.

'Couldn't cut the apron strings?' James laughed.

'It isn't like that.' Harry sounded sober.

'Kate's the same as me when it comes to parents, aren't you, darling?' James topped up the glasses.

Kate turned to them wearing oven gloves. She stared at James, expressionless. She didn't want to discuss it. Not being in touch with their parents had been one of the things they had in common when they met. But right now she wanted to know why he hadn't told her about the reason he'd split with his ex-girlfriend.

'It's better with your mum now though, isn't it?' Susie touched Kate's arm. 'Especially since your dad died.'

'It's bearable.' Kate nodded.

'It's Kate that makes all the effort,' James said. 'She went straight back when she heard her dad was ill.'

'How long since you saw them?'

'Twenty-five years.'

'Oh God, Kate, I didn't realise it was that long, what happened?'

'My mother, in her great wisdom, decided not to tell me that my father was not my real dad until I was nineteen.'

'That's awful. Why hadn't she told you?'

'To protect me, so she said. But what made it worse was that Dad didn't know either, although he suspected.'

'Your whole world must have collapsed.'

'She may as well have shot me in the heart. I couldn't forgive her. My dad went into himself, didn't take it well at all. I suddenly felt like a stranger in my own home.'

'That's so sad.' Susie rested her hand on Kate's arm.

'It's what you put in, how you bring your kids up.' Harry nodded.

'That's all well and good if you've got decent parents in the first place,' James said.

'Where are you two going on holiday next year?' Susie asked.

Kate was grateful to her for changing the subject. 'We're not sure yet, maybe back to California, do a bit of a tour. And you?'

'We're going to the Isle of Wight. It's very family friendly.'

'I've not been there for years. James, get the plates, please.' Kate whisked the salad dressing in a cup. She pictured the letter in her bag.

'Shall I do knives and forks?' Susie asked.

'Please.' Then under her breath: 'I can't think why you want James as godfather.'

'He'll come round; I know he will.' Susie gave Kate's wrist a little squeeze.

'You really think so?'

'He's one of my oldest friends. If it came to it and something happened to me and Harry, God forbid, he'd take in Lily as his own. Wouldn't you, James?'

'What's that?' James laid out the placemats.

'You'd take care of Lily if something happened to us, wouldn't you?'

For a second James froze, holding a placemat in mid-air. 'But Kevin and Belinda are your first choice, aren't they? I mean, they already have kids and their place is more... child friendly. They'd know what to do – if something were to happen.'

'Ja-ack,' Susie whined.

Kate sighed and took the moussaka out, her face burning from the sudden heat.

'We wouldn't have a clue where to start, would we, Kate?'

Shut up, shut up, shut up! She wanted to shout. She thrust the dish onto the table. Back at the sink, she slipped the gloves off and plunged her hands into cold water. She pulled out the salad leaves and shook them vigorously before dropping them into a bowl.

'Actually, we'd put you both as our first choice. We'd like you to be Lily's godparents too.' Susie appealed to Kate with her eyes. But she didn't see how they could change his mind.

'I'm sorry, I just don't think we're the right choice,' James said.

'I'm disappointed in you, James. I really am.' Susie crossed her arms.

Kate folded the oven gloves neatly and smoothed them over.

'Sorry, we're just not baby people, are we, darling?'

Kate drew in a breath and spun round, unable to contain her anger a second longer. 'Why do you have to be so bloody selfish?' The urge to break something overcame her, even if she appeared unhinged. She picked up the bowl of salad and hurled it at the wall, aware of their stunned faces as she stormed out of the room, slamming the door as hard as she could.

She stumbled into the front room, smearing tears across her face with her sleeve. A cloud like a sketch in charcoal hung low across the sky. She heard the kitchen door open and close.

'Are you okay?' James poked his head round the door.

'Go away!' she screamed.

A few minutes later, Susie came in and stood next to her.

'James is mortified; he hasn't got a clue why you flipped.'

Kate didn't answer.

'I said I'd come and see if you were okay.' She touched Kate's arm.

Kate shut her eyes, but the hot tears seeped under her lashes.

Susie reached up to the bookshelf for a box of tissues and offered her one. 'I can't bear it when the nights start drawing in so early.'

Kate sniffed and wiped her nose.

'It feels like all hope has drained out of the day.'

Kate drew her fingers through her hair.

Susie sat in the window seat. 'Shame about that dish, you won't be able to fix it you know.'

Kate tried to smile. After a minute she said: 'I want you to know I'd be very happy to look after Lily for you, to be her godmother... whatever he says.'

'That's really sweet of you.' Susie patted Kate's arm. 'He will change his mind you know.'

They fell into silence. Kate rubbed her stomach gently.

'You definitely want to keep it?'

'I think so. I didn't expect it to happen, not at my age. We agreed from the start, no children, and I know I should stick to that and have an abortion, but it's not that straightforward. I've been bleeding. I thought I was going to lose it. I might still.' Maybe because of what she'd done in the past, karma wouldn't allow her a healthy happy baby.

Susie held Kate's hands.

'I had to have an early scan to check it was still there.'

'And it is.' Susie smiled and gently squeezed Kate's fingers.

'Just when I didn't think it possibly could be. But I saw this... this tiny heartbeat, of *our* baby.'

Susie put her arm round Kate.

'And now I've seen it, I can't stop thinking about it. I can't get rid of it as though it's some inconvenience, when it's a living, growing baby. But if I tell James…' Kate reached for another tissue, '…what am I going to do?'

Susie gripped Kate's wrists. 'You have to convince him.'

'I can't see how.'

'He loves you and he needs you. He's different with you, believe me, and he won't want to lose you over this, I'm sure of it.'

'I had this silly dream of him playing in the garden with our child and I'm watching them from the sunlounger and I'm thinking what a fantastic father he is.'

'And he will be, he just doesn't know it yet.'

When they returned to the kitchen, the broken dish had been cleared up and the moussaka put back in the oven. James and Harry sat quietly at opposite ends of the table, drinking black coffee.

James stood up and directed a slight nod at Harry who waved Lily's soft toy rabbit in a show of solidarity.

'Kate, I'm sorry for upsetting you,' James said. 'Both of you.'

'We accept your apology, don't we, Kate?' Susie said.

Harry rested her rabbit next to Lily in the baby car seat.

Kate stared at James, wishing he could be as happy to be a dad as Harry was. Maybe Susie was right, maybe it was possible that James would accept a baby rather than lose her. But not if he knew who she really was. What she was capable of.

Chapter Six

Kate drove to the office on her own on Monday morning. James had left before her for a meeting with a telecoms company on the other side of Hemel Hempstead Industrial Estate. They were interested in their crime scene investigation package, so hopefully he'd come back with a booking.

She'd barely spoken to him for the rest of the weekend after Susie and Harry had left. She'd tried to stay a polite distance from him, pretending everything was fine, that she wasn't angry and hadn't lost it in front of their friends. But he wouldn't let it go and kept asking her what had made her lose her temper.

'I've never seen you fly off the handle like that before. I'm concerned about you, please tell me why you were so upset,' he'd pleaded. But she'd been determined not to give him any hint of what it was about. In the end he'd got annoyed and given up, stomping off to bed early.

At least Susie understood her. Telling her, telling *someone*, had been such a relief. James had gone out for an extra-long run on Sunday morning and she'd busied herself planning for the week ahead, all the time wondering when the best time was to break the news to him about the baby.

'Morning, Jane, anything urgent?' Kate asked before opening her office door. The aroma of freesias wafted towards her. A fresh bouquet was arranged in a vase on her spotless desk. It was the one extravagance she allowed herself every week. They provided lunch every Monday for all the staff and a bonus every Christmas. They worked hard and deserved to be looked after. When she'd been a junior, she'd appreciated little perks. It often made all the difference to how loyal she felt towards her boss and the company.

She took her jacket off, draped it over the back of her chair and grabbed her mobile and laptop out of her bag, half expecting another text demand to be filling the screen. Nothing.

Jane came in with her notebook and pen. They sat either side of the desk. Jane was five months pregnant and already showing. It was her third and likely to mean she wouldn't come back to work afterwards. Kate would miss her organisation skills and positivity and hoped to God she could persuade her to go part-time or at least become a homeworker. When they'd discussed it at home, James had done his usual eye roll at Jane's multiple maternity leaves. He'd pointed out to Kate that she was only as successful as she was because she didn't have a brood of kids dragging her down.

'How are you? Good weekend?' Kate turned her phone face down on the desk.

'Yes thanks, we treated ourselves to a spa weekend. My sister had the kids. I so needed it. I'm pleased to announce that I've got my energy back. How about you?'

'Good for you. You're glowing. We had friends over with their baby girl. We're going to be her godparents.'

'Aw, that's lovely.'

'I think so; James, not so much, but I'm working on it.' She smiled, wishing it were as easy as she made it sound. 'What have you got for me this morning?'

'Steve called about twenty minutes ago from the BM executive management meeting in Cambridge and wondered if he could check a couple of details with you about the team-building activities planned for this afternoon.'

'Okay, I'll give him a call.' She scribbled his name on her desk pad.

'And a woman from Shapeshifters PR called enquiring about a corporate team-building event for December. She's got Escape Rooms in mind. I said you'd call her back to discuss details. Her name's Izzy. I've emailed her number to you. That's it so far.'

'Great. Is everyone in?'

'Yes.'

'Good, can you let everyone know we'll have the team meeting at 11.30 and the usual buffet lunch will be laid on afterwards about 12.30.'

'Will do.' She stood up frowning.

'What's wrong, is my hair a mess?' Kate smoothed it with her hand.

'You look tired, stress-tired.'

'I'll be fine. It is Monday.'

'True.' They laughed. Kate wished she didn't have to brush it off. 'Can you call Sally in, please? And if you could stay and make notes then update the virtual whiteboard on where we're up to on the projects for the next week, please?'

'Yeah, course. Can I get you a coffee?'

'Please. Make it a big one.'

'Oh, and something arrived for you by courier.' She grabbed it from her desk and brought in a cardboard backed envelope addressed to Kate. There was a plain printed label on the front but no return address. It was probably samples from a printers touting for business.

When Jane had gone, she ripped the seal and took out a solitary sun-faded photo. It took a moment to sink in who it was. She peered closer. There he was smiling at the camera, no top on, already tanned, wearing swimming shorts and a straw trilby, lounging on a sandy beach in Spain with her next to him, wearing what had been her favourite red bikini, legs stretched across his, both licking ice-lollies, gazing into each other's eyes. She remembered the day, the exact moments before this was taken. How could she forget it? Her twenty-two-year-old self had been happy, excited. They'd asked the lovely old ice-cream seller to take their photo and he'd told them what a beautiful couple they were. A little over a year later and their lives together were in tatters. All because of her.

She turned the photo over and read his handwritten message.

DON'T FORGET, THIS WAS US
BEFORE YOU RUINED
EVERYTHING.

YOU OWE ME!

YOU DESTROYED OUR LIVES
TOGETHER AND I WILL DESTROY
YOUR PERFECT LIFE IN A
HEARTBEAT IF YOU DON'T PAY UP.

She ought to rip it to shreds, but she couldn't bring herself to. Maybe she should text him. And say what? That she didn't appreciate being dragged back in time? He knew, which was why he was doing it. She didn't want to add fuel to his mission.

'Knock, knock.' Sally stood at the door.

'Sorry, miles away. Come in.' She stuffed the photo and envelope in her bottom drawer.

Sally sat down. Jane brought in their drinks and sat next to her. For the next twenty minutes they ran through all the events they were organising over the coming week and what stage in the planning they were at. It took a surprising amount of manpower to make sure every event ran smoothly for each client. The photo flashed across her mind. The threat that he could bring her down so easily sent shivers through her.

Just as the buffet was being laid out, James arrived. He shut her office door and sat on the other side of her desk.

'How did it go?' Kate asked.

'Good. The Koreans booked the CSI event and we discussed a product launch they want organised in the new year. How's it going here?'

'All under control. Jane's updated the whiteboard if you want to add anything?'

'I will, thanks. So, how are you feeling?'

'I'm fine.'

'Are you?' He shifted to the edge of his seat. 'Susie called to thank us for dinner and hoped we're both okay.'

'Of course we are.'

'Are we? So explain to me the outburst?'

'Because you were bloody rude the way you dismissed being Lily's godparent.'

'But Susie's only asking me because... Oh I don't know. Why is she asking me? She must have known I'd say I wasn't up to the job.'

'She told me you left your last girlfriend because you didn't want kids.'

'You two were talking about me?'

'Why didn't you tell me about her?'

'What for? It was clear we weren't a good match. Fortunately, I found out in time. Anyway, we wouldn't have met, would we?'

Kate nodded. Jesus. So if she told him her baby news was he suddenly going to say they weren't suited?

Her phone buzzed on her desk. She picked it up feeling her face heat up as she read the message.

> Get my little present? A reminder to pay up, unless you want me to send a photo to your husband next time?

'Who's that?' James stood up.

'Nothing important.' She closed it and tried to slip it in her pocket, but it dropped to the floor. James picked it up and handed it to her. Thank God, the message had cleared from the screen.

'Are you coming to eat?'

'I'll be there in a second, you go ahead.'

What if she transferred a few thousand pounds to him, would it be enough to stop all this? But why should she give in to him? She could take this to the police, tell them he was blackmailing her. But that might backfire, open her up to their questions, although she could always deny his accusations. Was there any proof of what she did? What if that was why he was pursuing her after all this time? She thought she'd managed to run away from her past, but it had come back to haunt her.

Chapter Seven

On Friday afternoon, Kate sat across from her mother at the kitchen table in silence. She closed her laptop, took the cups to the sink and rinsed them while Elizabeth switched the radio on to a blast of *The Archers* theme tune.

In the dim hall, Kate stopped at the telephone table. Next to a vase of ostrich feathers was the photo of a young Elizabeth with soft tumbling curls as striking as a film star's. She'd always loved this photo. Noticeably pregnant, Elizabeth stood arm in arm with Kate's father in Trafalgar Square. They looked startled but were laughing at the cloud of pigeons taking off round them. She looked closer. Her face was already beginning to fill out like her mum's. She touched her bump and imagined how it would look when it got bigger, her waddling along, glowing and happy. She had grown up thinking how special it was, the three of them together before she was born, but it had all been an illusion.

'Dad's stuff is in his wardrobe,' Elizabeth called after her. 'I'll be up in a jiffy.'

Kate plodded up the stairs. The carpet had become threadbare in places. The once shiny brass poles were speckled and tarnished. She could remember kicking each step up to her room, sent there as a punishment for answering her mother back or getting in the way. A mahogany plant stand stood on the half-landing holding her dad's aspidistra, the once glossy leaves now laden with dust. She could picture him standing there whistling, shirt sleeves neatly rolled up, buffing cloth in hand.

In his bedroom, she could taste dust in the air. Everything was as she remembered it. The heavy brown curtains were drawn, bed made as if he would sleep there that night. On the bedside cabinet, his wire-rimmed glasses rested on a copy of *The History of Tom Jones*, by Henry Fielding. The new slippers she'd bought for his birthday a month before he died were tucked under the bed. A rush of air howled down the chimney, rustling the grasses in an earthenware vase.

Her mobile pinged in her pocket. She wanted to ignore it. If she didn't respond, would he give up? She doubted it. Knowing him, something was brewing. She took her mobile out and glanced at the screen.

I'm still waiting…

She switched it to silent and slipped it back in her pocket. From the solid oak wardrobe, she took out an open box. Her dad's brown trilby from the 1950s lay on top. Next to the other boxes stood his tan leather briefcase. She hoped her mother didn't intend to throw it out. She'd always thought it was beautiful. Her arms reached round it as she lifted it onto the bed, not letting go. She shut her eyes. The cold leather began to warm against her cheek just the way it used to when she'd curl up with it under his desk as he worked. *Oh Dad, I'm sorry I stayed away so long.* She should have come and spoken to him sooner. She'd thought about it many times, but after he found out he wasn't her real dad, he was different with her. She caught him staring at her once. Perhaps he'd wondered if she looked like her real dad, whoever he was. She hadn't been certain he would be as willing to forgive her.

She thought back to that final morning. It had been dark, and they were still in their dressing gowns when she dropped a carrier bag full of stuff she didn't want at her mother's feet and ran past her up the stairs.

'Where are you going?' Her mother's voice boomed after her.

'Spain.' They'd been living together in a bedsit for a month, all loved up, but next they planned to travel round Europe. She knew her parents had hoped she would come home, forgive them, but how could she when she was filled with so much anger and resentment? Her mother had lied to her all her life. It was her chance to make a stand. Show them they couldn't keep a secret like that and expect life to carry on as normal. Who was her real dad? She'd asked her mother, but she wouldn't say.

'Found something of yours?' Her mother had stood in the doorway, hands on hips, mouth drawn tight like a purse. Kate folded the wad of money and spun round, eyes flashing.

'That's mine, put it back,' Elizabeth shouted, her face pulled up by curlers packed into a hairnet.

'I'll pay you back.' Kate tucked the cash in her jeans without waiting for an answer. They faced each other in silence until Elizabeth's eyes flickered.

'When?'

'Six months, a year, I don't know. What do you care?' Kate laughed and pushed past her.

'You can't go, I won't allow it.' Elizabeth stomped back downstairs, but Kate was already outside in her boyfriend's camper van. He'd wound the window down, leaned his arm on the frame and grinned at them, triumphant.

'When are you bringing our daughter back?' Dad asked, his chin covered in shaving foam.

'How about never!' Kate shouted.

'She's stolen my savings,' Elizabeth's voice sounded alarmed and shrill.

'You'll telephone us, Katherine, won't you?' Dad called.

'You'll pay me back that money with interest, do you hear?' Elizabeth shoved herself in front of him, hands on hips, a scowl on her face.

Kate had closed the window, glowing in her victory, not realising that she had shut her parents out of her life for what would be the next twenty-five years.

As Kate pushed the box into the middle of the room, she stared into space. There had been several times when she'd considered asking for their help in those difficult first months. But after everything she'd said to them, everything she'd accused them of, she couldn't bring herself to give in. Before long, the years had stretched out and added up. It seemed there was no way back, until last Christmas, a few weeks after her health scare, when the lump in her breast thankfully turned out to be a cyst and she had decided to send them a card. A reply swiftly arrived from her mother telling her in her usual blunt way that her father was dying. Barely any pleasantries, no chit chat, but it was a start, a way back into their lives.

Everything of her dad's was precious now. She didn't want to get rid of any of it. He'd only kept beautiful things. She took everything out, one at a time: work logbooks; a collection of cigarette cards and a small pile of books with gilt-edged pages: *Moby Dick*, *Gulliver's Travels*, *The Riddle of the Sands* and *Oliver Twist*. Kate flicked through each of the leather-bound editions. When she came to *Oliver Twist*, two black and white photos fell out. A picture of a young Elizabeth was dated on the back: *May 1973*. The other was of a grand-looking old building beyond high gates, possibly a school: *June 1955*.

She looked closer at the photo of her mother: the pouting lips, soft curled hair and a flower print shift dress. Elizabeth would have been in her early thirties – an aspiring actress – yet Kate detected sadness in her eyes.

'Where are you?' Her mother boomed in the voice of a much younger woman.

How could she not have heard the tap of her stick on the stairs? She lay the photos upside down on the box, standing up in time to be greeted by her mother in the doorway.

'What have you got there?' She stamped her stick on the wooden floor.

'Some of Dad's old books.'

'Not those, what's that?' Her voice was lower now, each word spoken with laser precision.

'I found a couple of old photos.'

'Show me.' She moved forward, pivoting on her stick, her hand outstretched.

Kate picked up the top one. Her mother's Venus flytrap fingers snapped shut round the corner of the photo. Her sharp intake of breath was barely detectable. Kate pretended she hadn't heard it.

'Where did you find this?' Her mother's cheeks flushed crimson.

Kate shifted backwards. 'In the back of one of Dad's books.'

Her mother took it into her bedroom. Kate picked up the other photo and followed her. Elizabeth put on her reading glasses. She sat on the bed and seemed to slip into a trance, lost in another time.

'You know this place?' Kate asked softly.

'It's… it's a school now.'

'Your school?'

Her mother didn't answer. She turned the photo face down on the bed and cast her eyes over the lacy handwriting on the back. Her fingers crept over the date.

'There's another photo… of you.' Kate handed it to her.

Her mother took a close look at it. 'I'd not long found out I was pregnant.'

Her tone made Kate's heart stall.

'We married before I started to show.' For a brief moment, her mother's face lifted in its practised smile.

'Didn't you think about telling Dad the truth?'

'And have him leave me?' Elizabeth put a hand to her head as if to comfort a pain.

'But he had a right to know I wasn't his.'

'I was pregnant, unmarried. Do you know how shameful that was?'

'But you did love him, didn't you?'

'Of course I did.'

Kate gave a deep sigh. 'So tell me, who is my real father?'

'What does it matter now? I never knew mine.' Her mother propped herself up against a pile of silk cushions.

'It matters to me.' Kate longed to know something, anything about him. Were they similar in any way in looks or personality?

'There's not much to tell you. His name was John and he was a local greengrocer.' Elizabeth pursed her lips and fussed about throwing a shimmering quilt over her legs.

'Don't you have a photo of him?'

'No.'

Kate had always wished she had grandparents to talk to – the stories she'd heard at school from her friends, about how their granddad or nan had taken them on special trips and been given treats like ice-cream sundaes. It had always puzzled her why she didn't have any relatives on her mother's side. Her dad's parents were dead long before she was born.

'Well there you are. It couldn't be helped.' Her mother fanned her hand out round her neck.

'What couldn't be helped?'

But her mother unfolded the broadsheet from the bedside table and flapped the pages back and forth until it stood upright, blocking Kate out.

Back in her dad's bedroom, Kate sat on the floor. A familiar heaviness weighed in her stomach. As a child she'd imagined putting a stone in her mouth and swallowing it each time her mother ignored her, insulted her, or failed to consider her feelings. She'd always been aware that her mother wasn't the happiest person in the world. The truth was, she'd always had the feeling it was her fault. She remembered her dad saying once that Elizabeth had a difficult start in life and that sometimes she needed to be forgiven for the way she snapped at them and wasn't 'as warm as a mother should be'. When Kate was very young, she hadn't quite understood and suggested they buy her a coat for Christmas. Her dad answered by patting her on the head and making a strange shape with his mouth.

They'd been standing in the larder at the time, while she served her punishment for stealing a packet of biscuits. Her task was to re-label all the jars by teatime, writing out each word on a square of paper, sticking each label on the corresponding jar with clear tape. She loved the variety of colours, smells and textures of the ingredients: brown sugar, cinnamon, pearl barley and dried kidney beans. The space always seemed to shrink with her father there; it was barely enough room for one person let alone two. She remembered the tiny bobbles of wool on the undersides of his pullover sleeves and the holes unravelling at the elbows, visible only when he lifted the jars down for her. She didn't let on that she liked the job; it had given her the perfect opportunity to practise her handwriting and she had enjoyed organising the jars into a more logical order.

A loud tapping on the wall brought Kate back to the present. She dragged herself up and back to her mother's room. Elizabeth sighed as she closed the newspaper, keeping a finger inside to mark her place.

'You look a bit peaky. Stay for dinner; there's some leftover beef stew in the fridge. Too much for me.' A magazine was open next to her, showing a full page black and white photo of Katharine Hepburn in a pair of signature wide-legged trousers. 'Stay over if you want to.'

'I think I might, I feel exhausted. I was wondering what you want to do with Dad's ledgers?' Each item bought and sold in his auction business over forty years had been carefully listed.

'Can you burn them?' She opened the newspaper again, but it flopped forward.

'Really? It's his life's work.'

'What use are they now?'

'But Mum…'

'I don't want all those things cluttering up the house. What good are they except to remind me of something that's finished?'

'Would you mind if I kept them?'

'What do you want them for?' Her mother's throat rattled with laughter. 'It's all sentimental memories.' She brushed Kate away with a sweep of her hand.

Downstairs, Kate sipped a glass of water. Nausea was building again in her throat. Normally she'd be rushing off to meet friends on a Friday night. Always keen to get away. James wasn't going to be back from York until Saturday evening. What was the point in going out when she felt so sick? Anyway, she ought to help out more. She stared into the yellow light of the near-empty fridge. The smell of stew made her stomach rumble. She pictured herself standing in the same place more than twenty long years ago when all the plastic shelves were brand new. Now they were dull and scratched. She remembered taking out a joint of beef for Sunday dinner: a heavy, bloody lump of meat. It was the first time she had introduced him to her parents. He drank too much wine and told them why everyone should become vegetarian, trying to compensate for the lack of conversation. She could still hear the polite clink of cutlery on her parents' best china.

Kate took down the lidded Pyrex dish from the middle shelf, leaving half a bottle of milk and a small rectangle of cheese wrapped in greaseproof paper. She rattled out the bottom drawer and took the last two carrots. In the one-door freezer section, a hole in the centre of the ice-encrusted space contained a small bag of mixed vegetables secured with a wooden peg.

Elizabeth sat down, propping her stick against the table.

'Shall I warm it in the microwave?' Kate asked.

'Use the stove.'

She'd bought her mother a microwave a month ago, but Elizabeth never used it. Kate clattered about the kitchen pouring the stew into a saucepan and the mixed vegetables into a dish to go in the microwave.

'Was that note who I think it was from?' Elizabeth appeared colourless in the fading daylight.

Kate scratched the new patch of eczema flaring up between her fingers.

'You never said why you left him.'

Kate switched the hob on high. 'It's complicated.'

'We said he was no good for you.' Elizabeth pushed a cigarette into her silver-plated holder and lit it.

Kate swung round, a wooden spoon in her hand. 'I thought you weren't supposed to smoke?'

'One won't hurt.'

'Mum!'

'Don't think you can start telling me what to do.' Elizabeth blew out a funnel of grey-blue smoke. 'Do you know how difficult it's been for me?' Elizabeth's voice became shrill. She pressed her fingers into her forehead. 'All those years not knowing if you were dead or alive?'

Kate bent over the sink. This was it: she was going to be sick. She held onto the edge of the worktop and shut her eyes, hoping the room would stop spinning.

'We always celebrated your birthdays even though we didn't know where you were.' Elizabeth tapped the cigarette on the edge of a clean ashtray.

'Is that supposed to make me feel better?' Kate sank into her dad's high-backed chair. His filled pipe sat on the shelf in the little alcove as if he'd just stepped out of the room. She rubbed her palm up and down the smooth wooden arm, imagining all the times he'd rested his hand there. None of her memories would ever quite hold the same warmth; her mother had made sure of that.

'If only we'd known where you were.' Elizabeth gave the table a short sharp smack, jolting the cups, like she'd given Kate's legs on many occasions, leaving red hand marks. 'You broke our hearts. You've no idea.' She wiped her nose on a screwed-up hanky.

'I can't believe this.' Kate shook her head. 'You're the one who lied to me, remember?' She should never have come back. She scratched her fingers, prickly and cracked, opaque like a snake shedding its skin. 'Have you ever thought for one second how *I* felt?' Kate slumped back in the chair and imagined herself as a little girl, her dad's arms wrapped round her, shielding her.

Her mother squashed the cigarette butt in the ashtray and laid the ebony holder on the side.

'So why does he want money from you?'

'Leave it, Mum.'

Silence.

Elizabeth made a clicking noise in the back of her throat. She reached down to her carpet bag, picked up her knitting and started counting a row of stitches. Then she placed the knitting on the table and tried to push another cigarette into the holder. Kate sighed. The end of the cigarette buckled, and tobacco spilled out. The holder slipped from her fingers and rolled across the table. The stew fizzed and spluttered in the pan. The cloying smell of slow-cooked beef made Kate's stomach turn. She needed air.

Outside, the darkness had turned the back garden into a padded room with tall hedges and a black ceiling studded with lights. The brick walls were lined with deadly nightshade and the lawn spread right back to the orchard at the bottom in a rug of daisies. As a child, Kate had often hidden from her mother among the gnarly trees. She would pretend to be a fairy, dancing round the trunks, treading barefoot on fallen blossom, pretending she had whispered a spell and turned it into snow.

The crisp autumn air smelled of charred wood from a nearby bonfire. Closing her eyes, she imagined the sweet smell of melting marshmallows. She sat on the low wall by the side of the greenhouse where brambles had grown out of the jagged glass, smashed by red apples in a storm. All those summers when she'd played out here alone, never allowed beyond the garden gate, except the odd occasion when a friend was invited in. And here she was, a whole messed-up lifetime later.

She wandered down to the orchard among the acid-smelling apples and allowed herself to weep a little. But wasn't she just crying for herself, for what she'd lost?

Her phone flashed its piercing light through her pocket. Another text message appeared on the screen.

> Pay up by the end of the week if you don't want the truth to come out.

She couldn't ignore this one. If he told everyone what she did, her friends and colleagues would shun her, James would leave her, and everyone would know that her perfect life was built on lies.

Chapter Eight

Elizabeth switched off the main light and her bedroom fell into shadow. Shapes from the lamp formed on the walls and ceiling. She grimaced at the bones grating in her hip with each step she took towards her reflection in the black glass of the window. She shivered. In an instant she was back there: the rows of beds in the vast dormitory, children crying, muffled sobs into flat pillows, the strong smell of floor polish and starched sheets. Many nights she'd stared out of the tall curtainless windows at the lawn below and a whole world, she'd imagined, beyond the wall of cypress trees. What would she say now to the child she was then?

She closed the curtains. It felt strange having her daughter back, sleeping next door in her old room. She'd wanted more than anything to be a good mother to her, to give her the love and stability she'd never had. But it wasn't possible, she'd had no patience with her and no understanding of how to comfort a child. Instead, sharp words had sprung from her lips. Punishment and discipline were all she'd known and all she could pass on. Not one jot of love or understanding. Maybe she'd been too damaged to become a good mother to her. There'd been no one to show her how to care for someone else, how to love. She'd failed. She had to admit it. Her own daughter had left her, not wanted to be in her life. Not a word or a card until it was almost too late. She was only here tonight because she'd bullied her into sorting out her dad's things. Every day she lived with this dragging feeling in her chest of not being good enough. It had made her so impatient and judgemental, just like they'd been with her. Perhaps her punishment was a lifetime of regret and failure.

What about the note in Kate's bag? Why was he contacting her after all these years? And why send it here? Was he having a dig at her too? She'd give him what for. From the moment she set eyes on him she knew he was trouble. Had a shifty look about him she'd come across before. Always full of himself. Was Kate in danger? Trouble was she didn't confide in her about anything. But she had to get out of her what it was all about.

She picked up the photos from the dressing table. The grand old building full of secrets whispering along its corridors. The echoes of children laughing and crying. Alison and Elsie giggling as they pulled her along the floor on an old blanket, when they were supposed to be buffing and polishing. The gurgling screams from the bathroom. Fleshy arms wobbling as they scrubbed her with carbolic soap before dunking and holding her head under cold water. Each time her head came up, she'd focus on the tiles lining the bath, one decorated with a baby lamb, her silent witness.

Ray had taken her back there for a special tour after it became a school. It would help her move on, lay the ghosts and nightmares to rest, so he thought. No need to hide these photos, was there? Lately, she often found herself nattering to him out loud, as though he was still sitting in his reading chair in the corner. It helped to keep her going until reality hit her with a jolt. How was it possible that he was gone? Walking back in the house that first time without him, shutting the door, she'd felt a little gust of air on her cheek like his last breath.

She opened the drawer of the bedside table and took out a miniature Bible tucked away at the back. As the pages fell open, a small cutting from a newspaper floated out. John was only twenty-nine then, his face serious in his smart suit. Brown eyes and lashes as thick as a girl's. Ray standing next to him, best pals before this happened. Recently, there were moments when she couldn't help wondering what life would have been like with John if they'd married and grown old together. But that had been a fantasy because he wasn't the person she thought he was. Didn't she owe it to Kate to tell her about him? No. Enough damage had been done. She couldn't risk her going off again. She for one wasn't strong enough to bear it. She kissed her fingertips and pressed them to Ray's face before tucking the cutting back in its place.

She eased herself into bed and opened a folder of Ray's bank papers and picked up where she'd left off, checking each month for the same amount of £350 going out. Something to do with his car, more than likely, but it seemed an awful lot. Hadn't they finished paying that off a few years ago? Normally he'd have told her about something costing so much. Trouble was once the Alzheimer's set in it must have gone clean out of his head. She wished Kate had come back sooner, had a chance to see him before he became so ill.

She stuffed Ray's papers back in the folder and picked up a battered copy of *The Thorn Birds* from the bedside table. She leaned back on the pillows and opened the book, but before she finished reading the first page, her eyes fluttered shut.

Chapter Nine

The single bed faced the door, just as when Kate had lived there. A bookcase stood where the wardrobe had been. Her mother never read bedtime stories to her. If her father were home in time, he would sit at the end of the bed and read her Aesop's *Fables* or *The Chronicles of Narnia*. During the summer she hated being sent to bed when it wasn't dark outside. She would peep out of the leaded light window at children playing in the street below. Time seemed to swell with the heat, and she'd wondered if she would ever grow up.

A car turning in the street illuminated the room. She threw back the covers and sat up. Over the past couple of days the nausea had come on when she felt hungry or thirsty. She reached for a glass of water from the bedside table and drank a mouthful.

She wished she could tell James about the letter, the photo and countless texts, but the lie was too big for him to forgive her. She needed to put a stop to it all, but thirty thousand. Jesus. It would wipe them out. All their hard work building the business. They'd have nothing to fall back on. Why should she give in? But what was worse: risking him telling everyone what she did? He knew too much. Her mind ran a conversation she might have with James, trying to explain to him what sort of person he'd really married. She buried her face in the duvet over her drawn-up knees. She was a different person now, a better one, wasn't she? A sharp pain stabbed her groin. She pulled back from her knees, rested on the pillow, her hands to her tiny bump. The pain began to ease to the dull but familiar ache of her period. She sobbed into the pillow. She didn't deserve a baby and even less so because she'd wished it away. Curling into a ball, her thumb slipped into her mouth and she gently rocked herself to sleep.

When she jerked awake, the travel clock by the bed read three a.m. in green, luminous numbers. For a few moments she lay still as fragments of a dream pulled away from her. A baby in a pram rolling down a hill but no matter how hard she ran she couldn't quite reach it. The aching longing to save it lingered.

The pains appeared to have gone, but she became aware of a warm dampness at the top of her legs. She eased herself up and turned back the duvet. The sheets were soaked pink and smelt faintly metallic. Her hand shot to her mouth to catch the cry as it sprang from her lips. Cold air crept up her wet legs. She shivered as she dragged herself to the bathroom.

After a shower, she changed the bedsheets and collapsed in one of her dad's many reading chairs in the corner of her room. She pulled a blanket over herself. A small photo of her as a child stood on the dressing table next to the lamp. She must have been nine years old, grinning at the camera, showing her newly chipped front tooth. She could still remember falling from the swing and the sensation and taste of warm blood filling her mouth.

From a shelf above the bed, rows of her old dolls seemed to be watching her. Higher still were two jars of polished stones, like boiled sweets, used as bookends for her much-loved Enid Blyton books. She'd often read under the bedclothes to block out her parents' arguments.

A sharp pain etched through her groin. She cupped her tiny belly and rocked back and forth. Tears stung her eyes. She needed some more pads. Would her mother have any?

The smell of talc made Kate's nose tingle as she crept into her mother's bedroom. She called gently, but Elizabeth's slack face continued to process the air in long laboured breaths. After a few more attempts, she began to stir. Kate patted her arm and called her again, so as not to startle her. She didn't need to tell her what was wrong. It wasn't like there was anything either of them could do.

'Mum, sorry to wake you,' she whispered, wiping her eyes on her pyjama sleeve.

Gradually, Elizabeth appeared to understand. She gave a low groan and glanced up, but her eyes rolled and the lids fell shut.

'Mum, please,' Kate pulled at her arm, 'I need a pad.' She tried not to let the tears sound in her voice.

Slowly, Elizabeth's eyes opened again.

'Do you have any pads, something I can use?'

'Bottom drawer, a new pack.'

Kate rummaged round until she found them. StayDry for bladder weakness. She cringed. They would have to do.

'Something wrong?' Elizabeth's voice croaked with sleep.

'It's nothing.' Kate let a short breath escape. She silently sniffed back the tears.

'What is it?'

'I've started unexpectedly.'

'So why are you crying?' Elizabeth heaved herself up, so she was higher on the pillow.

'I'll be okay, Mum, it's just my hormones.'

'But is something wrong?'

'I… I think I'm miscarrying.' Her mother had always been bald with the truth: like the day she told her that their dog was dead, run over outside the house.

'Why on earth didn't you say?' Elizabeth frowned.

Kate took a deep breath. She wished she could explain how hard it was to speak to her. 'I went for a scan because I keep bleeding. I'm nine weeks today.'

'I thought you didn't want children?' Elizabeth's face softened.

'It was a mistake; I was sick and…' Kate rubbed her forehead.

Elizabeth blinked slowly as if the information had triggered a memory and she was watching it play out.

'Have you told James?' Elizabeth sank back in the pillow, a hand to her chest.

'Not yet, but he won't want it.'

Elizabeth breathed heavily.

'Are you all right?' Kate leaned forward.

'And it's his?'

'Of course it is.'

'Then he has to take responsibility. You can't erase a person just like that.' She clicked her fingers. The rows of white pin curls held together with clips threatened to break loose.

'But I'm losing it and, anyway, he won't see it like that.'

'Hmmf.' Elizabeth's face drew back as though she'd smelt something rotting.

Just once she wished her mother would reach out and hug her, tell her that it didn't matter because she'd be there to help her through it. How could she possibly be the kind of mother she wanted to be without one who could show her how to do it properly? In her head she reran for the thousandth time the moment on a train to Margate when she'd been sick all over mother's patterned dress. *Sorry mummy, sorry mummy*, she'd pleaded a dozen times. Her mother hadn't shouted at her for once. Instead, she'd pulled the same face she was pulling now as she silently removed Kate from her lap and ignored her for the rest of the journey.

'You have to tell him, that's all there is to it.'

'What's the point if I'm losing it?'

'He should know what his wife is going through, be there to support you.' She crossed her arms.

There were so many reasons why she shouldn't keep this baby but talking James into it wasn't the only part she was concerned about; the problem was she didn't know if she could trust herself.

Chapter Ten

Kate woke up early on Sunday morning. James was still asleep next to her, his calm rhythmic breathing more apparent with his mouth ajar. She pushed back the duvet, padded across the wooden floor and wrapped her silk gown round her body. In the bathroom, she pushed open the window as wide as it would go and inhaled the brittle icy air deep into her lungs.

In the kitchen, she checked her phone, but there were no more threats, thank God. She called the surgery and left a message for the midwife to say she was bleeding a lot more, then she switched on the kettle and took out a pan, two eggs and the last of the bacon. It was becoming a daily habit to check out of the window for any sign she was being watched. Was she being paranoid? An empty plastic bag blowing about on the green snagged on a branch high up in a lime tree across the road and billowed helplessly in the wind. No sign of him, but with every message she could feel him closing in on her. It was almost worse when he was silent, wondering what he was planning next. She had a sick feeling that sending him any amount of money was not going to be enough to stop his need to punish her. But this was the first morning for weeks she hadn't felt nauseous. Sometimes it was difficult to tell if it was anxiety or morning sickness. Could the pregnancy be over? Was it crazy to mourn something that had hardly existed?

She broke the eggs into the pan with a scrape of butter and a drizzle of milk. She pierced their yellowy centres. The opaque sliminess brought the sickness back to Kate's throat in an instant. This life force within her was strong, determined. Didn't it deserve a chance? She stirred the mixture until it started to catch in the pan then she tipped the scramble onto two pieces of toast. On top of it she arranged fine strips of bacon from the grill. After loading a tray with the plate and two mugs of tea, she carried it upstairs.

James was still asleep. Her heart beat with sudden strength as though she was about to confess a secret love. She put the tray on the bedside table. Sunshine stabbed her eyes through a gash in the curtains. She turned away and sat near her pillow, the laser brightness slicing the room in half. She shifted away so it fell across the bed in a line between her and James.

Perhaps it was the smell of bacon next to him that made James stir. Kate tried to control her breathing, going over and over how best to word what she needed to say, thinking of answers to all the questions he could ask.

'I made some breakfast for you,' she said, seeing that his sleepy eyes were opening, trying to focus on her. Could he guess her thoughts? She went round to his side and moved the mugs off the tray.

James sat up, his hair flattened on one side. 'What's the time?'

'Nine,' Kate said and laid the tray across his lap.

'It's not my birthday, is it?'

'Very funny. You've been away a lot; I thought you might like it.'

'Oh I do, very nice.' He opened his eyes wider to show his appreciation.

Kate took her mug and perched on the end of the bed. 'You're not having any?'

Kate shook her head. She sipped the scalding tea. 'What time did you come home? I didn't hear you.'

'About midnight. We got three more bookings. I can't remember if I told you. They said we had the freshest event ideas out of all the other companies they'd seen.'

Kate nodded, blowing steam from her mug. She swallowed a mouthful of tea too quickly, burning her tongue.

'How'd you get on at your mum's?'

'Yeah fine. Still some of Dad's stuff to go through. It would feel disrespectful if I chucked whole boxes away without looking at everything individually.'

James nodded as he chewed. Kate couldn't get comfortable. She hadn't squirmed in her seat like this since school when she 'borrowed' Tilly Brown's new pen and the teacher asked everyone to empty out their pencil cases.

'Is there something wrong?' James glanced at her.

She hesitated. It would be so easy to not say anything. 'You know I've not been feeling well…'

'I meant to ask if you think you should go back to the doctor?'

'Actually I have and there's something I need to tell you.'

'Fire away.' He filled his mouth from an overloaded fork.

'It's hard to explain.'

He nodded encouragement, his mouth busy chewing.

Kate finished her tea. 'I'm still bleeding.' A nugget of silence landed between them.

James wrinkled his nose.

'But it's not the normal sort.' She stood up and placed her mug on the dressing table.

'That doesn't sound good,' James said before shovelling in a pile of egg.

'Which is why I need to go to hospital again.' She stood with her back to him, stealing a glance at his face in the dressing table mirror, wishing he could be delighted with what she was about to tell him. He'd believed she was a good replacement for his last girlfriend, and it turned out she wasn't. They wanted the same thing.

'I thought everything was okay with the scan?' He reached for his tea.

She could stop right there, but she had to be honest with him.

'Go on, you went to the hospital about those… fibroid things?'

'Yes and I have to go again next week.'

'Oh right.'

She stared in the mirror at his puzzled face. The words were becoming a jumble in her head. She sat on the bed again.

'So do they know what's causing them?' He put his fork down, leaving the last mouthful of toast.

She pressed her palms together. He pushed the tray aside and stretched across the bed.

'Do they think it's serious?'

Kate began to cry. It was going against everything they'd agreed. She couldn't do this. He'd be so disappointed. She sniffed and wiped her eyes with a tissue from her pocket.

'Kate, tell me, please, what is it?' He climbed out of the duvet and wrapped his warm arms round her. 'You're shaking, darling. Tell me what's wrong.'

'I'm not ill, James,' she said, turning her face up to his.

'But something isn't right.'

76

'Maybe to you it isn't.'

'Now you're not making an ounce of sense.'

'It's a baby,' she said, closing her eyes, not wanting to see his reaction. But she felt it as he drew away from her.

'What… what are you talking about?' He sat back on his heels, his arms curling round his own body.

Please come back, please hold me, she wanted to say.

'I'm pregnant.'

For a few long seconds, James looked as though he'd be frozen in that moment forever. Then he let out a strange growl and gripped the hair on the sides of his head.

Kate stood up. 'I'm so sorry, it was a surprise to me too,' she said, backing away, her voice sounding more like a child's.

'It has to be a mistake,' he said, eyes wild.

'This nausea I've been having – it's morning sickness.' She leant back against the dressing table.

'No, no, that can't be right.'

Kate shook her head. 'I saw the baby's heartbeat.'

'But you're on the pill.'

'I forgot to take extra precautions when I was sick.'

'So hang on, how long have you known this?'

Kate looked away.

'Come on, how long have you been keeping this from me?' James raised his voice. He slapped his hand down hard on the bed. She flinched.

Kate couldn't speak, her whole body shaking.

'All this time and you've not said a word. Is this what the histrionics were about when Harry and Susie were here?'

Kate stayed silent.

'You know how I feel about children!'

'Which is why I didn't want to tell you.' Kate tried to hold in more tears welling up. 'I'm only telling you now because I'm bleeding, which means I'm probably losing it anyway.'

'How many weeks are you?' He shifted over to her side of the bed.

'Nine, but...'

'Well within time for a termination.'

'I can't do that, James. I've *seen* our baby. It's alive. It's real.'

He leapt out of bed and gripped her arms. 'This isn't going to happen,' he said through clenched teeth. He let go of her and strode out of the room.

Kate rubbed her throbbing arms and slumped forward on the bed and wept.

Chapter Eleven

Kate left work early on Tuesday for her second scan. She'd spoken to the midwife on Monday morning and they decided it was best to get her in again. It was mid-afternoon and the black clouds above had thickened with the threat of heavy rain. She parked the car and switched off the radio. James had refused to come with her. They'd barely spoken for the rest of Sunday; he'd gone out for another bike ride while she stayed in and wept. She'd thought about calling Susie but couldn't bring herself to share her pain. He'd made sure he was out all day Monday and by the time she woke up this morning, he had gone. He'd left a note to say he'd be back from York late.

In the waiting area, a schoolgirl sat flicking her nails on the wooden-edged seat while her mother knitted her fingers back and forth. The space between them was wedged with a handbag and an oversized school bag daubed with boys' names. The huge bump seemed so out of place on a girl wearing a school uniform.

When the girl was called in, she stood up and her mother give her a gentle nudge forward. A few minutes later, another midwife called Kate.

'So, you're nine weeks, three days,' the midwife said, looking at Kate's notes.

'I've been bleeding again.'

'All right, let's have a look to see what's going on.' She squeezed gel onto Kate's bare stomach and skimmed the paddle back and forth before pressing down on her skin.

'Husband at work?'

Kate nodded.

'Eldest at school?'

'This is my first.'

'Oh, sorry.' The midwife frowned, concentrating on the monitor. Kate dared not breathe.

'There we are, baby is moving nicely. Can you see?' She angled the screen so Kate could watch the baby tumbling over. Unbelievable it was still there, this innocent tiny miracle. Tears brimmed her eyes. In a matter of weeks, she'd gone from someone who almost never cried to being emotional about everything. There was no question she would keep it; this baby meant more to her than anything.

'It all looks fine. Here we are, can you see the arms and legs?' She pointed to the lighter shadows.

She wished James could have been there. She pictured his face when she'd told him she was pregnant. Surely, he would change his mind if he could see this? But what if he didn't? What if she had to choose between her husband and the baby?

The midwife wiped the gel away.

'You'll probably still be called for the twelve-week scan.'

Kate pulled her clothes back into place. Despite the unthinkable things she'd done in the past, this was her chance to show she could be a mother. Didn't she deserve a fresh start with this baby?

Outside in the waiting area, the midwife handed Kate the scan picture and her notes.

Walking back to the car park, she could see something bright red on her clean, white Mercedes. She broke into a trot and, as she got closer, the word *BITCH!* leapt at her, scrawled across her windscreen in lipstick. She shuddered and spun round, half expecting to see him standing there.

Her mobile beeped the moment she switched it on. A message flashed up on the screen.

> This is your final warning.

Shit. Was he watching her? She scanned the car park. A man was standing by a black Volvo. Was that him? No, it couldn't be, he was helping a child into the back seat.

> Leave me alone or I'll call the police.

She immediately wished she hadn't texted back.

A line of question marks and laughing emojis came straight back. He was crazy. She grabbed a pack of anti-bac wipes out of her glove compartment and wiped the lipstick off the glass as best she could. Then she jumped in, locked the doors and started the engine. She squirted several rounds of windscreen solution and set the wipers going to clear the smear that was left. She dialled James's mobile then thought about cancelling the call, but he answered straight away.

'I… I'm at the hospital, I've had my scan.' Her voice wavered. She was more shaken up than she'd realised. The silence swelled like a bruise.

'I see,' he said, then after a moment, 'I thought you'd be making an appointment at the clinic instead.'

'James, please… I can't do that.'

'We talked about this before; we agreed – no children.'

'It's not that straightforward.' The words caught in her throat.

'It's what *you* wanted too, remember?' His voice was calmer. 'We want to focus on our careers, be able to jet off on holiday at a moment's notice, not be tied down with those responsibilities.'

'I know that… I know…' She knew she was being unfair to him.

'So, come on, explain to me why. What's changed?'

Kate could picture his clenched teeth and the hammering muscle in his cheek when things weren't going his way. Why didn't she just go ahead with the termination, put an end to this fantasy? 'I… I…' she paused, not knowing what she was about to say. 'I want this baby. I can't explain it.'

She knew it was crazy going against him, but she couldn't help how she felt. Seeing the baby properly on the screen this time, not just the winking heartbeat but it's little body, had unlocked a need in her to nurture this tiny life they had made. It was relying on her. She wanted to be its mother; she wasn't sure how, but if she could put the terrible things she'd done in the past behind her and start afresh she could prove she wasn't a bad person. She waited for him to speak. Was he still on the line?

'You said,' he spoke more slowly now, 'if anything like this happened, you'd book yourself in for a termination… pronto.' He sounded irritated again.

Damage control. He was treating her like one of their projects, always a contingency in place, except he was struggling to pull this one back.

'I know all that, but I was younger then.' She rested the side of her head on the steering wheel. 'Maybe I've changed but hadn't realised until now. Can't you change your mind too?'

'I'm not going to.' He paused. 'I wish you'd tell me what's going on here – what's happened, what have I missed?'

'Nothing, nothing, I had no idea I would feel like this. Logically, I don't want this to be happening, because we agreed – but if you'd seen *our* baby moving, I'm sure you'd feel connected to it too.'

Silence.

'It's Susie, isn't it?' The tone in his voice had changed. Kate sat up. 'She's brainwashed you, hasn't she?'

'What are you talking about?' In other circumstances Kate might have laughed at the apparent non sequitur and James would have joined in, but he sounded serious.

'It's nothing to do with Susie.' Her stomach fluttered, remembering their conversation.

'But she knows, doesn't she? I bet she already fucking knows.'

'Yes, but no one else.' Had Susie betrayed her?

'And she told you to keep it, didn't she?'

'No.' But he wasn't listening.

'In case you have a horrendous abortion like hers.'

'What, Susie? She never said anything—'

'She agreed to it, it's what we both wanted,' James broke in, still not listening. 'The whole thing was a mistake from start to finish.'

'What are you talking about?'

'We both knew we should have stayed friends...'

'Are you saying you used to be together?' She felt as if she'd been dragged to the mouth of a volcano about to erupt.

'I've mentioned it before, when we first started going out, remember?'

She tried to swallow. 'Susie was pregnant with… *your* baby?'

'It was a million years ago.'

Kate struggled to take in what he was saying.

'We were both fresh out of uni. I told you about it.'

'No, you didn't.'

They both fell silent. Kate imagined the two of them together. Perhaps they were still secretly in love. *Stop it! Stop it!* She screamed in her head. How dare they not tell her.

'What can I say?' James spoke at last. 'I really thought I had. It was so long ago. It didn't mean a thing.'

The line crackled.

'So, Susie hasn't told you to keep it then?' he continued.

'Why would she do that?' Kate shouted. Everything she'd told Susie in confidence flashed through her mind – had she been passing it all on to James? But no, he hadn't known she was pregnant.

'I want to know who's put all this baby talk in your head.'

'You made Susie abort her baby, *your* baby?'

'Hang on, I didn't make her, it was a mutual decision; neither of us wanted to be parents.'

Kate let the silence push between them. So, he'd kept another secret from her. She shivered. First his ex, almost-fiancée, and now Susie. Perhaps he was keeping other

84

things from her. They'd been together for ten years, but how well did they really know each other?

'And now you want me to get rid of our baby?' she said.

'You actually really want it, don't you?'

'I'm not going to abort it, James.' The words slipped out by themselves, but she'd never been surer of anything. 'I can't and I won't get rid of it. It would kill me.' Her legs started to shake again but she meant every word, even if she ended up losing him. She could hear the rustle of his hand covering the mouthpiece. Someone was talking to him. Blood rose to her head. 'James, are you even listening to me?'

'I have to go.'

'What? Did you hear what I said?' she shouted.

The sound of him covering the mouthpiece again incensed her. She pictured Jasmine lounging against his desk, waiting to speak to him.

'I'm sorry, I can't talk now. I'll call you back later.' The phone line cut off.

Kate slammed the phone down on the passenger seat and stared at the rain battering the windscreen, washing away the last remnants of lipstick. James and Susie. A dull ache lodged in her chest. She'd never even guessed. She knew they'd shared a flat together at uni, but Susie always talked about other boyfriends, never that James had been one of them. Every smile, every touch between them flashed through her head in sharp relief. What if Susie was still in love with James? What if the story about his ex wasn't true and she'd made it up to try and stop her having his baby? A swirling sickness rose from her stomach. What would it be like now if they'd had their child? She couldn't imagine him and Susie as a couple, being intimate, getting pregnant. And he expected them both to abort the babies he'd fathered as if they were their mistakes, nothing to do with him. The trouble was, she had agreed not to have children; everyone who knew her knew that. So, he wasn't being completely unreasonable. But he needed to understand that something had changed in her that she couldn't explain. Her, of all people. The connection she felt with this baby was primal. If only James would try and understand.

When she reached work, half the office had already left for the day. She took a bowl of fruit salad out of the fridge and sat in her office with the door shut. She checked her phone. No more threatening messages. But what he'd done to her car sent chills through her. Maybe that's what he wanted. He'd attacked her property: was she next? She'd better send him something to shut him up. She took out her laptop and transferred five thousand pounds. Perhaps if she tried to explain exactly what happened that night, he'd leave her alone. She typed in his email address then stared at the blank screen, wondering what to say, where to begin. If she could go back in time and fix it, she would. She'd never meant to hurt anyone. She'd never forgiven herself for what she did, so how could she expect him to?

She stared out of the window at the rain-drenched street and the row of office units with their backs to her, until she was sitting in the dark.

Chapter Twelve

Kate sat in her office the next morning, wondering how she was going to persuade James to change his mind. What if she couldn't? Did she love him enough to sacrifice her baby? Give up her final chance of being a mother? She gently pressed her palm to her tiny bump. This baby was relying on her for everything. She closed her eyes and silently promised to never let it down. Sally tapped on her door and brought in the post. Kate opened her eyes.

'You okay?' Sally asked.

'I'm fine. How are the plans for the Shapeshifters escape room event coming on?'

'All good. Their marketing woman, Izzy, has had a look at the list you sent her and would like to have a look round Emergency Exit in Luton with you.'

'That's fine, I'll get in touch with Rupert and arrange it. Anything else?'

'James is still insisting we use this company, Wigwam, for some of our graphic design. Says he worked with the MD years ago and really rates him.'

'Fine, I'll let him have that one, but the decision about how much we use them is mine. I'd rather stick with the local company for our everyday work.'

'I agree with you. What happened to supporting small businesses in the community?'

'He probably wants to help a few mates out. They're welcome to do all our whizzy animations on websites and presentations, but that's it.'

'Is James coming in to the office today?'

'I'm not sure. He's gone to this meeting in London. I think it could take all day.' Had Sally guessed they were barely talking? Perhaps it was obvious when they weren't getting on. 'It's Mum's first "Lifestyle" appointment today, so I'll be leaving in about half an hour.'

'Oh, of course, I hope it goes well. I'm making coffee, want one?'

'Please.' She sifted through the pile of letters and picked one out that was stamped on the front with the blue NHS logo. She wasn't due any more appointments yet. Why would it be sent to work? She tore it open and took out a letter. A leaflet fell out of the middle: *All Your Questions Answered About Having a Termination*. What the fuck? She opened the letter: a hospital consent form for having an abortion. This must be James's idea. She ripped it in half.

'Here we are.' Sally came in with her coffee.

Kate scooped the papers into the envelope and stuffed it all in her bag.

'Are you okay?' Sally put the mug down.

Kate held her hands together to stop them trembling. She took a minute before she spoke, deciding what to do next.

'Sorry, I think I'd better leave now, pick Mum up before the lunchtime traffic.'

If James wasn't going to change his mind, this could mean the end for them.

—

'Sit yourself down, Mum, I'll warm us up some butternut squash and sweet potato soup.'

Elizabeth looked out of place next to the shiny granite surfaces and clean lines in Kate's kitchen. She tried to perch on a bar stool with the help of her stick, but it was too awkward for her, so she pulled a chair out from under the dining table.

'Are you all right?' Kate glanced over her shoulder. She ladled the soup into a saucepan. The round trip to the hospital and back had taken almost two hours. She'd been so tempted to text James about the leaflet and form but thought it would be better to save it until he got home. As soon as they'd had lunch, she would need to catch up on work emails, finalise details of a wine tasting event they were organising for a firm of solicitors.

'It's all going round in my head; everything they said, there's so much to think about,' Elizabeth said.

'You need to take one day at a time.' They'd given her mother the results of the ECG, which showed evidence of a silent heart attack a few months ago. Possibly around the time Dad died.

'Did you see some of the women in there? They looked so old. Do I look like that?' she said, patting her hair.

'That doesn't mean… look, you're relatively fit and healthy for seventy-nine.' Her mother looked tiny sitting at the huge table. No longer quite the ogre she remembered. 'You're as tough as old boots, Dad used to say, didn't he?'

Elizabeth smiled faintly. She shifted her wedding ring back and forth over the groove of hardened skin.

They sat in silence, listening to the ticking of the wall clock. When Kate was growing up, she could talk about everything with her dad, but rarely spent time alone with her mother for fear of saying something that would rile her or invite close questioning. She could never relax and enjoy her company. There was always something wrong.

'Have you heard from him again?' Elizabeth asked her. At least they were united in one respect, never wanting to speak his name, but for very different reasons.

'He's messaged me a few times, but I think I've put a stop to it.'

'Do you owe him all that money? Didn't buy a house together, did you?'

'Nothing like that, Mum. Honestly, it's nothing to worry about.'

'You never said how it ended.'

'Because it was so long ago and there's nothing to say.'

Somewhere in one of the quiet back lanes a dog barked. Kate stirred the thick orange mixture and inhaled the sweet, spicy smell.

Elizabeth cleared her throat. 'You've told James about the baby then?'

Kate looked up, picturing the ripped-up form in her bag.

'Didn't take it too well?'

'He doesn't want me to keep it, no.' Kate tasted the soup; it was only lukewarm.

'And you do, at your age?' Elizabeth's eyes shone, still enjoying an insulting dig.

'I can't bear the thought of…' Kate swallowed, 'anyway, why not?' She sliced a half baguette into chunks. The soup was developing a skin across its surface. She stirred it again.

'I think you should keep it, but it would have been easier having a baby when you were younger.'

'Yeah, thanks for that.'

'I lost a baby once.' Elizabeth hunched over.

Kate frowned.

'Five and a half months gone.' Her voice became so quiet Kate wasn't sure she'd heard her correctly.

'A few years after you.'

'You never said.' The photo in the hall of her parents in Trafalgar Square sprang to mind.

'It was such a surprise when we found out. We didn't think we'd ever be blessed.' Elizabeth gave a thin smile. 'But it wasn't meant to be. Ray so wanted a son. We'd have named him Edward.'

Blessed? That wasn't a term Kate ever thought she'd hear her mother use. She rubbed her forehead and tried to imagine a half-brother – taller than her, handsome, funny and caring. Her life would have been transformed. Elizabeth would have been so much happier. Perhaps her dad would have been more able to accept she wasn't his. A dragging sensation pulled at her chest. Her mother's words still chimed in her head as clear as the day she'd spoken them, sitting at the kitchen table smoking a cigarette. Ray in his chair opposite her, packing tobacco into his pipe and Kate coming in the back door with a basket of dried washing from the line.

'I need to tell you both something important,' she'd announced, tapping her cigarette on the cut-glass ashtray. 'I think you're old enough to take it in.'

Kate had frowned, side-eyed her dad for a clue, but he'd simply raised his eyebrows.

'You can stop worrying about cancer because Ray is not your real dad.' Her mother flicked the ash off her cigarette and drew in a lungful of smoke.

Ray stared at his wife as though she'd set herself on fire.

'What in heavens name are you talking about?' His throat caught on the last word.

'I'm sorry, but it's the truth and I can't let her carry on thinking she might die young like your sister. I wish I could have told you sooner, but I couldn't risk you leaving us.'

'What do you mean? I'd never have left you.' Ray stumbled on every word and Kate wished she could disappear. It had only been four months since her aunt had died from breast cancer and she'd thought about little else, worrying if that would be her future too. But now there was this new reality – her lovely daddy wasn't her dad at all.

'I was already twelve weeks pregnant when we got together. I had no idea, I might add.'

Kate would never forget the moment her dad looked round at her, frowning as though he didn't recognise her any more.

'Who is my dad then?' Kate's voice squeaked past the lump in her throat.

Her mum hesitated, glancing at Ray before she spoke.

'His name was John and he emigrated to Australia.'

Her dad's shoulders slumped; mouth lopsided as though he'd suffered a stroke.

'What do you mean, was?' Kate asked.

'I heard he died in a car crash soon after.'

Kate had sobbed and fled from the kitchen up to her room and thrown herself on the bed. All her life she'd believed she took after Ray. A father who was kind to her, gentle and loving with strong family values, but now she didn't know who she was. Did she have traits from her real dad – what was he like? Who was he? Why hadn't her mother stayed with him? Had she thought of getting an abortion, of not telling Ray about it rather than live with this lie?

During the days after, Ray had kept to himself, not speaking to either of them unless he had to. He didn't hug her as readily, and when he did there was an almost undetectable hesitation. She'd often caught him examining her face, no longer daddy's girl. Perhaps wondering how much she looked like her real dad. Her mother stomped round the house, clearly regretting telling them the truth, expecting them both to have accepted it without such a fuss. She withdrew from Kate too, hardly speaking, making sure the radio or the television was on in the background, telling her to shush if she uttered one word. Kate felt like a stranger, rootless. Leaving had been her only option.

'You look tired, Mum, why don't you have a lie down before we eat?' How much easier to share all this with a sibling. She tried to picture what her brother Edward would have looked like, standing with them now, comforting their mother. Why was her life full of longing for things she could never have?

They heard the shuffle of letters being pushed through the letterbox followed by a thud. Kate went out to the hall and picked up the post. She flicked through the pile as she walked back to the kitchen. Junk mail and bills. No NHS letters. Why get it sent to work?

Elizabeth tapped her nails on the table. 'I need you to contact the bank for me about your dad's account. I tried to get through but there are all sorts of numbers to choose and I ended up getting in a muddle then cut off. Why don't they have real people answering the phone anymore?'

'Haven't you closed his account?'

'I wrote to them to do that, but then I noticed a large sum has been going out of his account every month for the last few years. I want to know who and what it was for.'

'Dad must have said something about it?'

Elizabeth shook her head. 'Not a word. It's drained most of our savings.'

'Show me his statements when I drop you at home and I'll look into it.'

'I think I might go up.' Elizabeth followed Kate up to the spare room.

'There's a box of junk down here for the charity shop if you want to have a rummage through, see if there's anything you want.'

Downstairs, Kate gave the soup a final stir, put the lid on and turned off the hob. She checked her mobile. No new messages. It seemed that the five thousand pounds had satisfied him; for now, anyway. She stood still for a moment, thinking she'd heard an odd sound like a cat meowing. At the foot of the stairs, she half expected to see her mother standing at the top.

'Mum?' she called out, but her voice trailed off. She put a foot on the bottom stair, and hesitated. If she called again Elizabeth would complain that she couldn't move any faster. Kate slowly climbed the stairs. Halfway up, her head level with the landing floor, she stopped. There was a strip of bright daylight across the bottom of the spare room door but no sign of movement. Her gut told her something wasn't right. She reached the top of the stairs and barged into the room.

Elizabeth was sitting on the chair in the corner, her head hung low as if she'd nodded off to sleep.

'Mum, are you okay?' Kate rushed across the room.

Elizabeth raised her head. Her mother was crying.

'What is it, Mum, what's wrong?' Kate knelt next to her, but Elizabeth stared into space, her skin grey, eyes shadowy. The main box for the charity shop lay untouched, but a shoebox next to it, with all her old bits of jewellery and trinkets, was open.

'Mum?' She tried to rouse her again by squeezing her arm, but there was no response. A white satin jewellery box decorated with seed pearls she'd received for her tenth birthday was on top, the glue now discoloured yellow. It contained all sorts of odd earrings and chains.

Her mother was clutching something in her hand.

'What's that, Mum?'

Elizabeth snapped out of her trance and fixed her gaze upon Kate.

'You stole this from me.' Elizabeth shook her fist.

'What is it?'

Elizabeth opened her palm to reveal a tiny silk purse with the initials M.L. embroidered on the front.

'I... I don't remember seeing this before.' Kate's face felt hot. She peered at the tiny object, not much bigger than a box of matches.

'I've been wondering where it was for years, decades. I've searched everywhere.' Her mother's voice crackled. She was visibly shaking.

'I'm so sorry, I—'

'And all the time, *you* had it.' She pointed at Kate.

'But the initials...?'

'It's mine.' Her fingers closed around it.

'I don't know how it got there.'

But her mother wasn't listening. She opened the purse and took out a cream plastic disc with the number 23 carved into it. She smoothed her thumb across its surface, shutting her eyes.

'Mum?'

'Always stealing from me.' Her mouth made a drooping shape as though she'd eaten something bitter. 'Take, take, take.'

'That's not true!' Kate couldn't think what this was about. What did it mean?

Her mother put the disc back in the purse. 'And all that money I'd saved for a holiday. What made you think you deserved it more?'

'We've been through this and I've paid you back.'

'You can't erase what you did.' She jabbed her finger at Kate. 'You've no idea, do you…?' Her face contorted into a grimace. She caged her face in her fingers. 'This is the only thing…' She took her hands away and glared at Kate, '…the only thing I have from my mother… that I've ever had.'

A sudden chill ran through Kate.

'You're a spoilt, spoilt girl!' Her mother shouted.

Kate stepped back as if caught in the backdraught of a passing juggernaut.

'You had everything, everything handed to you.' Her mother glared at her. Kate had the urge to run down-stairs and out of the house, but her mother rose and came towards her. Kate backed out of the room; the door slammed in her face.

Kate stood on the landing wondering how she'd managed to upset her mother yet again.

The memory of a hot summer came to her. She was picking tomatoes in the baking hot greenhouse with her dad, the bitter smell of vines on her fingers. She'd asked him if Elizabeth was her real mum.

'Don't ask such stupid questions,' he said, showing a rare glimmer of anger.

'But why doesn't she like me?'

'Of course she likes you.'

'Why don't I have grandparents?'

'Your mother lost her parents when she was very little.' He hadn't looked at her when he said it, which left no room for further questions. But he made it clear that she must never ask Elizabeth anything. She remembered wishing for a breeze to roll in and carry away the sour stench of the geraniums under the workbench and how deceptively pretty they looked.

It wasn't until years later that Kate asked her father again about her mother's parents. He was digging a grave for her dog, Jerry, in a shaded corner of the garden. 'Were they old like Jerry?' she'd asked. 'We don't honestly know, love,' her dad had told her. But the unsatisfactory answer hung above their heads. She wondered why she couldn't ask her mum about it. She'd helped him wrap Jerry's body in his favourite blanket, then placed him in the grave with his collar on top. Tears dampened her cotton dress when he handed her Jerry's name tag then hugged her. She'd held him as tight as she could.

The bedroom door burst open, jolting Kate out of her daydream.

'Take me home,' her mother demanded.

'But lunch...'

'Now!' Her mother's hand tensed claw-like round her stick.

Kate made a hasty descent down the stairs.

She drove to her mother's house in nearby St Albans without either of them speaking. Kate pretended she was listening to the radio, but her mind kept drawing her away, tunnelling deeper into the slip of memories, trying to recall taking the silk purse.

When they arrived, her mother didn't want any help getting out. She took her time turning in her seat and pressing down on her stick as she stood up then slammed the car door. Not even a glance back or a thank you. All the old bad feelings and difficulties between them were still there. Their relationship had snapped in two on the day she took her mum's savings and left with a boyfriend they didn't approve of. James could spin it how he liked but the truth was things between her and her mum were worse than ever. Wasn't she kidding herself hoping they could repair it? Elizabeth was never going to be the mother that she needed. What if she turned out to be the same? She touched her bump. Where did that leave this little one?

She stayed in her car on the drive, making sure her mother got in okay. She rummaged in her bag for her mobile still on silent. There was one message emblazoned in capital letters across the screen.

I WISH YOU WERE DEAD!

The words pounced at her. Kate held her thumb on the pad to unlock her phone, hand shaking. First the word 'Bitch' emblazoned in lipstick across her windscreen and now this, taking it to a whole new level. It had to be him, didn't it? The photo he sent of them on the beach when they were a couple, the letter, all the text messages paled compared to this. All since she'd bumped into him at Sopwell House. But it can't have been a coincidence him being there; he must have hunted her down to demand a ridiculous amount of money from her. Maybe it wasn't enough. What was he going to do next? She shivered.

Hang on. How could this be? She didn't recognise the number. It wasn't his. Unless he was using another phone on purpose to disguise himself. Why would he bother? He hadn't cared so far.

> Who is this?

She texted. She waited a few moments, but no reply came, so she texted again.

> I know this is you, Paul. Stop NOW or I'm going to the police!

Little bubbles appeared as though he was about to reply, but nothing came up. No laughing emojis, no skull and crossbones. If it wasn't him then who was this? She pictured a finger jabbing each threatening letter on a keypad. Sod this. She pressed the call button. As soon as it connected she shouted down the line, 'What the fuck are you playing at, Paul?'

A digger or something rattled in the background.

'Paul say something. Come on. Why are you doing this? I said I'd pay you.'

The line went dead.

Shit. If it wasn't him then who the hell was this? Who had he told? Who else knew her darkest secret?

Chapter Thirteen

Elizabeth shut the front door and listened as Kate drove away. She collapsed into the chair at the telephone table until the pain in her chest had gone and her breathing returned to normal. Deep in her coat pocket, her hand clasped the tiny silk purse. The disc she'd carried with her every day of her life until she was fifteen. She pulled it out. Her fingers fell open, revealing its treasure. She brushed the purse against her dry lips. In another life, she had merely been a number: twenty-three.

For lunch she heated up a tin of hooped spaghetti in a saucepan. The tasteless pieces slid down her throat. Leaning into the wireless, she tried to catch the name of a piece of music she ought to know. *You can tell me, can't you, dear?* She pictured Ray sitting opposite her, hands dancing about conducting. *Serenade for Strings*, by Tchaikovsky popped into her head. She thanked him with a nod.

A loud banging gave her a start. She gripped her stick. Was it outside? There it was again. Ray must have forgotten his key. She shuffled to the front door but stopped dead. Daft, it couldn't be Ray. She reached for the wall to catch her breath. The impatient thumping started again. It'll be Kate. Come to say sorry. It was an effort to reach for the latch with the pain in her chest. A man was standing in the porch, grinning at her. Something about him scratched her memory.

'How are you, Liz?'

No one ever called her that.

'You look well.' He stepped over the threshold forcing her to move aside, unable to stop him.

'Got a bit of business to discuss with you, if you're not too busy?' He swaggered into the hall.

'Is it Paul?' Her voice came out diluted, as though she was only half there.

'That's it. You remember me then?' He towered over her, reeking of a sickly aftershave mixed with burger on his breath. He seemed bulkier, face rounder and darker than she recalled.

'She's not here.' Elizabeth's knees trembled. Her body prickled in a sudden cold sweat.

'Nah, it's you I came to see.'

'What do you want?'

'Let's sit down, shall we?'

She turned towards the kitchen and he strode ahead, opening the door.

'You put your feet up. I'll stick the kettle on.' He grabbed her elbow, fingers pressing into her thin flesh as he steered her into a chair.

'Sorry to hear about Ray.' He turned the tap on full and filled the kettle, splashing water all over the draining board.

Words gathered in her mouth. She clenched her teeth like a dog ready to bite.

'He was a decent sort. Always helped me out with my camper, didn't he?'

The pain in her chest had dulled to an ache.

'I'd have visited sooner, but you know how things are between me and Katie.'

'She left you. I knew she would,' she said triumphantly.

'Is that what she told you?' He roared with laughter. For a second, she saw his pock-marked teenage face, the cocky flick of his hair.

'What do you want?' Elizabeth ground her teeth together. Funny how some people never changed.

'She owes me a lot of money as it goes.' He switched the kettle off and poured boiling water in the teapot. 'That's a turnaround, isn't it? Bet you weren't expecting that.' He clapped his hands together in a single gunshot sound. Elizabeth jumped.

'What can she possibly owe you for? She's done very well for herself since she left you.' She clung to the top of her stick.

'Oh right. Best pals now, are you?' He stirred the tea then chucked the spoon in the sink with a loud clatter. 'Told you the whole story, has she?'

Elizabeth watched the pulsing muscle in his cheek, wondering what was coming.

'She's not being straight with you, Liz,' he said over his shoulder, a cheery note in his voice.

'I don't believe you.'

He spun round. 'That's right, she could get banged up for what she did.' His Cheshire cat grin slid up both sides of his face.

Her vision darkened at the edges. She blinked it away. 'You're lying!' she growled, the words scraping her throat raw.

He exaggerated lifting his eyebrows. 'No. Don't think so.'

'She would have told me if she'd done something serious,' she lied. Every image, conversation, thought and memory launched into a twister in her mind. What could Kate have done?

'You two were never close though, were you?'

Sweat collected under her arms, round her neck. He must have been waiting all these years to get back at her.

'Ray knew about it. I guess he didn't tell you either?' He took two mugs from the cupboard.

She hoped this was his idea of a sick joke because she couldn't for one minute believe that Kate *and* Ray would have kept something important from her. Lied to her.

'Yeah, I said to Ray he ought to tell you, but he didn't want you getting upset.'

A distant thunder was approaching in Elizabeth's head. She gripped the arm of her chair. 'What do you want?' Her voice was deeper now; she'd found herself.

'You need to tell Kate to pay up sharpish. She's dragging her feet. Tell her, if she thinks five grand is enough to keep me quiet, she's very much mistaken. That's it really. I'm guessing she doesn't want me to expose her secrets to everyone.'

'I think you had your pound of flesh long ago.' She struggled to keep her voice steady.

'No need to be like that, is there? I'm trying to do this the nice way. I could always take Kate to court instead.'

'Are you threatening me?' Her hands were icy stiff.

'I only want what's owed to me.' He leaned against the sink, wisps of steam from the boiled kettle rising next to him.

'You're lying. She doesn't owe you anything.'

'I could always tell you what she did, then you can decide.' He shrugged.

'Get out of my house.' She pushed down on her stick and stood up.

'All right, all right, keep your hair on.' He backed away.

'Get out!' Elizabeth shrieked, her whole body shaking. She held her stick up like a gun, following him all the way into the hall.

'Don't think this is the end of it,' he snarled, disfiguring his face.

He slammed the door so hard behind him it shook the house down to its foundations. Elizabeth struggled to catch her breath; the pain in her chest spread down her arm.

What if he was telling the truth and Kate had done something terrible? Maybe that was the reason why she had stayed away so long?

Chapter Fourteen

James's car was on the drive when Kate arrived home. She parked behind him and switched off the engine. She checked all her mirrors for any sign of movement. Brambles were beginning to choke the rose bushes in the front garden. Anyone could hide in there if they wanted to. She needed to get out here one afternoon and hack them down. They'd been lucky to find this house near the station in Boxmoor at such a good price. It was a safe area as long as you didn't have an ex-boyfriend hunting you down or whoever else he'd told. All the way home she'd tried to work out who could be threatening her if it wasn't Paul. His mother? Someone from the hospital? One of their old neighbours or friends? She'd moved away from the Isle of Wight, having only lived there for a short time with Paul, and she'd been careful not to keep in touch with anyone.

The car clicked as it began to cool down. She felt exhausted and still shaken by the anonymous message and the silence on the phone. It had been days since she'd felt this nauseous. Was it anxiety? It seemed different to morning sickness. She checked over her shoulder before opening the front door.

In the hallway, she could hear the shower on and was grateful for the few minutes' grace before she had to face James. Still reeling from Elizabeth's accusations, she couldn't bear another fight.

A sketchy memory of the purse on her mother's dressing table long ago came back to her. But perhaps she was imagining it. She didn't remember taking the thing and, if she had, she'd never have known its sentimental value. If only her mother would tell her what had happened to her parents and what the significance of the purse was. Maybe the initials M. L. were her grandmother's? But she didn't know her name, had never seen a photo of her.

The shower switched off. Moments later, the wet-room door opened, and a steamy waft of musky black pepper drifted towards her. She reached for a satsuma from the fruit bowl, dug her nail in and peeled it.

'Any coffee going?' James asked, wearing only his boxer shorts.

She shook her head, a piece of satsuma in her mouth. He switched on the kettle. Resting against the workbench next to her, he stroked her cheek with the back of his hand. She longed to put her arms round him. Instead she turned away.

'Are you in the office tomorrow?' He took a couple of satsuma segments from her.

'Of course I am.' She swung round. 'Why wouldn't I be?'

'It's not good all the chit chat in the office about the amount of time you're spending away.'

'What? I've been working from home on and off because of going to the hospital, you know that. They know that. We're equal partners in this business, so surely I can decide?'

'I know, but I'm worried it's not good for morale, especially when I'm out of the office as well.' He took two mugs out of the cupboard and scooped ground coffee into the filter.

'There's no one else to take my mother to her appointments.'

'I realise that.' He poured boiled water in and shut the lid. Kate passed him a teaspoon.

'If you let me explain to people what's going on…' She sat at the kitchen table in the hope that James would join her, but he stayed where he was, shifting his weight from one foot to the other. He poured the drinks and put hers on the table.

'You don't want people to know I'm pregnant, do you?'

He picked up his mug and blew into it. The steam rolled off and evaporated.

'Tell me I'm wrong?' She opened her handbag. 'I take it you're behind this?' She slapped the NHS envelope on the table.

James frowned at her and opened it, taking out the ripped-up pieces.

'Hey, hang on. I did not send you this.'

'No, the hospital did. But you gave them my name, didn't you?'

'No, I did not. I wouldn't do that.' He screwed his face up in disbelief.

'But you told me I should be going to the clinic.'

'It doesn't mean I rang them.' He sounded incredulous.

'Fine. So who else would it be? Only Mum and Susie know. Neither thinks I should abort our baby. Only you.' She twisted in the seat away from him. He reached out to her shoulder, but she jerked away.

'Look, I've been thinking about everything and…' His voice trailed off.

'Have you?' The words sprang out of her mouth. She wished she didn't sound so desperate.

'The thing is…' A faraway expression came over him as though imagining her reply. He gripped the work surface behind him. 'We need to think about who will step in for you when you have the baby and I thought Jasmine would fit the bill.' He stood with one foot on top of the other.

'So you've accepted the baby? I can't understand you sometimes.'

'You told me you're going to keep it, so what am I supposed to do?' He pressed his fingers on the counter so hard, the tips of his nails turned white.

She'd pushed him into a corner. It wasn't exactly the outcome she'd hoped for. She took a gulp of coffee. It tasted bitter, too much coffee, not enough milk. She'd seen the way all the men looked at Jasmine – her sleek hair that moved like a sheet of black satin, her neat exotic curves. Now James seemed to be falling under her spell too.

'The point is, Jasmine is easily the best qualified.'

'Is this negotiable at all?'

'We'll make the decision together, of course we will.'

'I won't be on maternity leave that long. I could come back after six weeks.'

'But it's still a whole six weeks and then there's the couple of weeks before it's born. The only other possible candidate is Steve.'

Suddenly Steve seemed like an excellent choice to fill her role. 'So does all this mean you've accepted we're having the baby?' Kate felt like she'd taken an impulsive dash across a bed of hot coals. She held her breath waiting for his answer. But James looked at her as though she'd spoken to him in Russian.

'Well, here's the thing, why don't we have a bit of space to think things over?'

Kate tipped her head and imagined her brain sliding along with it.

'Mac says I can stay at his for a while, until you… you know…'

'Come to my senses?'

'That wasn't what I was going to say.'

'No? But that's what you meant.' He may as well have thrown her in a washing machine on full spin she felt so dizzy. 'I can't believe you've discussed this with Mac before me.' She traced the route of a surface scratch across the melamine table. The depth of the groove was so slight it could only be seen when the light bounced off it at a certain angle. 'Is this anything to do with Jasmine?'

'Don't be bloody ridiculous.'

'Sounds like you've already made your decision.' She rubbed the scratch with her thumb in the vain hope of erasing it.

'I thought it would help if we had some time apart that's all.' He had the gall to smile.

'You're leaving me?' Kate raised her voice and sat upright.

'I'm *not* leaving you.'

'Sounds like it to me,' a sob escaped her lips.

'We both need to think this over carefully.'

'Are you serious? Is this anything to do with what happened with you and Susie?'

'Of course not.' He crossed his arms.

'So why did you keep that from me?'

'I didn't realise I had.'

'Being pregnant is not an illness. It's not going to go away.'

'See this as a little break from each other so we can both think about it clearly. We both need to be on the same page.'

'I could actually do with your support right now.' She willed herself not to cry.

'But you've still not told me what's brought all this on?'

'What do you mean, "brought this on"?'

'I thought we understood each other, wanted the same things in life, this not being one of them.' He finished his coffee.

'You're not listening to me!' Kate stood up.

'I am, it's just—'

'It's not some crazy notion I've dreamt up. I didn't plan it,' she interrupted. 'I'm pregnant with our baby. It's alive and already perfectly formed. Here, look at the scan picture.' Kate grabbed her handbag from the back of the chair and dug out the hazy black and white square of paper. 'We can't just get rid of it. This is our son or daughter. Part of you and part of me joined together.'

James glanced at the scan. She willed him to be amazed but he frowned.

'We talked it through, neither of us wanted children, so I don't understand where this change of heart has come from. You know our lives would never be the same.'

'And why does that have to be a bad thing? Why are you so against having children?' she shouted.

'Hang on, sorry to be harsh but it's you that's always insisted you were, and I quote, "definitely not cut out to be a mother".'

'Do not push the blame on me. If I can decide to give it a go, so can you.' She stormed out of the room.

Upstairs, Kate threw herself on the bed. Why wouldn't he budge on this? What if she couldn't talk him round? She heard him answer the front door. Minutes later he stood in their bedroom doorway with a box of flowers in one hand and a bundle of letters in the other.

'Secret admirer?' He raised an eyebrow and laid the box on the bed next to her. 'A letter here for you as well, from…' he turned the envelope over before handing it to her, '…who do you know on the Isle of Wight?'

Oh God, Paul again. She tried not to snatch the letter from James. She had no intention of opening it in front of him, so she tucked it under her leg. And flowers? What was he playing at?

'So when are you going to Mac's?'

'Today if that's okay with you?'

'Well it's not, obviously.'

'Look, I spoke to him earlier. He's going away on business for a few days. This will give us both time to consider our options.' He opened his wardrobe.

How could he have made plans without speaking to her? She tried to swallow the lump in her throat. They'd always been solid, hadn't they? Surely that counted for something in all this.

'How long do you think you'll be gone?'

'Let's see how we go, shall we?' He held up five shirts on hangers hooked over his fingers.

'I know it's a shock for you, it is for me too, but we're having a baby and we need to do this together.'

He strode into the bathroom and the door clicked shut.

She pressed her hands onto her hips. How was she supposed to handle this level of stubbornness? He was usually so open to trying new things, being flexible and considering all points of view. One of his mantras was, if something wasn't working, try a different way. But maybe that was the trouble: he loved their lives as they were, and he didn't see the need to bring a baby in to disrupt it.

When he came back out, his washbag was zipped and bulging. The telephone rang twice before the answerphone kicked in. The message couldn't be heard from upstairs.

'James, just listen to me a second.'

He threw her a cursory glance.

'I know it was really difficult for you growing up, but just because your parents—'

'Adoptive parents,' he cut her off.

'Okay, adoptive parents – just because you didn't get on with them doesn't mean—'

'Didn't get on? Are you joking me? Were you there? They were downright negligent.'

Kate sighed and raised her hand in submission. 'Okay, but I'm just saying that what happened to you doesn't mean you shouldn't have children of your own, that's all.'

He turned his back to her.

'Is that why you're so against having children? Is it something to do with Ben, why you don't see him any more?'

'Enough, enough! I do not want to talk about this.' He waved his arm aloft.

For a split second she imagined him as a child doing the same thing. She sighed and slid Paul's letter under her pillow.

'I'm going downstairs.'

She took the box of flowers with her and opened it in the kitchen. Inside, suspended in a plastic case and tied to a large bulb of water was a single dark purple rose. A card in an envelope was tucked inside with 'Kate' written on the front. She ripped the envelope open. On a small card she read the words:

Counting down the days until you die.

A gasp escaped her lips. The card dropped from her fingers and swept out of sight under the fridge. Was this Paul's sick idea of a joke?

She shoved the box and the flower into the bin then checked out of the windows and the spyhole in the front door. There were so many bushes and trees, he could be hiding out there and she wouldn't know. She checked her phone. Nothing. In the living room, she pressed play on the answerphone.

'Kate, call me back as soon as you get this.' That was it, a strident message from her mother. She would have phoned again if it was urgent, wouldn't she? She dialled her number and stood at the window. A light flurry of snow floated to the ground, melting on impact. She counted the number of rings before hanging up: twenty. She redialled, but still no answer. Fine. She slammed the receiver down. She could not deal with her right now. Better to give each other some space. She'd call back later and try to clear the air.

James dumped his suitcase next to the sofa. He wore jeans and a polo shirt she'd bought him on their last holiday to New York.

'Perhaps I should go over there.'

'Have you had another row?'

'She accused me of stealing something from her, years ago. She went a bit crazy.'

'And did you take it?'

'I've no recollection of it, but it was in our pile for the charity shop, so God knows how it got there.'

'What is it?'

'A tiny silk pouch, a purse she called it, with a numbered disc inside.'

James frowned.

'It's been a long time since I've seen her so upset. She said her mother gave it to her.'

'I'm sure she'll contact you again when she's ready.'

'Like you, you mean?' Kate tossed the phone on the sofa.

'You know you can call me any time,' he said, coming towards her.

She pushed him away.

'I don't want us to not talk about things, that isn't the idea.'

'So why go? Why not stay here so we can work it out?'

'Because I think the time away will help put everything in perspective.'

'I know we said if this happened I'd have an abortion, but the reality is, I can't. I simply can't do it.'

'This is so not you, Kate: being a mother. You told me so many times that it was the last thing you wanted to be. You said it was for other people, remember?' He knelt in front of her and stroked her arms. 'We won't be able to fly off somewhere at a moment's notice or go out for dinner several times a week. There'll be dirty nappies and toys all over the place, screaming, crying and sleepless nights. Not to mention the cost, the responsibility, the worry. It's not what we planned for our lives, is it? What about retiring early, living abroad? This will change everything we'd hoped to achieve.'

'But I'm not sure those things are important to me any more. Susie has changed, I've changed, why can't you?'

'What about us as a couple?' He turned back to his suitcase.

'We can get through it, become stronger bringing up our child together.'

'You think it will be easy?'

'Is planning every detail of our future really living? Surely this is an unexpected gift.' Perhaps he thought he could talk her out of it, but the attachment she felt to this life growing inside her was beyond her own comprehension. She pressed her hand to her bump. They were talking about the life of an unborn child – a person. It didn't fit in with his Ralph Lauren tops and Armani jeans or her Karen Millen dresses and Prada handbags – suddenly everything they owned seemed pointless, worthless in comparison.

Yet everything they'd built up together could be saved in the next moment if she changed her mind, but a surprising determination had embedded itself in her heart and couldn't be prised out, and anyway, she didn't want it to.

He picked up his bags and headed for the door. 'Nice single rose by the way. Who did you say it was from?'

'I didn't.'

'Why is it in the bin?'

'Because I don't know who sent it.'

'Maybe it is a secret admirer. Are you sure that baby's mine?' He grinned.

'I can't believe you just said that.'

'Sorry. Look, all I'm saying is take your time to think this through; it's not just about the first few months, it's about years down the line of responsibility and heartache.'

'You can't do this to me, James. I won't choose,' her voice rose as she followed him down the hallway. 'I want this baby and I want you too.'

After James had gone, the rattle of the front door rang in Kate's head; the invisible backdraught of all the words left unsaid swirled round her. Swallowing back the tears, she cupped her belly and reassured the baby that it was safe, Mummy could never get rid of it. She bolted the door top and bottom and checked the spyhole. There was no one around.

As she climbed the stairs she thought about the rose in the bin and the threatening note. Who other than Paul would write something so vile? What if they meant to do her real harm?

Chapter Fifteen

Upstairs, Paul's letter lay under her pillow like a sleeping bomb. She took it out, sliding a finger underneath the flap, tearing it along the seam. She paused before taking out a sheet of lined paper.

> *Kate,*
>   *I've been more than patient. I expect to see the*
> *full amount of money in my account by the end of*
> *the week or there will be consequences.*
>   *P*

Kate blinked at the words. She read it again and paced round the room. The same demand, but this time he was showing her he really did know where she lived. It was posted not hand delivered, but it didn't mean he wasn't lurking outside, watching her.

She thought of the time they'd lived together in a bedsit after she ran away from home, how exciting it was until they had to hide from the landlord when their rent was late. The flowery old bedsheet they'd used as a curtain had fallen down one evening. Paul pulled his boxers back on and they both laughed until they could hardly breathe as he climbed on a chair and tried to hang the sheet back up. A kitchenette and kettle in the corner of the room were their luxuries. The mattress on the floor and the shared bathroom up two flights of bare staircase were not so fun to get used to. Every night the front door banged followed by the loud voices of the other lodgers. A slippery path of junk mail littered the hallway and an arrest warrant for someone she'd never heard of was nailed to the wall. None of it had mattered because they'd been so in love. But she could never have imagined it would end so badly.

She'd have to dip into her own savings but how much more could she afford to send him?

Her mobile phone vibrated. James, thank God.

> Got here okay. Cat left a dead sparrow on the doorstep, not the best welcome. Hope you're okay, J xx.

He was treating this like one of his work trips, which strangely made her feel a little better. Should she tell him about the note with the rose and Paul threatening her? But then he'd want to know why, and she couldn't risk it.

She padded down to the kitchen, taking the mobile with her.

> Perhaps the cat thinks you need feeding

she texted. She poured herself an orange juice in a wine glass.

> Flat smells of cat's piss

came the reply.

Kate smiled.

Come home then!

She carried her drink into the living room. This time the mobile remained silent. She pushed it away and thought about texting Paul.

The mobile rang, making her jump.

'Kate…' James said.

'Have you cooked your sparrow supper yet? Or are you ringing for a recipe?'

'I prefer pigeon actually.'

'So, what are you having for dinner?' she asked, trying to stay cheerful and not let on how jumpy she was.

'A bottle of wine.'

'Oh.'

'Kate… I…'

'Come home, James.'

'I… I don't know how to deal with this,' he said.

'I need you here.' How could she admit she was nervous being in the house on her own? He'd want to know why and there was too much to explain, too much for her to lose.

'I do love you, you know that, don't you?' he said.

'Then don't do this, we can work it out.'

'Kate, this whole parent thing… I really can't do it.'

'You can, I know you can. We'll do it together.'

'I don't know. I'll call you tomorrow.'

'Please don't go.' She stopped short of pleading with him. If she admitted she was scared, wouldn't he come back straight away? The trouble was she'd kept this secret from him the whole time they'd been together. Telling him might have the opposite effect; he might leave for good, especially on top of struggling to accept the baby.

'We'll talk tomorrow.'

'Is it because you don't think I'll be a good mother?' she rattled out before he could hang up.

'Don't be silly,' he said, 'why would I think that?'

'You're sure?'

'How can you even ask that?'

'I just don't understand why you're so against it.'

Silence.

'It's difficult to explain.'

'Try, please.'

'I can't, I'm sorry.'

They said good night and hung up. Kate stared across the room with blurred vision. Her eyes rested on an early photo of them holding hands in front of a rhododendron at Kew Gardens. She'd already known then, after five intense months, that she was meant to be with James forever.

In the kitchen, she ripped up the note into tiny pieces and dropped them in the bin. She pulled the rose out and plucked each petal off one by one. Instead of smelling sweet they smelt sour, almost poisonous. Whoever it was trying to wreck her life, she needed to end it.

Chapter Sixteen

Elizabeth woke up on the sofa. The pain in her chest had left a dull ache. She pulled the sheets and blankets over her head to block out the noise of gushing tap water. She couldn't be sure if the man had gone. Had he helped her bring down the bedding? That was kind of him. The clock said eleven p.m. How could that be? It was safer down here. They wouldn't find her. The water slowed to an echoey drip, drip, drip. She plugged her ears with her hands and dragged herself up. At the window, she gazed at the stars in the plush velvet sky. One day she'd escape. Take Edward with her. She'd save him. Spilling through a seam in the universe came the sound of children singing, '*Silent Night*'.

She was standing in the death-cold church in her crisp white pinafore. Powder-puff breath streamed from their mouths. Edward's robin-red chest moved up and down as he belted out each verse.

She clung to the arm of the sofa and quietly sang along. The tears came hot and fast, but she didn't stop. Dear little Edward.

She pulled at the curtains until they covered the windows. A triangle of moonlight peeped through the crack at the top. She lay back down on the sofa and shut her eyes. Miss Dillard's face appeared so large she could see every pore on her flaky red-veined skin. Elizabeth gave a start, but her eyes wouldn't open. One by one the children marched to the side of the swimming pool. Joseph was first in line. He pegged his nose with his fingers, screwed up his eyes and jumped in. She shivered at the splash of cold water and prayed the line would never reach her. But each child followed in quick succession after him. A few were given a shove by Miss Dillard if they dithered too long. Elizabeth was last, as always, her knees knocking. She pressed her forefinger and thumb to her nose. The chlorine vapours smarted her eyes. Her baggy swim costume did nothing to prevent her shivering body turning to gooseflesh. Miss Dillard gave her a firm push, sweeping her clean off her feet. She entered the water with a stinging wallop. Water shot up her nose. The children's cries deadened as she sank deep underwater.

Time stopped.

She floated towards the surface and dared to open her eyes only to see a long stick prodded towards her. The hook end jabbed in her chest, pushing her so far down her hands touched the bottom of the pool as her mouth filled with water.

The loud ring of the telephone broke in. Elizabeth's eyes flicked open. She was sweating all over. She reached out and touched the soft lavender-smelling blanket and covered her ears until it stopped. But it started up again. Reluctantly, she climbed out of her warm cocoon, pulled the cable out of its socket in the wall and went back to bed to the quicksand of sleep.

A knock on the door woke her in an instant. She lay there unable to move. The knock came again, more forceful, in a little tune, rap-rap-rap-rap-rap. She sat up. Her eyes darted round the room. The triangle of sunlight cut through the darkness. Plates and cups were stacked on the table with half a loaf of bread and a butter knife. Had they been in while she was asleep? The knocks turned into thuds. The letterbox rattled followed by a woman's shrill voice shouting something. She sounded familiar. Elizabeth shouted back to go away. She started to shake and pulled the blanket over her head. When the noise stopped, she finally drifted back to sleep.

Chapter Seventeen

Kate was woken by someone knocking at the front door. After a few moments it started again, more urgently this time. She stumbled out of bed, glancing at herself as she passed the hall mirror: her face was net-curtain white, her hair a backcombed mess.

She opened the front door and squinted at Susie surrounded by a halo of sunlight.

'Oh, it's you,' Kate said. She had a nerve turning up uninvited. Why should she let her in?

'You look terrible, Kate. Do you know it's almost midday?' Susie pushed down on the pram handle and manoeuvered the wheels over the doorstep.

Kate had no choice but to step aside. She felt stupid standing there in her pyjamas, her hands lost in her nest of hair. Susie shut the door behind her.

'No work today?'

'I work from home on Fridays.' Kate spoke like a sullen teenager.

'Sorry, I didn't know.'

Kate didn't like her tone. If she expected her to be at work, what was she doing here? Hoping to see James on the sly? It had been almost two days since he'd left.

'I was working late and overslept if you must know.'

'You don't need to explain to me.'

Kate peered into the pram. Lily was fast asleep.

'I spoke to James this morning.' Susie fussed about with Lily's changing bag. 'I'll make some lunch; why don't you go and grab a shower?'

'You don't need to.'

But Susie was already in the kitchen taking a loaf of bread out of the fridge.

'It's no trouble, I want to help.'

'But I'm fine.'

'Kate...' Susie paused, bread knife in hand, 'I know James has walked out.'

'It wasn't like that. Is that what he told you?' Kate slumped into a chair and yawned.

'He said he's moved out for a while to give you both time to think, but sometimes that's a bloke's way of—'

'You make it sound worse than it is.'

'Did he tell you he's not eating?'

'Not exactly.'

'Well he's not. Anyway, I told him to grow up.'

Kate didn't answer.

'I think it's about time, don't you?' Susie examined Kate's face as she spoke. Probably hoping for a reaction.

'I need to ring my mum.' Kate forced herself out of the chair.

'Okay, but you know you can't bury your head.'

'Don't tell me what to do.' Kate glared at her.

'Oh.' Susie stopped. 'I'm sorry, have I upset you?'

Kate sloped off to the living room with Susie's words trailing after her like bad breath. She dialled the number. The monotonous dialling tone made her head throb. She rang off and tried again. It wasn't like her mother to ignore the phone for this long, especially when she'd asked her to call. She should have tried calling again sooner. What if she'd fallen over and couldn't reach it? She'd have to go round there.

After her shower, Kate went back to the kitchen in search of food. A mug of peppermint tea was ready for her on the table next to a plate of toast soldiers.

'Sorry. Automatic pilot.' Susie grinned. 'I was helping out at a toddler's party this morning, I'm still in little people mode.'

'I have to go out in a minute.' Kate turned the plate of toast to find a piece which wasn't soaked in butter.

'I need to go into town anyway. I promised James I'd call in on you.'

'He asked you to?' Perhaps they had other secrets between them.

'Well sort of. I called him to see if he would make it to badminton this week and he said he didn't have his kit with him, which is when he mentioned he was staying at Mac's place.'

'So you're checking up on me?'

'It's not like that.' Susie tidied away the butter and loaf of bread. 'Aw, did he send you flowers?' She smiled, pulling the cardboard box out of the bin and placing it next to the recycle box. She peered inside and took out the cellophane wrapping. 'Oh, do you know the flower is still in here?' She pulled out the remnants of the long-stemmed rose.

Kate wanted to scream at her to stop interfering. 'It wasn't from James so don't ask. And as you can see, I'm absolutely fine.'

'Okay.' She pushed the stem back in the box and closed the lid. Susie had her back to Kate now, hands deep in soapy water, washing Kate's dishes from the night before.

'I think it's good that you told him,' Susie said.

Kate swallowed a mouthful of tea. It tasted like a boiled sweet. Her palate seemed to be changing; she couldn't bear the smell of anything sugary.

'I mean he's going to have to make a decision now, isn't he?' Susie carried on.

'You told me he'd change his mind.' Why had she confided in her?

'He will, when he realises what he'll lose.'

'You don't know that. Why is he so against having a baby?'

Susie's hands stopped washing. 'Something happened to his brother Ben when they were kids. I know he blames himself for it.'

'I knew they'd fallen out, but he hasn't told me why.' Kate bit a toast soldier in half. Yet again, a shared secret between them.

'I'm sure he will when he's ready. He will come back to you,' Susie said over her shoulder, 'I promise.'

'So he's told you what happened?' Rage flared through her. Was there anything she didn't know about James?

'Years ago, yes.'

'How can you be so sure he's going to accept this baby when—' The cloying taste of cold butter was stuck to the roof of her mouth. She wanted to retch.

'I can see him now, being amazed at the sight of his own baby.' Susie gazed out of the window.

'Can you really?' She chucked down the piece of toast.

'It's so different when it's your own; the love is over-whelming.'

'How can you have the front to say all this?' Kate shoved the plate away.

'I'm sorry, have I done something wrong?' Susie twisted round, hands dripping.

'You and… James… were expecting a baby and he made you get rid it.'

A plate fell from Susie's hands and clunked into the sink. 'He told you that?'

'You never even mentioned you dated.' Kate pushed the plate further across the table.

'I couldn't see any point.'

'You both kept it from me. Pretended you were only friends.'

'We were young; it was a long time ago; there didn't seem any reason to bring it up.' Susie wiped her hands on a tea towel. 'It didn't mean anything.'

'Getting rid of a baby was easy, was it?'

'No, I didn't mean that. We agreed it was a mistake. He didn't want it and I didn't feel anywhere near ready or willing to be a mother.'

'So you happily told me he'd change his mind knowing full well he wouldn't want a baby, that he'd leave me if I didn't have an abortion,' Kate shouted.

'That's not true!' Susie came towards her, arms outstretched.

'Why are you always defending him?'

'I don't know, he's my friend. I care about him.'

'You mean you still have feelings for him?'

'Not like that. Honestly, Kate.' She wiped her nose. Was she crying?

'Okay, so tell me what really happened with his ex. Was it him that gave her the ultimatum, not the other way round?'

'No, what I said was true.'

Kate backed away. 'I think you should go.'

'Kate, please, I really think he'll be okay, given time. You should see the state he's in.'

'You've seen him this morning?' She blinked in disbe-lief. Another cosy little chat.

'He called in on his way to work. He's in a bad way.'

'And he sent you to check up on me.'

'He loves you more than anything.'

'Did he love you?'

'No not really, we thought it was love at first, of course we did, but we were kids, it wasn't serious.'

'But you got pregnant.' She ground her teeth. Her jaw clicked. The thought of James being intimate with Susie sent needles of jealousy searing through her. And they were still keeping each other's secrets. Susie knew more about James than she did.

'We both knew straight away that it wasn't what either of us wanted.'

Kate wanted to believe her, but why hadn't she told her sooner?

'I've not even told Harry.' Susie cast her eyes down at her trainers. 'You won't mention it, will you?'

Kate shook her head. She wasn't exactly the best person to preach about honesty. The truth could hurt people as she knew too well. If only she could talk to Susie about Paul, ask her what she should do. But how much could she trust her?

Their conversation was interrupted by the telephone ringing. Kate strode into the hallway.

'Mrs Marshall?' She recognised the voice but couldn't place it straight away.

'Speaking.' Kate pressed the receiver closer to her ear.

'It's Mrs Connell… your cleaner.'

'Oh yes, hello.'

'I've been on your mother's doorstep for the last fifteen minutes.'

'Oh, I'm sorry. Isn't she there?' Kate walked into the living room.

'She's in all right.' Then after a pause. 'Your mother won't let me in, Mrs Marshall.'

'Oh goodness.' Kate tried to grasp what Mrs Connell was saying. 'How odd. Are you sure?'

'I'm *very* sure.' Mrs Connell sounded exasperated.

'And she's definitely there?'

'I called through the letterbox and she told me to go away; how's that for you?'

'Really?' Strange, her mother had been pleased with the extra help.

'Well I never, I said to myself. How rude. Quite uncalled for, and she said a certain word – something I'm not able to repeat, I can tell you that much for nothing,' she paused, 'in all my years—'

'I'm so sorry,' Kate cut in. 'I can assure you this is not like her at all. It's very odd indeed. Look, you go home, Mrs Connell, and I'll come over to see what's going on.'

'Will I still be paid for today? I mean I've been standing here for quite some time and before that I was standing at the bus stop for at least twenty minutes all in all. It's a waste of my day. I could have been cleaning another house.'

'Yes, yes, don't worry, I'll still pay you and I'll be in touch again shortly. And thank you for letting me know, I do appreciate it.'

'Much obliged to you,' Mrs Connell said and rang off.

Kate took her coat off the peg and returned to the kitchen where Susie was finishing her drink. 'I have to go.'

'I need to get on too,' Susie said. 'I'm sorry you had to find out. I don't know what James was thinking. It's not something either of us is proud of.'

For a second their eyes met and the air round them dragged time to a halt.

'It's my mother,' Kate said, going back into the hall. She opened the cupboard under the stairs and pulled out James's badminton kit.

'I hope she's all right.' Susie took the bag from her.

Kate threw Susie a glance to tell her she wasn't about to share the details with her.

'I am really sorry.'

Kate held the front door open while Susie backed the pram out with Lily still asleep.

'I'll tell James you're fine then.'

'Tell him what you like,' Kate said and followed her out.

She locked the front door, got in her car and drove off.

Chapter Eighteen

A light rain suddenly became stabbing and drenched Kate as she ran from the car to her mother's porch. She closed the noise off behind her and took out the front door key. It seemed strange that her mother had let the angel's trumpets wilt and not mopped the chequered tiles. They were normally gleaming.

'Mum,' she called as she unlocked the front door. She stood and listened for an answer. The faint sound of music was coming from the kitchen. 'Are you here, Mum?' She took off her coat and hung it up, running her hand down the arm of her dad's tweed jacket next to it. Was her mother keeping it? In the mirror, she ruffled her wet hair in a half-hearted attempt at shaking off the rain.

Slowly, she opened the kitchen door. The sound of an orchestral version of Debussy's *Clair de Lune* filled the room, but her mother wasn't there. She switched off the radio and called out again. The shroud of silence gave no clue as to where she might be. Then, as if roused by the lack of noise, Elizabeth emerged from the living room, stooping in a strange shape over her stick, as if weighed down by a yoke across her shoulders.

'Mum, are you all right?'

'Careful,' Elizabeth whispered, putting a finger to her lips, 'they'll push your head under the water again.' She pointed to Kate's wet hair. 'Come in here with me.' She beckoned.

'Who are you talking about?' Kate checked round them. The living room felt too warm and stank of body odour and unwashed clothes.

'They'll be looking for you. Best stick with me.'

'Who will?'

'Don't be silly now, you're already soaked through.'

'That's because it's raining outside.' Kate had never seen her act so strangely before.

Her mother turned to her, finger to her lips. 'No need to be afraid. We're all in this together.'

They sat on the sofa in the darkened room, the strong musty smell hanging in the air. A hairline of light seeped through the velvet curtains. The trailing ivy on the plant stand in the corner looked half dead.

'They're all bullies.' There was fright in her mother's wide eyes.

'Who is? Who are you talking about?'

'The nurses of course.'

'There aren't any nurses here, Mum. Look, I'll show you, we'll go round the house together.'

'No,' Elizabeth grabbed the hem of Kate's skirt in her fist, 'you can't go up there, they'll try and drown you.'

Kate stood up.

'I won't let you!' Elizabeth shouted, holding on to Kate's arm.

'I'll be all right, I promise.'

'But that man might still be here.'

'What man? Mum, look it's okay, I'll stay with you, but I think I should call a doctor.'

'Not the doctor, not the doctor.' Elizabeth's eyes became wild and roving.

'Mum I need to use the phone.' Kate eased herself away from her. In the hall she picked up the telephone. The line was dead. She traced the wire under the table. It had been pulled from the socket. 'Why have you unplugged this?'

'It wouldn't stop ringing,' Elizabeth whispered, gripping the door frame.

'I was trying to ring you. You left a message asking me to call you. You said it was important. Don't you remember?'

Elizabeth didn't answer.

'This is silly. I'll call the doctor in my car.' Kate slipped on her coat, picked up her handbag and took the battered old address box with her.

In the driver's seat, she took out her mobile and pressed the letter 'D' in the line of alphabet tabs. The lid popped up revealing an ancient sheet of paper full of names and numbers underlined or crossed out. 'Doctor' was at the top of the second page. She dialled the number and asked for a GP to come to her mother's house.

'Is the patient mobile?' asked the morose voice on the end of the line.

'You mean can she walk? Then yes, I'd say so,' Kate said.

'So is she able to come to the surgery?' said the voice.

'Not really. I think she's… well it's hard to explain because she's not herself, she's not making sense, like she's delirious and her movements are restricted.'

'The doctors are very busy today, Mrs Marshall. I can put a request in for Dr Maltby to come out to your mother at the end of surgery, but bear in mind he has other visits to make—'

'Which will be what time?'

'This is assuming he is not called to a higher priority case.'

'But *this* is serious. How long will we have to wait?' Heat rose from her neck to her face.

'Surgery ends at five thirty p.m. He has scheduled visits until six thirty p.m., so anywhere between then and eight p.m.'

Kate looked at the car clock: 1.52 p.m. 'That's far too long.'

'There's no one else available.'

'Fine, don't bother.' Kate hung up and chucked the phone on the seat.

Back in the house, she tried to persuade her mother to get in the car so she could take her to A & E, but Elizabeth refused to leave. Kate went into the kitchen and shut the door. Should she ring James? Would this count as encroaching on their break from each other? But who else could she call who would understand? She dialled his number. The line was engaged, so she hung up. Damn, now what? A few seconds later, her mobile rang.

'You called?' James asked.

'Sorry, I didn't want to bother you, are you in a meeting?' She tried not to sound in a panic.

'About to go into one. Is everything okay?'

'It's Mum, I don't know what's wrong with her. I think she's delirious. She keeps talking about a nurse trying to drown her and something about a man being in the house.'

'Kate, Kate, stop a sec, have you called a doctor?'

'Yes, of course, but he wouldn't be able to get here for two hours, maybe more and she won't get in the car.'

'Call an ambulance.'

'But she won't leave the house.'

'You need to call an ambulance. They'll know what to do. I'll meet you at the hospital.'

'Will you?' A lighted fuse zipped through her body along with the ridiculous thought that perhaps she could persuade him to come home.

'I'll get there as soon as I can.' The line cut off.

Kate looked at her mobile and dialled 999.

–

When James arrived at the hospital, Kate waved him over. She was sitting in a side room of the emergency unit waiting to hear the doctor's verdict.

'She'll be all right.' James wrapped his arms round her.

'It was like she didn't know who I was.'

'Whatever it is, we'll deal with it.'

'When she didn't answer my calls, I assumed…'

'There's no point going over that now.' James covered her hands with his.

'But I should have called back sooner.'

A nurse walked into the room and crouched in front of Kate. She sat up and looked searchingly into the nurse's eyes.

'We suspect your mum has had a heart attack, which has triggered pneumonia.'

'Oh God. Is she going to be all right?' Kate clenched James's hand.

'We're still assessing her condition. Her temperature has gone sky high, which is why she is delirious. We need to stabilise her first.'

'Can I see her?'

'For a few moments. She may not recognise you.'

They followed the nurse into the emergency room and were ushered behind a curtain. Elizabeth's eyes were barely open on her stark white face, her body sunken and frail in a lightweight gown. Kate placed her hand next to her mother's. Elizabeth's fingertips touched hers.

A doctor spoke to them and pointed to a lightbox on the wall opposite the bed, showing the shadows on Elizabeth's lungs, partially filled with fluid.

'She's had pneumonia before, when she was ten,' Kate told him.

'We'll need to keep her in for a few days. As soon as we've got her temperature under control, we'll let you know.' The nurse showed them back into the waiting room.

Kate sat down and covered her face in her hands. 'This is my fault; I must have upset her so much.'

'Stop it, Kate,' James said gently, crouching in front of her. He rubbed his hands up and down her arms. 'You said you don't remember taking this purse, and you didn't know what it meant to her.'

'I had no idea. I wish she'd told me about her mother. How could I have known how important it was when she hasn't told me anything?'

'So, stop blaming yourself.' He kissed her forehead and held her in his arms.

It was gone midnight when the nurse came back to tell them that Elizabeth's condition had stabilised, and they could come back in the morning.

James walked Kate back to her car.

'Are you okay to drive?' He touched her arm.

She nodded. 'Thanks for coming.' He was always there when she needed him. When she reconnected with Mum and Dad, he was so good to them, they loved him straight away. And when Dad died, he was the one who helped them make the arrangements for Dad's funeral.

'I'll follow you back.'

'Don't you have a cat expecting you?'

'I think the cat can wait,' he said. 'I want to make sure you get home safely.' He hugged her and she nestled in the warmth of his soft wool jumper.

'I'm going to see if the cleaner will go to Mum's over the weekend. You should have seen the state of the place. Anyone would think we hadn't seen her for a week. She can't come home to it like that.' She shut her eyes, but the image of her frail mother wouldn't shift from her mind. Why did she think nurses were trying to hurt her, and who was the man she was talking about?

–

A cold wind whistled round the corner of the house, making the leylandii wave its languorous welcome. James wheeled the recycle bin up from the pavement to its place by the side gate. Kate checked her phone then unlocked the front door. She'd not had any more malicious messages in the last few hours and the silence was unnerving. Maybe now was the time to trust James and tell him about Paul, explain everything that had happened? Was it possible he'd understand? But if he didn't, if he found it impossible to forgive her, their lives together would surely be over, and she'd be left bringing up this baby on her own. He might even take the baby away and have it adopted. She glanced over her shoulder. Keeping him here tonight had been too much to hope for. James was already walking back to his car, one hand raised in goodbye.

Chapter Nineteen

Kate came home from work early on Monday so she could go to the hospital to see her mum. She was sitting at the kitchen table finishing an event plan on her laptop when the doorbell buzzed. The long insistent noise sent a bolt through her body. Her head tilted up like an automaton. Before she'd even risen from her seat, the rasping buzz sounded again. She wasn't expecting a delivery and it was too late for the post. A darker reason skidded across her mind. It couldn't be, could it? All this way? She rose and crept to the front door, spying in the hole only to see the back of a man's head. Her car parked on the drive would have given her away instantly. Could she pretend to be asleep? Out for a jog? She wished she had a dog who would bark incessantly so he'd think no one was home.

She peered in the spyhole again. It *was* him. Had he been watching the house? He could have seen her come in; knew she was on her own. He blinked back, making her jump, his all-seeing eye distorted in a tiny sphere. He continued to stare as though he could see the worst things about her deep in her soul; he knew everything. Her pulse pounded in her ears. James could have been here. What would she have done then? Why hadn't she paid him off when he'd given her the chance?

He pressed the buzzer again. Then it stopped. Would he go away? No doubt he'd return and then it could be when James was back. A thump rattled the front door giving her a start. He called out her name. She'd keep her hand on her mobile in her pocket, just in case. Taking in a shallow breath, she slid the chain across and opened the door an inch.

'What are you doing here?' she hissed, wondering how strong the metal links were that separated them.

'Let me in.' His flat tone demanded no answer.

'What do you want?'

'Come on, Kate, you know what it's about.' He pushed the door until the chain was taut. Any harder and it would snap.

'I've not had a chance to sort out any more money.'

'You've had plenty of time.'

A woman walking her dog across the street glanced over at them. Kate rose on her tiptoes and thought about calling out to her. But there was no way out of this. He knew too much. She unhooked the chain.

Paul shoved the door open and shouldered past her. Kate let out a silent trail of breath. Her lungs seemed to have stopped working. Thank God James was at Mac's.

'Stick the kettle on, I'm parched. You remember how I take my tea, don't you? Two sugars and a splash of milk.' He filled most of the kitchen doorway.

Silently, Kate followed him in. The musky scent of him filled the air. He sat on her chair, peering at her laptop. She slammed the lid down and shifted it out of his reach onto the counter behind her.

'Nice gaff. You've done all right for yourself.'

Kate knew better than to take it as a compliment. The quicker she could get this over with, the better.

'I could get comfortable here.' He grinned and put his feet up on the table. His football-style trainers, laced down one side, looked brand new.

'Aren't you working?' she asked.

'I am as a matter of fact. Run my own gardening business in Sandown. Plenty of work from all the retired people. You should send your mum down.'

'She's in hospital.'

'Oh. Sorry to hear that.'

Heat flushed over her. He had a bloody cheek coming here after everything he'd been putting her through.

'Didn't you get my note?'

'Yes, and the photo of us on the beach, the single rose with the nasty message.' She crossed her arms. It was still under the fridge.

He laughed. 'Hang on, I didn't send you any flowers. Must be from your secret lover.'

'Very funny.' Of course he would deny it. But it couldn't be anyone else. 'And what the hell were you doing daubing lipstick all over my windscreen?'

'You what?' He laughed, eyebrows raised.

'Oh yeah, pretend you don't know.'

'What are you talking about?'

'How dare you call me a bitch,' she shouted. 'You've sunk pretty low to write something like that.'

'I didn't.' He took his feet off the table.

'I don't believe you.' She pointed at him.

'Funnily enough I don't own any lipstick.'

'Don't mock me. I could go to the police.'

'Why don't you then if you're so fucking sure it's me?'

'And you've been sending me malicious messages from a different phone. Think you're clever disguising yourself, do you?' She picked up her mobile, opened the message

'I WISH YOU WERE DEAD' and shoved it under his nose.

'I don't know that number. I don't *have* another phone.' He'd dropped the mocking expression and actually looked serious.

'Call it.'

She pressed the number half expecting it to ring in his pocket, but it didn't. No one picked up, then it clicked off. No answerphone.

'But you sent this one, didn't you? "This is your final warning". And it was at the same time as the writing on my car. It can't be a coincidence, Paul. You're not fooling me.'

'That was about the money. What happened to your car has nothing to do with me, or the rose and the note.'

She sat in the chair opposite him. He had no reason to deny it, did he? If he was out to scare her, he'd be happy to admit it. Be pleased that his efforts were upsetting her. Who could it be then? There was no one else.

'What do you need so much money for anyway?'

'It's nothing compared to what you left me to deal with. I could ask for a whole lot more.' He gave a cheeky smile. He still knew how to play her.

'I told you I haven't got any more money ready.'

'You've kept me waiting so I'm afraid it's gone up to thirty-five grand now.'

'What? You can't do that. I don't have that sort of money just lying around.'

'Can't you sell a few designer handbags? What about your husband? He must have a bit tucked away.'

'Leave him out of it. I'll sort something out.'

'Ha!' He pointed at her. 'Not told him, have you?'

Kate didn't want to answer when he already had so much against her.

'Poor bloke doesn't know what he's got himself into, does he? Perhaps I should have a quiet word with him.'

'I said I'd pay you.'

'How long you been married?'

'A long time.'

'Good to you, is he? Could have been us. We were the perfect pair, remember? Everyone said so.'

They had made a striking-looking couple in the early days when they were carefree twenty-year-olds. Her with long dark curls and short skirts and Paul with his George Michael designer stubble and permed hair.

'I remember the first time you told me you loved me. Said you'd never love anyone else. What an idiot I was believing you.'

She remembered too, but she wouldn't admit it to him. They were in the Algarve on a beach in the warm early evening sun, noisy seagulls their only company except for a few late sunbathers. They'd walked backwards holding hands, the gentle waves lapping their ankles as they marvelled at their footprints washing away all evidence of them ever being there. Paul had pulled her to a halt, so their feet sank in the wet sand, then he'd kissed her and told her he loved her. She'd said it too and thought she meant every word. He'd been fearless, exciting, creative. They travelled round Europe in his camper van; made friends wherever they went; found work wherever they stopped. But it didn't last. They soon ran out of money and had to sell the van, come home and get proper jobs.

She tried not to look at him. Part of her loathed him but she hated that she was still drawn to him too, as though they belonged together and she'd simply been marking time for the last twenty-odd years, waiting for the moment they would be reunited.

'Can't deny how good you look, Kate,' he said, rubbing his palms together.

She stood at the sink turning her back to him and rinsed the mugs, hoping if she didn't rise to the bait, he'd take the hint and leave. What would he say if he knew she was pregnant? He must never find out. She had to get him out of her life before she really started to show.

'I bet he's not enough for you, is he?' Paul whispered behind her ear, smoothing his hands across her shoulders and down the sides of her breasts. Her back stiffened.

'I remember what you like.' He pressed himself against her and licked her neck.

She caught her breath, body buzzing, sinking into a long-forgotten place her body remembered.

'You know you want to,' he murmured, his hands reaching under her T-shirt. She cursed herself and twisted round, trying to push him away, but he held her arm and kissed her lips, reaching between her legs with his fingers.

'Get off me!' She pulled away and shoved him hard, wiping her mouth on her arm.

A satisfied grin swept across his face as he adjusted himself.

'You need to go.' She wished he hadn't aged so well and wondered how her body could betray her so completely.

'Empty-handed? I don't think so.' His frown deepened and his penetrating stare became menacing. Silly of her to forget how quickly he could turn.

'I… I can give you ten, but that's all I have, so don't come back for more.' She rummaged through the letter rack for her chequebook. She couldn't believe she was doing this, but she had to get rid of him. What if James came home early? He must never know about any of it. And he wouldn't need to. It was her money.

Her hand trembled as she wrote the words: 'ten thousand pounds'. As soon as she'd signed it, he snatched it from her fingers. A small price to pay to preserve her dignity and her life.

Chapter Twenty

On Saturday morning, after visiting Elizabeth in intensive care, Kate and James drove to her house. As Kate opened the front door, the same musty smell hit her. In the living room, she opened the curtains and as many downstairs windows as she could. James stripped the bed Elizabeth had made on the sofa and stuffed the sheets in the washing machine. On top of a stack of unopened post on the dining table were the two photos Kate had found before.

'Is that really Elizabeth?' James asked.

'Hard to believe, isn't it? I think this is where she went to school.'

He took the other photo. 'Look at the clock tower, it's very upmarket. Were her parents well off?'

'Not that I know of,' Kate said.

'This looks like a private school to me.'

'Well I only went to the local comprehensive. I'd like to have had that choice.'

'You said her parents died when she was very young, so perhaps they left money to pay for her education.'

'That would make sense.'

Kate answered the firm tap-tap on the front door.

'Well, I say, this is a state, isn't it?' Mrs Connell said. 'No wonder she wouldn't let me in.' She tut-tutted as she took off her puffa jacket, which looked more suitable for a teenager than a sixty-year-old woman.

Kate led her past the living room and into the kitchen. Mrs Connell shook her head as she looked in.

'As I said on the phone, Mrs Connell, my mother is very ill, which is why she was acting so strangely when you last came here. And why she hasn't been able to—'

'I get you,' Mrs Connell said and waved her hand next to her head as if wafting away a fly. She put on an apron and rubber gloves from her bulging shopping bag.

James carried a tray of glasses, cups and bowls he'd collected and brought them into the kitchen.

'Good morning, Mrs Connell,' he said, sliding the tray next to the sink.

She looked up from the dishwasher and tutted again.

'Do you want me to bring the clothes in from the line?' he asked Kate.

'Yes, please. They'll need rinsing through again. They must have been out there for a couple of days by the look of it.'

He followed her back into the living room and pushed the door until it was almost shut.

'She's a happy camper, isn't she?' whispered James.

Kate nodded. 'Ssh, she'll hear us.'

'These can go in recycle, can't they?' He picked up a pile of newspapers from the coffee table next to the sofa.

'Hang on, I'm not sure,' she said, more serious. She picked up the one on top. 'They're old – why would she have kept them?'

'For the crossword puzzles?'

'No, I mean they're really old, look at this one – 1955. It looks like she was reading them before she went to sleep.'

'I'm coming in to dust,' Mrs Connell called, not waiting before she barged in.

'No problem, Mrs Connell, we'll get out of your way.'

'Are we keeping them?' James asked.

'Mum must have kept them for a reason. Could you take them out to the car, please? I'd like to have a closer look.' Kate trudged upstairs to collect a few essentials for Elizabeth. The bed was made but there were papers strewn across it. Had her mother even gone to bed after their row? She picked up a fanned-out pile of bank statements. In each month over the last few years, the sum of £350 had been circled in red. Why wouldn't Dad have told Mum about this? A prickle of unease crept through her. She folded one up, slipped it in her pocket and tidied the rest away in a drawer.

She opened the wardrobe and took out a dress for Elizabeth to come home in, whenever that might be. She gathered a couple of nighties, underwear and toiletries and laid them on the bed. From Elizabeth's bedside drawer she took a tube of hand cream, a copy of *The French Lieutenant's Woman* and the latest issue of *The Lady* magazine. From the bottom of the wardrobe, she dragged out an old leather case her mother used for weekends away. She emptied the contents of old shoes and handbags and packed in Elizabeth's belongings.

Her thoughts turned to the silk purse. After causing such upset, she was ashamed she couldn't remember looking at it before. If she had stolen it as a child, it must have been because it fascinated her.

Her eyes were drawn to the black strongbox tucked under the bed. It must be in there, under lock and key. She had a strong urge to look at it properly. She glanced at the door as if her mother might appear. James's voice drifted up from the living room followed by the dulcet tones of Mrs Connell. Silently, she opened the jewellery box and felt inside the front edge of the bottom tier for the key. Her fingertips couldn't find it. She peered inside, but it wasn't there. Her mother must have hidden it.

'When I'm done down here, do you want me to carry on up?' Mrs Connell called from halfway up the stairs.

Kate came out of the bedroom carrying the case. 'Yes, please, when you're ready. It's not so bad up here, just needs a quick going over.'

—

Back at home, Kate hung her coat in the hallway. This time James followed her, hanging his in its usual place next to it.

'Do you think Mum will recover?' she said, in the dimness of the hall.

'I really hope so.'

Without another word, they moved into each other's arms. She listened to his heart beating and imagined the baby's heartbeat too. He kissed the tip of her nose and she squirmed leisurely in his arms.

He smiled and planted a kiss on her lips.

'Let's have a drink.'

'There's that bottle of white still in the fridge,' she said, eyes darting round for any sign of Paul's visit.

'Will you have a drop?' He took out a glass and hesitated at taking down a second.

'I'll have sparkling water, thanks.' She took both bottles out of the fridge. James pulled out the cork.

'Susie came to see me,' she said.

James gulped down a mouthful of wine and followed her into the living room with the bottle.

'She told me she would call in,' he said.

'Did you ask her to?' Kate sat on the sofa and put her feet up on the beanbag. James sat next to her.

'Only if she was passing; I needed my badminton kit.'

'She thinks you walked out on me.'

'You know that's just Susie being dramatic.'

'Well it felt like it,' she said, cradling her glass. 'I couldn't sleep.'

'If it makes you feel any better, neither could I.' He finished his wine and refilled the glass. He wasn't giving much away.

'Are you going back to the cat tonight?' Kate stared at the bubbles in her drink.

'Not with Elizabeth still so ill; it's been a shock for you.'

'So you're going to leave me again when she's better?' She put her glass on the coffee table and switched on the CD player. A classical compilation thundered out of the surround sound speakers. Her fingers lingered on the volume dial.

'I think we can work this out.' His words were followed by the rolling drums.

'I'm not having an abortion, James.'

He seemed to be waiting for the wave of music to fall back to the sound of plucking strings. 'You've made that very clear,' he said.

'And?' She touched her bump.

His eyes fixed on her hand there. He swallowed before he spoke. 'I've thought of nothing else. I respect your decision, despite our agreement.'

'But?'

'But nothing, Kate.'

'So what do you mean you respect my decision?'

'Susie told me it's time I grew up.' He stood over her. 'Yes, she said.'

'And Harry told me I'm a bloody idiot.' He bounced his palm off his head to demonstrate. 'He told me I'd regret it forever if I didn't stand by you.'

'Harry's a good man.' She pressed her fingers to her lips to hide her growing smile.

'He told me he'd kick me into next week if I didn't.'

'Does this mean…?'

James sank to his knees. 'It means…' he took her hand in his, 'that I can't live without you, Kate.'

She blinked, her eyes filling with tears.

'Whatever you throw at me.' He smiled.

Kate laughed and wiped away a tear. 'Are you back for good?'

'If you'll have me?'

She cupped his face and kissed him.

'And I know you don't want to hear this,' he continued, 'but this whole pregnancy thing has made me think about the baby that might have been with Susie: how old it would be now; if it would look like me, be like me. I've tried not to think about it over the years, but this has made me face it and… well… what we did makes me incredibly sad.'

Kate ripped up the tissue in her lap. Now would be the perfect time to be honest with him about her past. If she told him everything, it would take away Paul's power over her before he had the chance to expose her or bleed her dry. But she couldn't risk losing James now he'd finally accepted they were having this baby.

Chapter Twenty-One

On Monday, Kate arrived home from work before James. She'd bought a quick dinner of fresh pasta, sun-dried tomato sauce and a salad from the village shop.

Upstairs, she lay on the bed and stroked her tiny bump. Eleven weeks, two days. The last scan photo lived on her dressing table, so it was always in view. Their little baby. Almost the size of a plum. It was still so hard to take in that she was pregnant, especially when she'd spent most of her life being so against the idea. So far though, she was enjoying the thought of parenthood and was determined to do everything she could to be the best mother possible. But she couldn't ignore the tiniest niggle in the back of her mind. What if she woke up one day at nine months pregnant and changed her mind? Or worse still, after it was born? All these years she'd told James she wasn't cut out for it because she was focused on doing well in her career. So was she kidding herself and him that she could see it through?

She sat up and took her dad's bank statement out of her handbag and Paul's letter from the bedside drawer. Right now she needed to eliminate a different kind of niggling doubt. She placed both pieces of paper side by side: Paul's account number scribbled on the back of the note next to the typed list of income and outgoings. That couldn't be right. She followed each number with her finger and checked it again. How was this possible? Paul's account number matched the one on her dad's statement. Her dad had been paying him three hundred and fifty pounds a month – for years according to her mother. Jesus. Paul must have been blackmailing him. Which meant he'd told her dad… everything. A shudder ran through her body. God, what must he have thought of her? He'd probably been glad he wasn't her real father. She lay back on the bed and ran her hands down her face. Her poor dad had been paying for her mistakes. No wonder he hadn't told Mum. She had to thank him for that. The torture he must have gone through keeping it to himself. How would she explain any of this to her mother?

The crunch of tyres on the drive made her sit up. She glanced at the clock. It was already half past six. Out of the window she could see the corner of James's silver Mercedes as it pulled onto the drive. She tidied the papers away. The front door opened as she reached the last stair. She clung to the bannister a little out of breath.

'Are you okay?' He pecked her on the cheek.

'I completely lost track of time. I need to get dinner on. We have to be out of here in half an hour, otherwise we'll miss visiting time.'

James followed her into the kitchen. 'Why don't we call in at the drive-thru takeaway?'

'Are you sure?' She held a pan in her hand, poised under the cold-water tap.

'Yeah, come on, let's go.'

–

Elizabeth had been moved to a ward on a different floor. When they found her, she was sitting up in bed. She welcomed them with a weak smile.

'How are you doing, Mum?' Kate asked and indicated to James to pull up a second chair.

'I brought you some things,' Kate said. James lifted the case onto his knees. Kate took out the paperback and magazine and put them on the table that stretched across the bed. 'There's underwear, nighties and a cardigan.' She tucked the toiletries bag away in the bedside cupboard. 'There's a dress in here too, for when you come home.'

'Goodness knows when that will be,' Elizabeth said. 'It's enough to make you ill all the tests they put you through.'

'They say you have pneumonia, Mum, brought on by a mild heart attack. You'll have to take it slowly.' Kate sat down.

'You were in quite a bad way,' James said.

'You kept telling me a nurse was trying to drown you.'

Elizabeth reclined onto her pillows and gazed at the ceiling.

Kate glanced at James who shrugged one shoulder. They all sat without speaking for several minutes.

A tea trolley rattled onto the ward. A man in a plastic apron and gloves offered tea to the patient in the bed nearest the door. He dropped two cubes of sugar into the cup, making the liquid splash into the saucer. He stirred it, dropped in a straw and placed it on the table next to the woman's bed.

Elizabeth continued to stare at the ceiling. James flicked through *The Lady* magazine.

'Do you know what it was about?' Kate asked.

'Hmm?' Her mother closed her eyes.

'You thinking some nurse might be trying to drown you?'

Elizabeth crossed one hand over the other on her chest.

'Don't you remember?'

James glanced up from the magazine. Elizabeth's eyes and mouth remained closed.

'Whatever it was,' Kate hesitated, 'you're going to get better now.'

The trolley pulled up at the end of the bed.

'Can I get you a tea, coffee or hot chocolate?' the orderly asked with an overstretched smile.

Elizabeth's eyes opened. She eased herself upright. 'Hot chocolate, please.'

He spooned two heaps of brown powder into a cup and poured in boiling water, stirring the grainy-sounding mixture at the same time.

'Anything for my visitors?' Elizabeth asked as he set the cup down and manoeuvered the table nearer to her.

'Sorry, darling, no can do. There's a machine near the entrance they can use.'

'Don't worry about us.' James put the magazine down.

'How are you two?' Elizabeth blew a hole in the brown froth.

'We're fine, Mum.' Kate smiled and caught James's eye.

'Pleased to hear it.'

James smoothed his trousers with his hands.

'This baby needs both of you,' Elizabeth and Kate exchanged a look, 'more than you realise.' Her hands began to shake as she tried to put her cup down. Kate steadied it and helped her rest back on the pillows.

'There's something I'd like you to bring in for me. A large brown envelope from the strongbox under my bed at home.'

'Where's the key?' Kate didn't want her to know she'd been snooping round for it. She probably wanted to check over her will.

'It's in the top tier of my jewellery box.'

'I brought your book and reading glasses.'

Her mother gave a weary nod.

'We've tired you out. I think we'd better be off.'

'I'll bring the car round.' James said goodbye to Elizabeth and strode towards the exit.

'Is there anything else you need?'

Elizabeth grabbed Kate's wrist with a sudden surge of energy, her eyes fixed wide. 'Paul came to the house,' she whispered.

Kate stopped breathing.

'Pushed past me, forced me into a chair, scared me half to death. He still wants money from you.' Elizabeth squeezed Kate's hand.

'Did he say what for?' Kate tried not to sound desperate.

'No, but he said some terrible things about you.'

'What exactly?' Kate's heart pounded.

'Tell me it's not true.' Elizabeth grasped Kate's wrist again. 'I didn't know what to do. He wouldn't leave. What's it all about?'

Kate's heart stopped. 'He didn't tell you?' She blinked at her mother, trying to appear calm.

'No, but he said Ray knew as well.'

He could easily have told her everything. This was clearly a warning. She gently removed Elizabeth's hand, pulled the sheets up and tucked her in.

'Why don't I know about all this?'

Kate swallowed hard before she spoke. 'It's nothing important. Try not to worry yourself, Mum.' But she couldn't bring herself to look in her mother's eyes. It was impossible to erase what she'd done, but no matter how hard she tried to suppress it, her deepest fear always reared up as a phantom in her mind – was she capable of doing it again?

Chapter Twenty-Two

After Kate had gone, Elizabeth wondered if she should have asked more questions. What if it was true? Or had Paul been exaggerating when he said Kate could be in trouble with the police for something she'd done?

But Ray. Paul said Ray knew. *Why didn't you tell me?* Paul must be up to his old mischief. Still as cocksure as ever. Ray wouldn't have kept something from her if it was serious.

Dinner arrived under a plastic dome. She gave Sheila a little wave. An orange curl was hanging down from her blue hairnet.

'Extra pudding for you, my love,' Sheila said, waving back with her see-through gloves. No doubt the same sort they used to examine patients' intimate places.

Elizabeth tried to pull on her best smile, despite the waft of boiled cabbage and some sort of meat with gravy so thick it wobbled in its own skin.

Food was the first thing she'd been aware of when she first came round, before she'd even opened her eyes. In an instant, she was back in the sanatorium. Seventy-odd years vanished in a second. The smell, the clatter of plates and shuffling of nurses in their thick stockings and starched uniforms. She used to wonder if the doctor caring for her was her father. His handsome Errol Flynn face with its neat moustache emphasised his kind smile.

He'd put a cool, soft hand on her forehead and told her she was making good progress. Once she'd said 'thank you, Daddy' instead of 'thank you, doctor', by mistake. He'd given her the biggest smile which made his eyes twinkle. He made her want to get better for the first time since they'd told her about Edward.

–

The meds trolley rattled into the middle of the ward. Her favourite nurse, Josie, brought over a little pot of coloured pills. Elizabeth tried not to stare at her silver scars.

'How are you doing today?' Josie passed her a glass of water.

Elizabeth tried to smile as she swallowed a tablet.

They had these strange little chats together that sprang out of nowhere, when they came straight out with secrets they'd barely told a living soul. Josie had told her about the time she cut her wrists after she gave birth to her stillborn baby. Her mother had found her in the bath and saved her. And Elizabeth had told her all the things she wished she could say to Kate about her own childhood and Kate's real father.

'Has your daughter been in?' Josie asked in her sing-song voice.

Elizabeth nodded and swallowed another tablet.

'You sorted things out with her?' She picked up the empty pill pot.

Trouble was, telling Kate the truth could send her packing again. She'd be so ashamed of her. She could see her now, standing there with her arms crossed trying to work out how they could even be related. But wasn't it better than her finding out after she was dead and gone?

And after the last few days, she didn't honestly know how long she had left.

'Don't leave it, my darling, remember what we said?' Josie brushed a tear from Elizabeth's cheek with the back of her hand. 'You have nothing to be ashamed of, do you hear me? Just be yourself.'

Josie was right. Ray had been right too. By trying to protect Kate, she'd pushed her away. But there was also the matter of Kate's real dad. Should she have told her everything or would it have made things worse? Perhaps it was too late to put everything right.

Chapter Twenty-Three

Kate called into her mother's house on the way to the hospital on Friday. She'd still not worked out what she was going to say if she asked again about Paul. What was he doing turning up at her mother's house? What if his sudden visit had made her ill? It must have been a shock for her, and then him saying Kate had done something terrible. And what about the money Dad was paying him? How could she tell her the truth about that?

The angel's trumpets in the porch were giving off their fragrance. She unlocked the front door, cracking open the silence. All the curtains were closed, leaving the house under a veil of greyness. The faint smell of furniture polish mixed with citrus enveloped her as she opened the living room door. Everything was back in its place, but she missed the smell of fresh flowers and the familiar hum of voices from the kitchen radio.

As she stood absorbing the silence, memories pushed in on her: arriving home from school for the summer holidays; her dad coming home from work, hanging up his jacket with leather elbow patches, whistling a tune as he untied his laces. And the aroma of warm honey cake wafting from the kitchen. Kate would watch through a crack in the door as her mother beat the mixture, but if she was seen, Elizabeth would shoo her away.

Kate climbed the stairs. She crossed her mother's room to the dressing table and searched for the little key. There it was, hidden in the upper tier, under a string of pearls. She knelt by the bed and, reaching under, pulled the black strongbox towards her. Her hand smoothed across the lid. As she turned the key, the lid popped open and a pile of papers slid out onto the carpet. Kate tidied the bundle to one side. She lifted out a wad of fifty-pound notes secured with an elastic band, followed by documents relating to the house and the brown envelope her mother had asked for. Beneath all of these was the silk purse.

Kate took the tiny object out and stood at the window to examine it. The initials M.L. were embroidered with a delicate feather-like stitch. It must have been red when new but now it had faded to an uneven pink. She took out the disc of yellowing plastic with the number '23' carved in the centre. It was the sort of thing a mudlark might find washed up in low tide along the River Thames.

Years ago, Kate and her dad had collected stones together on Chesil Beach. On the way back to the car they'd been weighed down with their haul – two plastic bags half full. Her dad bought a machine to tumble them to a high polish using various grades of grit. When they returned from the holiday, Elizabeth accused them of deliberately leaving her out, of Kate keeping her dad all to herself, even though it had been Elizabeth who'd encouraged them to go without her, to give her some peace. Kate had silently withdrawn to her bedroom and had sat on her bed staring at the pebbles. That was when she'd first imagined swallowing them: dropping them in her mouth one by one, and when she shut her eyes, she could almost hear the rattle as they landed in the depths of her stomach.

Kate put the disc back in the purse then peeped inside the unsealed brown envelope. She was surprised to see a birth certificate: *Molly Liddle; born 24th March 1939.* She frowned. That was her mother's birthday. She picked up the purse again – the initials fitted. Did her mother want to tell her that she'd had a twin sister?

Kate picked up the papers from the carpet, shuffling them together into the box. There were several black and white photos of Elizabeth as a young woman in the late 1950s, including two of her with Ray on their wedding day in 1973, both cutting a modest-sized cake. Elizabeth's hair, fashionably short and curled under, revealed pearl drop earrings and matching necklace. Apparently only a matter of weeks after Kate's real dad had died. Yet not a hint of the pregnancy and no sign of grief in her mother's eyes.

She wondered what her real dad had looked like if part of the reason her mother was always angry with her was because she reminded her of him. She pictured Elizabeth as she was now, in the hospital bed, her body withered beneath the flimsy white gown. It was time to ask her again.

–

There were no nurses at the desk when Kate arrived on the ward, so she carried on along the corridor until she came to 'G' bay. It wasn't until she'd reached halfway into the room that Kate realised her mother's bed was empty. It had been stripped back to the plastic covering the mattress. Her 'get well' cards had been collected and left in a pile on the bedside cupboard. Kate clutched the brown envelope a little tighter to her body. Could they be letting her come home already? That would explain it. She gave an uneasy smile at the woman sitting in the bed opposite, but she frowned back.

'Waiting for my mum,' Kate said to her.

The woman continued to concentrate on her elaborate set of knitting needles with three shades of blue wool.

'Did they say if she'd be long?'

But the woman didn't look up again from the rhythm of her tapping needles.

Kate sat in the chair next to the empty bed and gazed out of the window at the miniature rooftops below. Soon she'd be having her twelve-week scan. At last she'd be able to share the special moment of seeing the baby with James.

A pigeon flew straight at the glass with an almighty thud, making her jump up. The bird fell away, and she pressed her face to the window, imagining it hurtling to the ground. Shaken, she hugged the envelope to her body.

'Do you know if they are letting her come home today?' Kate's shadow fell across the woman knitting. She glanced up, but Kate couldn't be sure if there was a slight nod or if she imagined it. The clicking needles seemed to speed up.

'Mrs Marshall…' A nurse in full stride was heading towards her, hand in the air as if hailing a cab. 'Mrs Marshall…' came the nurse's insistent tone as she stopped in front of Kate, 'could you come this way, please?'

She followed the nurse along the corridor into a room the size of a cupboard. The nurse bowed her head and arranged her fingers so they linked in front of her.

'We tried to call you this morning, but there was no answer.' Her delivery was chillingly formal. A hundred needles pressed into Kate's chest.

'It was very sudden and unexpected.' The downy hair on the nurse's top lip moved in slow motion as she spoke.

Kate blinked. She wanted the nurse to repeat herself. Sudden? Unexpected? She clutched the envelope tighter but her hot fingers were melting into the paper.

'Your mother had another heart attack early this morning.' The nurse closed her eyes for longer than a blink. 'Like I said, we tried to call you, several times.'

Kate dropped into a chair, hand to her forehead, black dots blotting her vision. This couldn't happen. Not now. When they were finally starting to understand each other. Her mother still had so many things to tell her about her family and her real dad. How would she find out about any of it now? She didn't want her mother to die.

Chapter Twenty-Four

Kate gripped the arm of the chair.

'She's stable,' the nurse said, 'but it was touch and go.'

Kate tipped her head back and let out a stream of air. 'Can I see her?'

'For a moment or two, she's sleeping.'

Kate followed the nurse into intensive care. The sounds of the machines the patients were wired up to whirred and clicked to their own rhythms. Like all the beds, Elizabeth's faced the wall. The nurse went off to deal with a woman crying out in the bed opposite, leaving Kate standing by her mother's bedside.

Elizabeth's eyes were shut. Her face had a waxen sheen and her body a childlike form under the thin sheet. Kate moved closer. Would she even be aware of her? The skin on her mother's arm barely covered the bones and gave a little too much under her light pressure. She crouched down so she was level with Elizabeth's face.

'Please don't leave me,' Kate whispered, 'I need you, Mum.'

Elizabeth gave no response, but Kate hoped she had heard. A few minutes later, the nurse came over and ushered her out.

Back in the car, Kate telephoned James.

'I just can't believe this has happened. We were here only yesterday, talking to her. I thought she was getting better,' she said.

'I know, so did I. It's such a shock,' James said. 'Maybe she knew more about her health than she was letting on.'

'I was convinced she'd be coming home soon. You should have seen her, James, all wired up to machines.'

'Shall I come and pick you up? I'm not sure you should drive in that state.'

'I've got a coffee. I'll sit here for a few minutes.'

'Okay, but if you don't feel up to it, call me back. Either way, I'll wrap up here and come home.'

Kate sipped her coffee. Her phone buzzed. A message popped up on her screen.

> You've got four days left to give me the
> rest of the money.

She stared at the words. What did he mean? She'd given him ten thousand pounds, fifteen in total. This was the end of it as far as she was concerned. She pushed her phone into her bag and drove home.

—

Kate opened the fridge. Under a heart-shaped Post-it note James had left her a piece of baked cheesecake. She slid it onto a plate and took a dessert fork from the draining board. If she could only talk to Susie about Paul, but a pinprick of doubt penetrated Kate's mind; this would be too big a secret for Susie to keep to herself. She wasn't certain she could trust her. Her loyalty would be with

James over her. She wished she had other close friends she could confide in, but she wasn't very good at opening up to people. It was so hard to trust anyone completely, especially with something as big as this. Her life with James and the business took up all her time and that suited her; she felt comfortable keeping people outside of that.

Still, she should invite Susie and Harry over, clear the air and show them that she and James were very much together, working things out.

She put the plate down and stood with her palms flat on the table, her head stooped as a wave of nausea hit her. The cheesecake didn't taste the same today. She scraped the remains into the pedal bin. It fell with a thud to the bottom, taking the empty liner with it. She stood there looking in, having second thoughts.

Her phone buzzed. She dug it out of her handbag. A message was emblazoned across the screen.

> YOU'VE FUCKED UP MY LIFE, BITCH,
> SO I'M COMING TO GATECRASH
> YOURS!

What the hell? It was from the other number again. Who was this? Paul must have told someone. Had he given them her mobile number and home address? She switched her phone to silent and turned it face down on the counter.

She took out the newspaper they'd brought back from her mother's house and opened it out at the article her mother had been reading.

Ashlyns School's history dates back to 1740 when the first children were received into the London Foundling Hospital. A retired sea captain, Thomas Coram, was concerned at how many infant bodies were being abandoned on rubbish tips. His campaign for a hospital to accommodate the so-called foundlings was successfully granted a Royal Charter in 1739. Three years later, work started on the first permanent building at Lamb's Conduit Fields in Bloomsbury, 1742.

The sound of James's car as it pulled onto the drive broke into her thoughts. When he walked in, he tossed his keys onto the table and put his arms round her.

'I'm so sorry about your mum,' he whispered into her hair.

Kate couldn't speak.

'Hey, are you okay?' He drew back and kissed her forehead. 'We'll get through this, I promise you.'

Kate nodded, her eyes brimming with tears.

'What's this?'

'One of the newspaper we found at Mum's.'

'What's a *foundling hospital*?' He pointed to the words in print. 'Sounds more like a school than a hospital. Hang on, here we are,' he read aloud: '"*For the maintenance and education of exposed and deserted young children. In 1926 Governors of the hospital decided to realise the value of the London site (which was sold for £2 million) and to build a new hospital on the Ashlyns' site at Berkhamsted.*" It's not far from here. Maybe your mum's interested in the local history. "*The children were sent to temporary premises in Redhill until 1935 when the Georgian-style buildings in Berkhamsted were ready for occupation.*"'

'I came across a birth certificate with Mum's birthday, but for someone called Molly Liddle. I wonder if she had a twin who died when they were children or was sent to this… foundling place.'

'Quite the detective, aren't we?' James patted her hand.

'Not a very good one. I googled the name but nothing much came up except for the Twitter account of someone who's never tweeted and a tattoo artist on Pinterest. I think it could be what Mum wanted to talk to me about. But we might not get the chance now.'

'I'm sure you will.' James picked up the newspaper and folded it. Kate's mobile was underneath. 'Who's this?' he asked, looking at the screen as another text popped up of a waving hand emoji and the words:

Call me!

Kate's heart thudded. 'Just someone I went to school with,' she said, snatching it up.

'An old boyfriend?' He smirked.

'An old friend.' She willed her skin not to blush. 'Actually, he wants me to go and visit him on the Isle of Wight, meet up with our old gang of friends.' She wasn't sure where that came from, but it wasn't a bad idea. Confront Paul and put a stop to this.

'Oh, nice.'

'Do you have a problem with that?'

'Not at all. Why don't I come with you?'

Kate clung to the door handle. 'It would be boring for you, all our school chat.'

'Oh, I don't know, it would be fun talking to someone who knew you back then.'

Kate flashed her eyes at him.

He laughed. 'It's all right, I'm joking. Why don't you try and coordinate it for when we're in Southampton for the boat party?'

'Good idea.' Kate pretended to smile as she tried to compose herself and change the subject. 'I was thinking of asking Susie and Harry over for lunch on Sunday. We can go and see Mum in the evening.'

'OK, if you want to.'

'I need to clear the air with Susie. It will be easier if you and Harry are here.'

'As long as it's not all baby talk.'

'It won't be, I promise.' Then after a pause, 'Do you think Harry knows about you and Susie?'

'I don't know, why?'

'You've not mentioned it then?' Kate took a packet of risotto rice from the cupboard.

'No, why would I? It's up to Susie.'

'She says she doesn't want him to know. He'd be shocked, wouldn't he?'

'But relieved that Susie did the sensible thing.'

'Sensible?'

'At the time it was – for both of us.'

Kate took out a saucepan. James started chopping an onion.

'Just as well anyway. I couldn't see Harry playing stepdad to a twentysomething,' he laughed.

'I think he'd be very accepting.'

'Not a chance. He told me he was with a woman years ago who had a couple of kids, now what was her name?' He squeezed his forehead with his finger and thumb. 'Janet, that's it. She had two teenage daughters, and, in the end, he couldn't deal with all the problems of their dad turning up then not turning up, as well as the usual roller coaster of emotions you girls...' He grinned, teasing her.

'Maybe Janet wasn't the right woman for him. I'm sure he would do anything for Susie.'

–

It was dark when they arrived home from visiting Elizabeth again later that day. James switched off the engine, but they remained in the car. The security light in the porch drew her eye to next door's Persian Blue slinking across the doorstep. She touched her tiny bump. It still felt strange to think of herself as pregnant and happy about it. Didn't that prove it was possible to change?

'I wish I could talk to Mum. Do you think she'll be in intensive care for long?'

'I don't know. They said she's making slow progress.'

'I wonder if she'll be well enough to come home for Christmas.'

'Let's wait and see.' James kissed her cheek.

She became aware of the confined space they were in and the heat disappearing as the car cooled down. The stubble on James's face made him look older but more laid back than the usual clean-cut face he presented at work every day. This was her James. The James who always put her first, believed in her unconditionally. When she'd been unsure of herself, he'd helped her to knock down obstacles and not be afraid of success. She'd almost become a different person. But what kind of wife keeps secrets from her husband? Her mother did and look at the devastation that caused. What other secrets was she keeping? Who was Molly Liddle? If Elizabeth could lie about Kate's paternity, she could lie about anything.

Chapter Twenty-Five

The rain on Sunday morning started slowly at first, undetectable, like the hushed rustle of leaves, until it grew steadily to the white noise of a downpour. Kate stood in the kitchen eating porridge, her dressing gown wrapped over her satin pyjamas. These dark mornings made it impossible to imagine how they might resurface into spring. She'd called the hospital as soon as she'd woken up. Elizabeth was still in intensive care, awake at last, her condition stable.

The front door clicked open and shut. She knew it was James, but the sound still made her jump. She needed to pick the right time to call Paul. It was proving harder than she'd imagined. She only had three days left. The day before, she'd got as far as dialling two numbers when the postman knocked, scaring her rigid. Today, they were going to Susie and Harry's. Susie had suggested they go there this time and Kate promised to take a homemade chocolate mousse. Somehow, before that, she had to speak to Paul, find out who else knew and put an end to these threats.

James peeled the cycle helmet from his sweaty head. She thought he always looked ridiculous in Lycra shorts, but she wasn't about to tell him.

'I'll grab a shower,' he said, pecking her on the cheek before going off to the wet room.

The radio beeped nine o'clock. The news headlines were announced as she crept into the living room. She picked up her mobile and stared at it, but she couldn't bring herself to call him. Shit. Still a coward.

Back in the kitchen, she opened her recipe book to a page splattered with the browny-yellow of an indistinct sauce. She always checked the recipe first, in case she missed one of the vital ingredients. Reaching up to take out a bag of sugar from the cupboard, she felt the tiniest flutter of movement. But wasn't it too early? Her hand smoothed across her small bump. She must be imagining it. 'There, there, little one.' She smiled, surprised at her own soothing tone.

James came in, rubbing his hair with a hand towel, leaving it spiky. A larger towel was wrapped round his waist.

'I've run out of eggs,' Kate said without thinking. If she didn't call Paul soon, he'd ring her and then James would start asking more questions. 'We need them for the mousse,' she lied, picturing the box of six in the cupboard as she said it. 'You couldn't pop out to the shops, could you?'

James drank a glass of water in one long mouthful. He nodded, wiping his lips on the back of his hand. 'How many do we need?'

'Half a dozen.'

Kate broke a slab of dark chocolate into pieces and dropped them in a glass bowl over a bain-marie.

'Anything else while I'm there?' James came back dressed. He picked up his wallet and keys from the table.

'I don't think so.'

When he'd gone, Kate waited a couple of minutes in case he returned then took her phone into the living room. She wanted to be able to move on without any reminders of her old life, her mistakes. Look forward to a fresh start with James and their baby. To being a mum. Her new little family. She sat on the arm of the sofa staring at the phone before pressing in Paul's number. As soon as the dialling tone kicked in, her head began to thud from a sudden rush of blood. She'd come this far, rehearsed what she would say, but now her mind went blank. The answerphone clicked in.

'Leave me a short message and I'll call you back as soon as I can.' Paul's voice was softer, casual, more as she remembered him in their early days. When the silence came for Kate to speak, she was at a loss.

'Paul, it's me…' She stopped. 'Kate, that is.' She wished she could start again but the silence began to swell, so she continued, 'I'm calling like you suggested… Why don't I come and meet you, so we can sort this out properly? Please don't call me back, I'll call you.' She put the receiver down then covered her mouth. Damn, she'd put too much emphasis on the word 'please', making her sound needy. In her head she could hear Paul's voice, the confident yet casual tone. It had thrown her completely. She pictured them together, curled up on a mattress on the floor of his old bedsit. She shook the image from her mind.

'Are you okay?' James's voice startled her. He stood in the doorway, holding up a carrier bag from the local farm shop. 'I thought it would be quicker than going into town,' he said.

She grabbed the bag from him and marched back to the kitchen.

'I bought a tray of twelve; they were on special offer and you said—'

'I said I needed six,' her voice too sharp. Had he heard any of her message?

'Yes, you said. You're making chocolate mousse, Susie's favourite.'

'Is it?' She lifted the bag onto the bench and took out the tray. Her finger ran over each egg, checking for cracks.

'You really do want to make it up with her, don't you?'

Kate didn't answer. She broke an egg into a bowl.

'It's pointless allowing the past to dictate the present.'

'What are you going on about?' She cracked the next egg, watching the albumen slide out followed by the plump orangey yolk.

'I read it somewhere. A motivational quote.'

Shame he didn't take his own advice.

'We're different people now, aren't we?' He started massaging her shoulders. 'God you're tense. Are you all right?'

'Are you saying you have no regrets?' She cracked another egg on the side of the bowl and stacked the shells in a line.

'About the abortion? None at all. You must have done things in the past you're not proud of.'

She flinched. The yolk split and oozed over her fingers. She should tell him everything. If he couldn't deal with it, that was his lookout. She'd had to live with what she did. 'How would you feel if there was something...'

But James had stopped listening. 'I quite fancy a fried egg sandwich,' he said, taking out a small frying pan. 'Do you want one?'

Kate threw him a look of disbelief.

'Sorry, did I miss something?' He switched on the hob.

'It doesn't matter,' she said, chasing a piece of shell round the bowl with her fingertips.

'Come on, what did you say?'

'How would you feel if I'd done something I regretted before we met?'

James shrugged. 'I don't know. I'd assume it couldn't be that bad, otherwise we wouldn't be having this conversation, would we?'

She didn't know how the egg slipped from her fingers, but it landed on the floor with a crack; the insides oozed out. They both bent down at the same time to mop it up. James reached it first. Kate straightened up.

'You're shaking.' He held her wrist. 'Are you okay?'

She rubbed her back.

'Come and sit down.' James took her hand. 'Have you had breakfast yet?'

'Only a piece of toast.'

'Let me get you something. You must eat,' then after a pause, 'the baby needs you to eat.'

A smile blossomed on her lips.

'You're eating for two, isn't that what they say?' His face disappeared inside the open fridge.

Kate silently exhaled a breath and looked up at the ceiling. Could she tell him? Did he love her enough to accept her, forgive her for what she did? For the tiniest moment she imagined the relief telling the truth would bring her. But it terrified her too; the huge demon shape of it rose in her mind. She wasn't ready for another battle yet.

Chapter Twenty-Six

Kate and James arrived at Susie and Harry's at midday. Their sprawling 1930s house in Tring was hidden behind a wall of mature laurels. Harry's vintage MG was tucked away in a carport next to an equally immaculate Morgan.

Susie stood in the doorway holding a half-dressed Lily. Kate tried to read the look in her eyes as she handed Susie a Jojo Maman Bébé bag. 'It's just a couple of little outfits.' She linked her arm through James's.

'Thank you,' Susie let the bag fall open and peeped inside, 'they look gorgeous.'

'I've been doing a bit of window shopping myself.' Kate missed Susie. She could do with her advice on cribs and these multiway prams.

'You must tell me all about it.'

Harry appeared behind Susie, wearing dungarees and wellingtons. 'Been doing a bit of planting. I'll go and get cleaned up.'

'Don't mind us.' James handed him a bag containing the tub of chocolate mousse and a bottle of wine.

'Look at us all standing here – come in, come in.'

They followed Susie down a long corridor to the kitchen at the back of the house.

'Right, what can I get you?' Harry rubbed his hands together in front of the wine rack.

'A large glass of red for me, please,' James said.

'Australian Shiraz OK for you, sir?'

James nodded his approval.

'What about you, Kate?'

'Water with ice and lemon, please.' Kate sat at the huge wooden slab of a table. She loved the naturally occurring knots and dips in its smooth surface. Almost everything in their kitchen was handcrafted from solid oak by Harry and his dad, the humble beginnings of their bespoke furniture business. She stole a glance at Susie, but she had her back to her.

'How's business?' Harry handed Kate a glass of water.

'More than we can cope with at times,' James said.

'Victims of your own success eh?' Harry popped open the bottle and poured James a glass.

'What can I say, we're good at what we do, and businesses love team-building events more than ever. What about you?'

'We're not usually that busy in the weeks leading up to Christmas. I'm having a week off this year, so it works out well as Dad still likes to keep his hand in making the more bespoke pieces of furniture.' Harry took a mouthful of wine and sat next to Kate. Susie continued to fuss about with Lily on the sofa in the new extended part of the kitchen.

Harry nudged Kate gently. 'Look, whatever it is, can you two please kiss and make up?' He raised his glass.

Kate's face flushed. She hated that Harry had no idea what their fallout was about.

'I don't know what you're talking about, we're absolutely fine.' Susie smiled at Kate.

Harry laughed.

'How's your mum?' Susie came over and handed Lily to her.

'Not good. She had another heart attack.' Kate sat Lily on her lap, the soft chunky legs dangling over her arm. She held her close and kissed the warm downy head of hair.

'That's awful, I'm so sorry.'

'Yeah, sorry to hear that,' Harry said.

'We're going up to the hospital again later. It's been a bit touch and go.'

'Must be a dreadful worry for you.' Susie took the knives and forks out of a drawer.

'Harry, take these.'

Harry laid the table then drained the vegetables while Susie took the dinner out of the oven. Kate's mobile rang in her bag. Shit. She held Lily up to pass her back to Susie while she tried to reach for her phone.

'Shall I get that?' Without waiting for a reply, James took the phone out and answered it. Her heart thumped up to her throat. Too late. She froze. His voice sounded higher than usual, indicating that he was talking to someone he didn't know. She exchanged a quizzical look with him.

'Is it the hospital?' she mouthed at him. He shook his head.

Susie peeled the oven gloves off and took Lily from her. James handed Kate the phone. 'It's someone called Paul?'

Heart pounding, she tried not to snatch it from him.

'I hope this is a good time?' said the voice in a clear, measured tone.

'Hello, yes, yes, it's fine…' Kate beamed at everyone but was silently screaming inside. 'Can you hang on a second?' She could feel her face burning up. Clamping her hand over the mouthpiece, she left the kitchen, pulling the door shut behind her.

'What are you playing at?' Kate whispered through clenched teeth. She stood by the window in the living room.

'How are you, Kate? Was that your husband?' Paul laughed.

'I said I would call you back.' Kate paced in a circle. She'd broken into a sweat.

'You mentioned about meeting up. I think it's a good idea. Should have thought of it myself.'

'Okay, but then you need to leave me alone. And whoever you've got sending me threatening texts.'

'What are you going on about?'

'You know what I mean.'

'I haven't got the foggiest. Don't think I'm letting you off lightly. I've told you how much I want, and you've not even paid half yet.'

Silence descended as fragile as burnt paper. She'd hoped to change his mind, come to some other agreement.

'I told you that was it. I don't have that any more.'

'You expect me to believe that when you run your own business? Live in a posh house with brand new Mercs? Perhaps I need to have a word with your husband.'

'You leave him out of this. Why do you need so much?'

'I don't think a grand and a half a year is anywhere near enough, but it'll do. I'm sure we can work something out between us.'

'When?' What did he mean it would do? Was he going to keep coming back for more? She'd have to make it clear that was the end of it: he couldn't go on blackmailing her.

'Whenever suits you.'

'We're running an event in Southampton on Friday the seventh of December at the Town Quay Marina. I could meet you the morning after?'

'Yeah, sounds good for me.'

'Okay, I'll text you a time.' Kate swallowed hard. A sudden headache pain stabbed her eye. 'There's something I've been meaning to ask you.'

Silence.

'Do you ever... talk about me?'

Silence.

'I'm not going to answer that.'

'I know, I'm sorry, I shouldn't have said anything.'

Silence.

'I'll see you in Southampton then,' Kate said.

'I'll be there.'

James looked round the door. She waved him away, but he wouldn't budge so she turned her back on him.

'Okay good, I have to go now.'

James had gone but he'd left the door open. She could hear laughter from the kitchen, meaning he'd be back again any minute.

Paul didn't answer, probably chewing over her question. Wondering how she'd found the cheek to ask.

James looked round the door again.

'I really do have to go now, goodbye.' Kate put the phone down and pressed her hand to her eye.

'Are you coming?' James called from the hallway.

'Give me a minute.' Kate shook her head, scattering memories like grains of sand, but the pain remained.

In the kitchen, Susie was holding a ladle over the casserole. 'Are you ready for me to dish up?' she asked.

'Yes, sorry, please do.'

'She's going to see an old school friend from the Isle of Wight,' James said, as Harry topped up the glasses. 'I offered to tag along, but...' James smiled and shrugged in an exaggerated, rejected way.

'There's a small group of us that used to hang out together. I'm meeting them on the Saturday morning in Southampton.'

'They're bound to know all sorts of juicy secrets about Kate.' Harry winked at her.

She stood next to Susie and handed her a plate. She could feel them all watching her, but she concentrated on the three thin lines painted round the rim. How had her life come to this? Lie after lie to James about Paul and about her past. And his lies to her and Harry about Susie and their baby, his ex-girlfriend and whatever had gone on with his brother Ben. If she walked out, would any of them really care? She was so sick of it all, she felt like blurting out the truth then storming off, going into hiding for a while so she didn't have to deal with the fallout.

'More reason not to go I'd say.' Harry raised his glass to James. 'The less I know about my wife's past the better to be honest,' he said, his nose already a glowing beacon from too much drink.

'Really?' James said. 'I'd rather know every last detail.' He caught Kate's eye and without meaning to, she shot him a look of panic.

'You can't change the past so why worry about it?' Harry said.

Kate glanced across at Susie, who kept her head down. Harry clearly had no idea about his wife and James. Did it matter? They hadn't had the child.

'No, you certainly can't,' James said, 'as long as it doesn't affect the here and now.'

Lily's sharp cry filled the momentary silence.

'I'll go.' Susie handed the ladle to Kate. 'Do you mind? I'll dish mine up when I come back down.'

'Don't you want us to wait for you?' Kate said.

'No, don't be silly, you all eat.'

Kate passed a plate of food to Harry.

'So, are you spending the whole day with these school friends while we're down there?' James asked, holding up the next plate.

'I'm not sure what the exact plans are yet, or if everyone can make it.' Kate couldn't look at him. If he knew who the friend really was, their lives together would be over. She submerged the spoon into the rich, dark sauce and began to stir.

Chapter Twenty-Seven

After work on Monday, Kate strode down the hospital corridor, James following close behind. She'd barely slept, worrying about meeting Paul, wondering how she'd raise the rest of the money without James noticing. Maybe she could borrow it from the business? But how would she explain it to James? He was sure to notice and she wasn't sure how or when she could pay it back. And the other thing she couldn't shift from her mind was whether she should trust Paul to come alone, keep their secret between them. What if it was a trap? The malicious messages popped into her head. He'd clearly already told someone. She needed to find out who.

Elizabeth had been moved out of intensive care and onto a ward.

'She's been calling for you ever since she came round,' said a nurse at the desk, pointing to the bed nearest the door. That was the last thing Kate expected to hear.

Elizabeth's eyes were shut, face white, reminding Kate of her dad the day before he died. She'd stood next to her mother, hoping she'd hug her or squeeze her hand, but she never did. If she'd been brave enough to make the first move herself, her hug would have been greeted with a stiff response or her mother's hand pulling away. As if he could read her thoughts, James came closer and put his arm round her waist. She rested her head on his shoulder.

A nurse came over and called Elizabeth's name. 'I'm going to take your temperature, all right, my love?'

She held the electronic thermometer in Elizabeth's ear until it beeped then she took her pulse.

'How is she today?' Kate asked.

'Stable, but still fragile.'

'Hello, Mum.' Kate brushed her fingertips across the parched skin on the back of her mother's hand.

Elizabeth's eyes half opened.

'Mum, it's me, Kate, and James is here too,' she said pulling James's arm, so he was in view. But Elizabeth's eyes fell shut again.

'She needs to rest,' said the nurse.

Kate tucked the brown envelope inside her mother's bedside cupboard.

On the way out, she stopped at the nurse's station to ask more about her mother's progress.

'She's better than she was, put it that way,' said a nurse with bleached hair. 'There was one point in the night we thought we might lose her.'

Kate swayed as if someone had swept past her in a hurry. James put his arm round her. She wasn't ready for this.

-

The next day, James drove Kate straight from work to the maternity unit for her twelve-week scan. In the waiting area, she drank from a bottle of mineral water. She'd been lucky hardly suffering from morning sickness. James leaned forward, eyes scanning all the health posters. He looked a little overwhelmed. *Smoking For Two? Quit Now; You're Pregnant, Who Do You Tell?* – next to a picture of a sad-looking schoolgirl on the phone. *Are You Group*

B Strep Aware? The most common cause of serious infection in newborns and meningitis in babies under 3 months. And another, *Baby or the Bottle?* About the importance of not drinking alcohol during pregnancy, shown through the silhouette of a woman drinking and the alcohol going straight to the umbilical cord. James rubbed his eyes and picked up a *Country Life* magazine.

A notification from Kate's Twitter account pinged up on her mobile. Someone called @BammerGirl had tagged her in a tweet. She opened the app and clicked on the notification. A GIF of an evil woman with yellow eyes and spiky hair sliding out from behind an ordinary office girl was headed with the message:

> Stop pretending to be something you're not.

She glanced at James. His eyes were shut. She checked BammerGirl's profile picture. It was an adult blow-up doll. Was this someone she knew? Whoever it was must have only just set up the account because there were zero followers and the only account BammerGirl was following was Kate's. Could this be the same person who'd been texting her? Who'd scrawled 'Bitch' on her car and sent flowers with a cruel note? She clicked on the ellipsis icon in the top right-hand corner and blocked the account.

When James opened his eyes, she squeezed his arm and gave him a reassuring smile. She wanted to tell him how pleased she was that he was there with her, but she didn't want to overdo it.

The time for their appointment came and went. James tapped his watch face. The waiting area started to fill up.

A woman held onto the back of the seat next to them before manoeuvring herself into it. She wore a cropped T-shirt showing stretch marks across her bump.

'Twins,' the woman explained.

'Did you hear that, James?'

James sat up from his stupor.

'It was meant to be my last one,' the woman continued.

'How many do you have?' Kate asked.

'These two make four. I was hoping to go back to work after, but no chance now.'

James rolled his eyes. Kate elbowed him.

A midwife called Kate's name. She led them into a scanning room.

'Take a seat,' the midwife said to James when he lingered by the door. He perched on the edge of a chair, brushing his palms together.

Kate climbed onto the couch.

'Let's have a look. No more bleeding?' The midwife spread gel across Kate's belly.

'Only a bit now and again.'

James's eyes were fixed on her.

She held her breath while the midwife pushed the scanning paddle across her skin. It was several minutes before she spoke.

'There we are the baby is moving nicely.'

Kate pointed to the monitor on the wall opposite, unable to speak.

James stared up at the shadowy profile of their baby on the screen.

'Having a good kick about,' the midwife said, 'and there's the heartbeat nice and strong.' She looked over her glasses at them.

Kate reached for James's hand, but he seemed to be in a trance, staring at the screen, eyes wide. He took her hand and squeezed it gently. It was real. They were going to be parents. She was going to be a mum. How amazing was that? What sort of mother would she be? A huge canyon opened up in front of her. Could she really do this?

A snow globe of a family caught her eye on the shelf behind the monitor. She had only ever pictured her and James travelling the world, growing old together with no children. But now she could see that it wouldn't have been enough; something would have been missing. She thought of her aunt Karen, not a real aunt, but a friend on her father's side, forever travelling to exotic places on her own; always a visitor looking in, but never part of a family. That life had appealed to her once.

'That's all the checks I need to do at this stage; everything seems to be in order.' The midwife switched the main light on and opened the door. 'I'll fetch a printout of the scan for you,' she said, 'back in a minute.'

Kate pulled her top down and sat up.

James drew his hand through his hair, leaving it messy and sexy looking. 'I didn't know it would look so much like... a little person already.'

'Don't you remember Susie and Harry's scan photo?'

James shook his head.

'I suppose you weren't that interested.'

'It makes it so... real.'

'Do you see now why I couldn't get rid of it? A baby is fully formed at twelve weeks.' She swung her legs off the side of the couch and stood up.

'I don't know what I was expecting.' He shook his head and stood up too, hand clamped to his forehead.

'There we are,' the midwife bustled in, 'it's quite a clear picture.'

At the reception desk, the midwife went through the baby's measurements and the expected due date. James examined the scan picture.

'What do you think then?' Kate couldn't stop smiling.

'It's hard to fathom that this living thing, this person, is right there growing inside you.' He touched her belly. 'We must think about names.' He took her hand and they strolled back to the car. 'Let's draw up a list.' He put his arm round her shoulders, gently drawing her closer to him. 'We should go shopping, shouldn't we? For a pram, car seat, cot...'

'Hey, slow down, it's a bit early for that,' she laughed, 'we can wait another month or two.'

'Well there's no harm in looking, is there?'

'True. But we need to decide if we're going to use disposable or washable nappies and if we're going to buy a crib or a Moses basket. Susie said we might be able to borrow some of their things.'

'Oh, okay.'

'And we'll need baby wipes and muslin cloths.'

'What are they for?'

'Wiping up dribbles after feeding, mopping up sick, dirty bottoms, that kind of thing.'

'Good thing you know all this stuff.' James switched on his phone.

As they left the building, Kate walked fast ahead of James while he checked his messages. How would she explain it if there was another cruel message daubed on her car? As she approached, she scanned round for anyone looking suspicious. She took out her key, almost as a weapon, just in case.

'I should think most women know something about baby stuff. We pick it up from girlfriends and magazines. Anyway, it's not long ago that Susie was pregnant.' She pressed the button then dug the key into her palm.

'Just as well because I wouldn't have a clue.' James laughed, squinting at her in the low winter sun.

They waved at the woman from the waiting room as she drove out of the car park.

'We're not having any more after this though, are we?' James asked. 'I think one is more than enough for me.'

Kate didn't answer.

'I'll drive, you look tired,' he said.

She tossed the keys to him and he caught them in one hand. She had no intention of buying anything for this baby until she was sure that nothing could go wrong. Because right now, if she didn't raise another twenty thousand pounds, her life as she knew it would be over.

Chapter Twenty-Eight

Kate's heels clicked an echoing tune along the low-ceilinged corridor the next day, past a pile of soiled sheets on a trolley and towards bay four. James had stayed on at work to organise an animal feeding team-building event at a zoo for a new client. She was glad of some time alone with her mum.

Her mobile buzzed in her pocket. She couldn't ignore it in case it was James, so she tentatively took it out and glanced at the screen.

> HEY SELFISH SLUT, WHY NOT DO US
> ALL A FAVOUR AND DIE?

Kate almost dropped the phone. Who was doing this? If it wasn't Paul, then who? How had they got her mobile number? Was it on their website or listed in their Companies House details? It could be anyone who had a grudge against her. She was so tempted to call or text back, but she'd tried that, and they didn't speak. Engaging in a conversation might make it worse. Wasn't the advice to ignore trolls? Not give them the oxygen they craved? Although perhaps she ought to report it to the police. But hang on, this was from another different number. What did that mean? Was there more than one person trying to attack her? She switched her phone off and zipped it in her bag.

The curtains around all the beds were drawn back and Elizabeth was sitting in a chair next to hers, legs covered with a blanket, hands on top of a folded newspaper. Her hair had been washed and combed, giving back its candy-floss fluffiness.

'You look well, Mum, how do you feel today?' Kate pulled up a chair. The bed to the left nearest the door was empty and the woman opposite was snoring.

'Not too bad, you know, considering.' Her mother seemed tense, possibly because she'd been waiting for her.

'I brought you grapes and clementines.' She laid the bulging bag of fruit on the bedside table.

Elizabeth's face lit up momentarily. 'Thank you. I'll have some after my tea. Did you bring that envelope for me?'

'I put it in here.' Kate opened the bedside cabinet's magnetic doors and took it out. She handed the envelope to her mother, who motioned to her to pull the curtains round.

'There's something I need to show you. Something I should have told you long ago.'

Kate waited while she shuffled through the papers and pulled out a single sheet. She hesitated with it still facing her as if she might change her mind and whip it back at the last minute.

'This is my birth certificate.' She passed it to Kate.

Kate took it but when she glanced at the paper the name danced about: Molly Liddle.

'Mum?'

Elizabeth stared blankly at her.

'This isn't you.'

'It's my real name.'

'Real?' She pushed it back into her mother's hand. 'What are you talking about?'

'The name I was born with, that my mother gave me.'

'I don't understand, why would you change your name?'

'I didn't.'

'Mum, you're not making much sense.'

Elizabeth shuffled through the papers and pulled out another certificate. 'They changed it.' Her hand trembled as she passed her another piece of paper.

Kate could see it was another birth certificate with the name she knew her mum by, but headed: *The Foundling Hospital*.

'Why were you in hospital? I don't understand.'

'It wasn't a hospital in the modern way, it meant "hospitality" in those days.'

'You mean like a hotel?'

'More… an orphanage. A safe place for people to leave their babies if they weren't able to look after them.'

'Oh.' Kate frowned, trying to take in what her mother was saying. 'So where were your parents?'

'They weren't married so couldn't keep me. My mother left me there as a baby. That's all I know.'

'Why have you never told me this before?'

'I didn't know how.'

'What right did this Foundling Hospital have to change your name?'

'It was all well intentioned. They helped all the babies that were left there to start a new life, which included a new identity.' Elizabeth tried to put the certificate in the envelope, but it wouldn't go back. Her tears dropped and soaked into the paper. She took the pages from her and slid them back in place.

'I wondered for years why she abandoned me, got rid of me just like that,' Elizabeth snapped her fingers, 'like you might give up a dog because it bites.' She took a sharp intake of breath. 'I was a tiny baby and my mother… didn't want me.'

Kate reached for Elizabeth's hand, causing the whole pile of papers to slide to the floor. 'I'm so sorry. I wish I'd known.'

Elizabeth's lips trembled. Kate handed her a hanky. Neither of them spoke for a moment.

'You have to understand, back then, we were made to feel ashamed because our mothers were unmarried, so we weren't allowed to forget where we'd come from, that we were second-class citizens. Before I started at The Foundling Hospital, I was first placed with a foster family who lived nearby until I was five years old. The woman was cruel to me. She had half a dozen children of her own and would lock me up in the chicken coup. I'd chatter to the chickens, gather them round me and tell them stories.'

'Did you never get to meet your mother or father later?'

'Never. The only connection I have is that tiny purse and the disc – my identifying number. I found out my mother's name was Edith Liddle. It conjured up an image of a woman with bobbed hair.'

Kate sank to her knees and collected up the papers from the floor. For the first time in her life her heart ached for her mother. In the last few minutes, she understood her more than she'd done in forty years. She wanted to ask her whether that was why she'd never shown her any affection, because she didn't know how to. Did this mean she would be like that with her baby too? 'I wish we'd talked about this before.'

'It's not the sort of thing we were encouraged to do – talking about ourselves, our problems, feelings or anything personal, we just had to button up and get on with it.'

'What was it like living there?'

'It was often savage, especially at bathtime in the early years. Nurse Bell was normally in charge. We were all terrified of her. She'd press my head under tepid water and if I cried, she'd dunk me in again or give me a wallop. She called us all dirty little urchins who needed a jolly good scrub – "you'll never be clean", she'd say. We all had to learn not to react, to keep our emotions deep inside us.'

'That's so cruel.'

'The boys had it worse. The first I knew there were boys living there was one day when we were sitting in silence learning our times tables. The Master in the next room screamed a boy's name. The crack of his cane was followed by the boy crying.'

'That's horrible, like something out of a Charles Dickens story. Did you have friends though?' Kate put the papers away.

'Making friends wasn't encouraged, but I had one good friend: Alison.'

'The whole experience sounds horrendous, but there's no shame in it, Mum. It wasn't your fault.'

'Ray was the only one I told about it all.'

Kate sat back down.

'I think deep down he suspected he wasn't your real dad when you were little. I was terrified of him turning his back on us if he found out you weren't his. I didn't want to be an unmarried mother – repeating history.'

'I can understand that. Can you tell me more about what happened to my real dad?'

'I was told he was in a car crash. We'd gone our separate ways. He went off to Australia on a ship to start a new life.' Elizabeth was gazing at the ceiling as if the whole episode was projected up there.

'Where is he buried?'

'In Australia I expect.'

'Did he know about me?'

'I didn't have the chance to tell him I was expecting because we'd already split up when I found out, and he'd left the country by then. There didn't seem any point tracking him down. I thought it was better for everyone. It was a shock when I found out though, I can tell you, because I was with Ray by then. I was about twelve weeks gone. As time went on, I thought it would be cruel telling a child that her daddy wasn't her daddy at all. But then I had to tell you when you were older, so you knew you weren't related to your aunty. To me, Ray was your dad. He was always there for you, as he was for me.'

'I would still like to have known more about him.'

'I didn't want to upset Ray any more than I had. I thought you would take it better than you did, I have to say. I didn't expect you to go running off with that layabout. But I suppose there's never a right time for these things. I often think that honesty is overrated. Look at all the damage it did. And as for Ray... sometimes I wonder if I should ever have told him. He never got over the fact that you weren't his own little girl.'

'He was never the same with me after that. He'd hesitate for a millisecond before hugging me, then I think he hated himself for reacting like that; I could see it in his face. Telling the truth has painful consequences. Are there no photos of my real dad?' Kate still couldn't help wondering if she looked anything like him.

'No.' Elizabeth darted a glance at her.

'Ray took me back to Berkhamsted years later after the place closed down. It brought back terrible memories for me. I had nightmares afterwards – even seeing the little lane we used to walk down on Sundays, although it was generally the best day of the week. We'd have to crocodile march along the country lanes to chapel for Sunday service, and pray for all the brave men who'd gone to war. When the choir sang it was so uplifting. Once, a woman with a pram and a little boy stopped to watch us go by. I'll never forget how she put a protective arm of her cloak round him, like an angel's wing, pulling him close to her and tipping his chin up so he could see her smile down at him. She whispered into his corn-blond hair. I could only imagine what she said. It gave me an insatiable longing to have *my* mother cup my face and kiss my forehead, or simply hold my hand walking down the street. I wondered why I couldn't have those simple pleasures.'

Kate struggled to think of a time Elizabeth had ever given her a hug.

'I didn't realise until I left how much every moment of our lives was regimented. It took some time to adjust to normal life.'

'I'm so sorry about the purse. God, if I'd known what it meant to you…'

'It was something to hang on to, that's all.' Elizabeth clutched her hanky. The lined pattern of the blanket seemed to stab at Kate's eyes.

'Your dad was all for filling you in about my childhood, but I wouldn't let him. I didn't want anyone to know about it, not just you. The shame of it all was too much.' Elizabeth smoothed her hand over the envelope.

The clatter of the food trolley interrupted them. Kate put the papers back in the cupboard and moved the table across the bed. She sat reading the newspaper while her mother ate meat in gravy with an ice-cream scoop of mashed potato and sticks of boiled carrot.

'Anyone would think they didn't want us to get better,' Elizabeth said. She pushed the plate away, half the food uneaten.

'You'll be able to come home soon.'

Elizabeth put her head back. 'I don't know. They said I was lucky to survive this one.'

'That doesn't mean you will have another heart attack though, does it?'

'There's more chance I will, especially in these early days.'

'Don't talk like that. You'll be home for Christmas, you'll see.'

'I dearly hope so.'

'I'm going to meet up with Paul.'

'What for?'

'I need to sort things out with him, put an end to it.'

'I thought you'd done with him.'

'I had, but there's something I need to deal with.'

'What's all the money for?'

'I can't say.'

'Whatever it is between you two, be careful. I don't trust him. Have you told James about him asking for money?'

'I will, but now is not the right time,' Kate lied. She rubbed her bump. The thought of telling James about any of it made her head swim. She couldn't let herself think about what she did, or it would make her feel sick to the stomach. She'd spent so long trying to block it out, but now Paul was digging it all up again. He wasn't going to let her forget. And nor was whoever was sending her the nasty texts.

The main ward lights went off, leaving the individual lamps on above the beds.

'I think they want you all to rest,' Kate said, standing up.

'Katie…' Elizabeth reached out, '…you will be careful, won't you?'

'I promise.' Kate dipped down to kiss her goodbye on the forehead. She detected the faint smell of rose water. The lines on her mother's face seemed softer now she'd released her weight of secrets. If only she could do the same.

Chapter Twenty-Nine

It was a fresh chilly morning when Kate and James arrived in Southampton the following Friday. They drove straight to the marina to host a boat party event they'd organised for the local business community. All the way down Kate had been going over in her mind what to say to Paul when they met the next morning. How she could persuade him to let her off the full amount and end it now. If he didn't, she'd have to look into taking out a personal loan. The money would never make up for her mistakes, but at least she'd sleep a little easier at night knowing she'd paid her fair share. The only problem was she had the feeling it would never be enough for Paul, that he'd keep coming back for more.

James parked at Town Quay and they walked along the pontoon to the *Princess Caroline* moored a few metres away. The crew showed them round to make sure everything was in order before the guests started arriving. The upper deck had been closed off to the elements and the middle and bridge decks, where the restaurant and stage area were set up, were already laid out and decorated with fresh flowers. Kate visited the galley to check the food for the brunch buffet had been prepared. Flute glasses were lined up on the bar for the welcome drinks of Prosecco, Buck's Fizz and orange juice.

On her way back up to greet the guests she checked her phone was on silent, but immediately wished she hadn't. A notification was on the locked screen. @BammerGirl21 had tagged her in a tweet. She couldn't help clicking on her notifications. There was a GIF of a drunk girl crying to another girl: *why am I so ugly?* in dancing words underneath. The message read:

> You're so ugly how can he bear to look at you every day?

This wasn't random. It felt personal, like they knew her, but maybe she didn't know them, which meant it could be anyone. She immediately blocked the account and switched her phone off.

The first guests arrived at 10.45 a.m. promptly. James invited each guest on board, shook hands with them, then ticked the business off his list. A crew member showed them to a table full of business name badges. Kate shook their hands and introduced herself. She scrutinised their faces for any sign of someone who was out to get her. The waiter offered them a drink from his silver tray. By 11.15 a.m., almost everyone had arrived, except a few who'd had to cancel due to sickness. But minutes before they were about to begin the first speech, Kate spotted a man in a navy suit hurrying towards the boat. She alerted James, who rushed over to greet him.

'P. L. Gardening Services,' the man said, looking past James, straight at Kate. She blinked back at him and slowly the penny dropped who it was. Paul. Hair slicked back, designer stubble, just like he used to have it. Shit. How could she not have realised he was on the guest list?

Of course, his business would be in this county: Hampshire and Wight. It hadn't even occurred to her. Part of her had assumed he'd been exaggerating about owning a gardening business, that he was more of a casual odd-job man. But here he was, grinning at her, looking almost unrecognisably dapper in a sharp suit, gold cufflinks and a crisp white shirt open at the neck.

'Are you okay, do you want to sit down?' James asked as he rejoined her on the small stage.

'I'm fine,' she whispered and passed him the microphone.

'You look very pale,' he said before he spoke to the audience.

And she felt it – as though all the blood had been sucked out of her. How was she going to survive a whole day with Paul here? Somehow she had to keep him away from James. What was he up to?

After James's speech welcoming everyone and announcing the details of the day ahead, he introduced the local mayor who had joined them for brunch. The plan was to set sail around the Solent and moor off the coast of the Isle of Wight for afternoon tea. There would be an opportunity for guests to have a ride in the speed boat, if they were feeling brave enough, which Kate wasn't.

When everyone had finished brunch, the mayor stood up and thanked them all for coming then spoke about the value of the local business community. He thanked Hampshire and Wight Council for organising such an excellent business networking event. After a few minutes, Kate zoned out, her mind too scrambled with the next phase of the trip and trying to fathom how to manage Paul being here. Every time she glanced in his direction his eyes were fixed on her.

Despite the cold weather, the day was bright, sunny and calm. Kate and James mingled with the guests as they set off on the mini cruise, making sure everyone was fed and watered and in good spirits. All the time Kate tried to watch where James and Paul were, ready to spring between them if they got too close. Paul seemed to know several of the other business owners, so he was suitably occupied chatting to a group, glass of bubbly in hand.

Once they'd moored off the Isle of Wight, some of the more adventurous guests took rides in the speedboat, including Paul who was next in the queue for a ride. She imagined herself jetting towards the beach, Bond style with a briefcase of cash, and Paul standing at the water's edge wearing Speedos, arms crossed waiting for her.

As soon as Paul had gone in the speedboat, Kate left James in charge of who was next in line for a ride, while she went to the galley to check on afternoon tea with the chef. The finger sandwiches were being freshly made, but when she checked the numbers, there weren't enough for the eighty or so guests. She went through the checklist again and the chef offered extra mini cheese scones and slices of quiche and fruit loaf.

By the time she got back to the queue, the last person was climbing into the speedboat. Where had Paul gone? And James was nowhere to be seen. A feeling of unease crept through her. She searched up and down, politely checking on the guests as she frantically looked for James. She asked a couple of the crew, but no one had seen where he'd gone. Then at the far end of the deck, she spotted Paul's head and shoulders, his back to her, deep in conversation by the look of it, although she couldn't see who with. She squeezed through the groups of people chatting and drinking, a fixed smile on her face, hoping to bump into James on the way. How could he just disappear and leave it all to her? Maybe he'd gone to the bathroom. Afternoon tea was being brought out at any minute.

But as she got nearer to Paul, she heard James's laugh. Her body turned to ice.

'There she is.' Kate heard James say. And then she saw that he was the one who'd been keeping Paul so animated all this time. He'd been shielded by Paul's body so she couldn't see him, deliberately she was sure of it. Paul had literally cornered her husband. What the hell had they been talking about?

'You didn't tell me your Isle of Wight friend Paul was here,' James said.

Kate glared at Paul. He grinned back, hand shading his forehead, squinting at her in the afternoon winter sun beaming through the window.

'Oh I get it; you didn't know he'd be here either?' James laughed. 'Paul tells me you dated each other when you were teenagers. You didn't say, darling.'

Kate squinted. She wished she could disappear. She did not want to have a conversation about this or anything with either of them.

'I'm sure Kate will tell you all about it. My lips are sealed. Never spill an ex-girlfriend's secrets.' Both men laughed. Kate wanted to throw up.

'I need your help, James,' she said with as little emotion as possible. She about turned and walked off. James followed behind, but she couldn't speak until they were on their own on the top deck.

'Why are you talking about me? What has he been saying?'

'Nothing really, what are you so worried about? So you have secrets too, now we're even.' His smirk enraged her even more.

'I don't like the way he's cosying up to you, talking about me, plus you're leaving everything to me down-stairs.'

'Oh, I get it, you don't like me catching you out. I told you about me and Susie, but you denied Paul was an old boyfriend. Why didn't you want me to know? Any other dark secrets you want to share with me?' He looked genuinely amused by her outrage.

'Like what?' For all she knew, Paul had told him everything about their lives together.

He laughed. 'Nothing.'

Kate swished past him, unable to contain her anger. As she stomped back downstairs to the galley, she bumped straight into Paul.

'You all right, Katie? You look a bit upset.'

'Excuse me.' She tried to squeeze past him, but he stuck his arm out to stop her.

'You're not worried I spilt the beans, are you?'

'I don't know, have you?' She tried to calm herself, smooth back her hair, but she was flushed and sweating. He could have told James every detail, although she doubted it because he was still talking to her, laughing at her.

'Come on, I'm not a bastard, am I?' He stroked her cheek.

'You can forget about meeting up tomorrow, I'm going home.'

'Ah that's a shame, because I was prepared to let you off the rest of the money.'

'Oh. Really?' Kate did a double-take, frowning at him. Did he really mean that or was there a 'but' coming? Perhaps she'd misjudged him. She searched his eyes for clues he was joking.

'You need to meet me in the morning at 10.45 a.m. sharp, because we've got another boat to catch.' He smiled and rubbed his hands together.

'Have we?' A shiver ran through her.

'Yeah. I think you can guess what the deal is.'

Part of her wanted to pay him the money and get out of there as soon as possible.

'There's someone special who's dying to meet you.' He grinned, watching her as the words sank in.

She started trembling uncontrollably as though she'd stepped onto a vibrating exercise machine. Now she could see clearly what he was doing, making her face up to what she did, what she'd been running from for two decades. The details of that day were filtering back to her every time she saw him, and it made her more ashamed of herself than ever. The passing of time hadn't eased her guilt or shame: it had only amplified it.

Chapter Thirty

On Saturday morning, Kate sat at the front of the ferry, watching it skim through the water, Paul dozing across three seats next to her. She couldn't sit still, shifting this way and that, checking her phone, zipping it up in her handbag then doing it all again a few seconds later. She'd hardly slept, going over and over in her mind how she was going to handle today, this meeting. Her stomach, in fact her whole body, was full of jitters. She scratched the eczema between her fingers. Paul was going to enjoy watching her squirm. It would be like one of those meetings set up after a crime, the chance for a victim to confront their perpetrator for the first time. Find out what made them do it, if their remorse was real or just for the benefit of reducing their sentence. Who'd get the most out of it? Could it really help a victim, or did it add the one detail that was missing from their nightmares? – the face of the monster that caused them harm.

Her mobile beeped. She grabbed it from her bag and read the message:

> You don't deserve to be a mother!

Her body jerked forward as though someone had stabbed her. This was from a different number again. Clearly not from Paul as he was asleep. Who was it? Were they here on the boat? She scanned round her. Lots of people were on their phones: was it from one of them? She picked up her handbag and walked up and down the aisles. A woman glanced up from her phone and frowned. Was it her? But who was she?

Kate moved to the lounge bar. The queue wrapped right round the corner, and every time she saw a frosted glass of wine or beer, she mentally moved a little closer to joining the line. What prevented her, apart from being pregnant, was knowing that the alcohol would make her sleepy and she needed to stay alert.

She bought the last copy of *The Times* and tried to read, but her mind kept jumping from the words on the page to an image of Paul's smug face, knowing he had the upper hand whichever way she turned. She thought of James in their hotel last night, talking so innocently about his school days and who he'd like to meet up with again and the worst person he could hear from.

'If these people were your best friends, why didn't you keep in touch?' he'd asked. Always so trusting of her. Believing that she was going to a school reunion with Paul. She'd said as little as possible, that she couldn't remember why, not wanting to complicate her lie any further, but now the question of why she hadn't maintained some sort of contact floated untethered in her mind like a lost balloon.

The Isle of Wight seemed an idyllic place to live. Paul always said he loved growing up near the beach. She remembered her fascination with the different coloured sand layered in anything from a miniature glass lighthouse to a teddy bear. The first time she'd visited was with her parents when she'd been about nine years old. The bed and breakfast they'd stayed in had neatly set tables, each with cotton napkins and a glass dish of butter curls. Every morning for two weeks, they greeted a woman who sat with her husband by the unlit fireplace. She couldn't stop staring at Kate. On their last day, she handed Kate a small package and her parents allowed her to unwrap it at the table. Inside was a red purse with a long shoulder strap. On the front, printed in gold lettering was the name 'Jennifer'. Elizabeth had squeezed Kate's thigh under the table as a threat not to open her mouth. Kate smiled and nodded her thanks at the couple. The husband had passed his wife a cotton hanky and patted her hand while she dabbed her eyes. Kate hadn't understood why she couldn't tell them Jennifer wasn't her name.

By the time the ferry docked, it was approaching midday. The greyness of the sky and sea had merged into one. A seagull screeched overhead. The salty damp air and the faint aroma of fish was strangely reassuring. She followed Paul past a ruddy-faced man with an Asian woman, whose childlike frame was balanced on razor-sharp heels. Behind them were three elderly ladies in walking boots, each gripping their hiking sticks.

'Let's eat,' he said over his shoulder, striding ahead of her. He pointed to the end of the causeway. Kate's stomach wobbled at the thought of food, but she refused to let him know how nervous she was. She checked her watch for the hundredth time. What if she didn't show up? She might have decided against coming or never had any intention of seeing her. But a tiny niggle she'd tried to ignore crept into her mind. What if she was the one sending the malicious messages? Maybe it was part of Paul's plan to scare her. She felt the baby flutter. She lightly touched her bump, well hidden under her loose-fitting dress and swing coat. Was she safe coming here on her own with both of them out for her blood?

They crossed the road and walked in silence to the bottom of Union Street, to the Italian restaurant on the corner. They had a good view of Ryde Esplanade and the sea beyond. The waitress greeted them as though they were family. She showed them straight to their table. Another couple about their age were sitting by the window sipping wine and chatting. Every sill was decorated with colourful bags of different shaped pasta and tall elegant bottles of olive oil.

'Can I get you some drinks?' the waitress asked.

'Bottle of red?' Paul nodded to Kate.

'I'm not drinking; could I have sparkling water, please?'

'Thought you'd be wanting a stiff one.' He raised an eyebrow, took his suit jacket off and draped it over the back of his chair.

'I'm fine with water, thank you.'

The waitress came back with their drinks and a basket of bread then took their food order. Kate could only manage soup of the day.

'Cheers.' Paul held up his glass.

Kate wasn't sure what they were meant to be celebrating. The waitress brought his starter of deep fried calamari. Strange to be eating a meal with him again. It felt too intimate, his feet bumping into hers, the way he piled food into his mouth and wiped his lips on the back of his hand. The lightly spiced aftershave radiated from the warmth of his body. She thought of all the weekends she'd spent with him when they first moved in together, whole mornings in bed, and afternoons visiting galleries and exhibitions. She would make them a sandwich each, wrapped in foil, hidden in her duffle coat pockets so they could take a bite as they walked round and spent as much time as possible absorbing the paintings and sculptures. Most people spent about thirty seconds on each one before moving on to the next. But they would sit on the floor or a bench and examine them in detail, making notes on brushstrokes, use of colour and light and the uniqueness and beauty of each piece. Their passion for art had connected them so deeply it had run through their veins. How could this man have once been her whole life? Part of her missed the young girl she used to be, when life had been simpler because she was unafraid of being herself. Now she'd reinvented herself as a businesswoman with a practised public face, careful not to let the mask slip and reveal the real her hidden underneath.

'Is this settled now, no more demands?' She took a slice of crusty bread and ripped it into small pieces.

'Up to you, isn't it?' Paul said, a huge grin on his face.

'What else do you want from me? Can't you let me get on with my life after this?'

'Wow, still a hard bitch, aren't you?'

She walked straight into that. Her nerves were beginning to show. She needed to stay composed.

'I want you to face her, look her in the eye, maybe even say sorry.'

'How is she? You haven't told me anything.' Kate found it hard to say her name aloud after so many years of suppressing it.

'You can ask her yourself soon enough.'

'And you think meeting her will make up for it all?'

'Of course not, but it's a start.'

The waitress brought their mains. Paul tucked straight into his venison steak in peppercorn sauce. Her tomato soup smelt rich and delicious. In other circumstances she might have enjoyed it. She scattered the pieces of torn bread on top and dipped her spoon into the well of red liquid.

'Hasn't she ever asked about me?' She blew across the spoon and stared at the streaks of white above Paul's ears which stretched further than she remembered all those weeks ago in her house.

'No,' he said with his mouth full.

Kate's jaw tightened. So, she hadn't been dying to meet her at all. Of course she hadn't. The malicious messages popped into her head again. She blew harder on the spoon, splaying soup over the edge onto the table. She fixed her eyes on Paul. 'You still haven't told me what the money was for.'

'Are you serious? Do you need me to spell it out? Have you contributed anything in twenty years?'

'That's not quite true though, is it?'

He frowned.

'My father was paying you a tidy sum every month until he died. That's why you started coming after me, because his payments stopped.'

'What he gave me was a minuscule amount. He was trying to make up for what you should have been paying. Did you think we were going to survive on fresh air?'

'So there you are, you've had your money. Why were you expecting more?'

'I just told you, because it wasn't enough, especially for what you put us through. It will never be enough for what you did!' He shoved his plate, crashing it into hers. The couple by the window looked in their direction.

'Oh, you want compensation as well, do you?' Kate placed her spoon down and wiped her mouth with the serviette. She watched him glug down his third glass of wine. She should end this now and go home, but she was curious to meet her, see how she'd turned out.

'You still need to tell me who else you've told. I'm receiving more of these texts.' She took her phone out and showed him one of the messages. 'Do you recognise the number?'

His smile broadened. 'We've been through this. I told you before, I haven't told anyone. I don't know that number.'

'There have been different numbers and messages on social media too.'

'All I know is there was only one other person there that night. So you better ask her yourself.'

She reran the messages in her head. If Paul was telling the truth, then there was no one else it could be.

The door jangled open and a young couple walked in surrounded by a flurry of snow. The woman's skin was pale except for pink cheeks and bright red lipstick. She wore a parka and long boots and walked with a stick. The man behind wore a snow jacket and beany hat, his arm round her. The woman pulled her hood down and shook out her long dark hair. She looked straight at Kate.

'Hello, Mother,' she said.

Chapter Thirty-One

Kate tried to speak but it felt as though something was stuck in her throat. Only a croaky sound came out. As she stood up, her legs suddenly became weak, her breathing shallow. She cleared her throat.

'Francesca… Frankie.' She felt the shape of the name in her mouth. This was her *daughter* talking to her for the first time. She could hardly believe it was really her, standing in front of her. Her head pounded. How could she have left her baby girl and not gone back? She felt sick with shame. Frankie's gaze fixed on her. Kate could barely meet her eye, but she searched her face for traces of the baby she remembered. The soft hair, just a tuft then, the dark-lashed eyes and face shape were like her own. Paul's chin and ears. Their daughter had turned into a beautiful young woman and she'd missed out on it all.

Paul stood up and kissed Frankie on both cheeks, all the time watching Kate.

'Meet your daughter. Twenty years too late.'

'I'm so sorry,' Kate said, and covered her mouth. Guilt stabbed her hard and threatened to overwhelm her. She'd imagined this moment for so long, dreamt about it many times, but never thought it would happen. She looked from Frankie to Paul and back again, trying to read their thoughts. *Francesca.* He had chosen her name and she'd loved it straight away. One of the few things they'd agreed on. She should have stayed and faced the consequences of her actions, but she'd been too ill, too cowardly.

Frankie held out her hand, head tipped, inquisitive.

Kate took it and with that one touch felt the gravity of everything she'd missed. Shame swept through her like a ghost of herself. She wrapped her arms round her daughter, eyes squeezed shut to block the tears. Frankie stiffened.

'Careful, my back...' Frankie pulled away, frowning.

'I'm sorry, did I hurt you, are you okay?' Kate stood back, not knowing what to do.

'It's an old injury,' Frankie said.

Paul asked the waitress for two more wine glasses and ordered another bottle of red.

'This is my fiancé, Matt,' Frankie said. The tall, smiling man behind her stepped forward and shook Kate's hand. She was grateful for his friendly face.

'Nice to meet you, Matt. And what do you both do?'

'I'm a plumber. Frankie's an artist.' They pulled up chairs next to Paul.

'Oh really? That's fantastic.' Kate raised her eyebrows at Paul not mentioning it. He smiled back.

'Do you want to see Frankie's work in progress?' Matt pressed a button on his phone.

'I'd love to.' When she had been expecting Frankie, they'd day-dreamed about her becoming an artist like Paul. But imagining their lives as a family had been the easy part. Living them had been so much harder. How different things could have been if only she'd asked for help. Her behaviour had been shameful. Because of her, this beautiful young woman had grown up without a mother.

Matt showed her the tall, half-painted canvas set up on an easel in what looked like a living room.

'That's beautiful, reminds me of *The Three Ages of Woman*, by Gustav Klimt. It's incredibly accomplished.'

The light in Frankie's eyes glimmered. 'Do you know Klimt's work well?'

'He's one of my favourite artists.'

'Really? Dad never said.' She elbowed him playfully.

'What a wonderful talent you have,' Kate said.

Frankie took a sip of wine. 'Call it my homage to Klimt. I'm about to work on the older woman just here.' She pointed to the blank space on the left of the canvas. 'Did Dad tell you he used to sit with me as a kid? We'd draw together for hours. He says it's the only way he could get me to concentrate on anything.' She burst into laughter. 'Every time I said I couldn't draw something, he'd draw it first and get me to copy it.'

'She exhibits all over the place now,' Matt said. 'She's even been invited to exhibit in a London gallery next spring.'

'It's no big deal.' Frankie blushed.

'Of course it is,' Matt said. 'You're starting to be recognised; your mum should know you're going to be famous one day.'

Frankie stopped laughing. Kate looked out of the window, hoping a hole might open up so she could fall through it. The word 'mum' rattled round in her head like a bead from a broken necklace she couldn't quite reach.

'Let's call everyone by their first names, shall we?' Frankie said.

Paul poured Frankie and Matt a glass of wine each then tipped back his last mouthful and refilled his own glass.

Kate tried to read the look that passed between him and Frankie.

'Had a nice meal?' Frankie asked, taking off her coat. She was speaking to Paul, not her.

'Yeah, I think so.' Paul rubbed his palms together. 'Do either of you want something to eat?' He passed Frankie the menu. His leg brushed against Kate's, bringing back the memory of his hands on her body, his lips over hers. Her head began to swim.

'I'm not hungry, thanks,' Frankie said, passing the menu to Matt, but he put it straight down on the table.

Paul took an envelope out of his jacket pocket and pushed it across the table. The flap was unstuck. 'I brought you these photos, so you can see what a good job I've done.'

The photo he sent her of them both on the beach immediately came to mind. She'd told him she was pregnant just minutes before it was taken.

She took out the photo on top: Francesca, aged about eighteen months, holding a rag doll under her arm, giving a toothy grin straight into the camera. Peering closer at her daughter's face, she touched it with her fingertips and looked up at her now. She couldn't believe she was sitting opposite her. She struggled to conjure a clear memory of her as a newborn, but she remembered the first time they'd taken her out in the pram, she'd cried all the way and Kate couldn't work out why. She'd been certain everyone was staring at her, wondering why she was such a bad mother.

She eased the rest of the photos out of the envelope. They were mostly holiday snaps: catching crabs on Stee-phill Cove beach; riding on a merry-go-round at The Needles; digging up fossils from muddy sandbanks at Alum Bay. The loss of every moment she'd missed snagged like an old scar. She'd abandoned her own daughter. The shame and guilt of her actions had eaten away at her every day since. For all her own mother's faults, at least she'd been there for her. She vowed to do everything right for this little one. She secretly touched her bump under the table. Paul had been both parents to Frankie. He'd done everything she should have. Despite his recent behaviour towards her, she had to acknowledge what an incredible job he'd made of it. But his success only showed up her failure all the more.

'Remember when you thought you'd picked up the wrong baby at the hospital?' Paul's laugh cracked the silence.

'Only because she wouldn't stop crying. She'd been so quiet those first few days.' Every time she'd held Frankie, her baby face would screw up in one of those end-of-the-world cries. Whatever Kate tried to do to calm her made no difference.

'You can't deny the resemblance,' Paul said.

It wasn't so apparent in the younger pictures. She looked at another, of Francesca aged fourteen, where the likeness to her was a little clearer: the wavy hair loosely plaited framed her bronzed face, holding a floppy hat on her head against a sea breeze. The sunshine had made her half squint, half smile but the pose was casual, comfortable. She wore cut-off jeans and a bikini top with shells draped round her neck, strung together haphazardly on a shoelace. The shadow of the photographer, probably Paul, elongated across the sand dunes beside her.

'Your dad didn't tell me you'd hurt your back,' Kate said.

'You mean my accident? No, he wouldn't; he says people should look beyond appearances.'

'Accident?' Kate glanced at all their faces waiting for an explanation from one of them. 'Can you tell me what happened?' Kate sipped her glass of water.

Frankie didn't answer.

'She fell off a horse.' Matt sat back in his chair. Frankie finished her wine and crossed her arms.

'That's terrible. When?'

'I was fifteen,' Frankie said.

'Seven years ago?'

'Two weeks after my birthday. I broke my back.'

'She couldn't walk at first; they thought she was paralysed,' Matt said.

'Why didn't you contact me, Paul?'

'Hang on a minute, he didn't know where you were.' Frankie pointed her finger at Kate.

'He knew where my parents lived; in fact, my dad was sending him maintenance payments for you for years.'

'Here we go,' Paul said, crossing his arms.

'That doesn't even make sense.' Frankie scraped back her chair as if she was about to leave.

'Why doesn't it?'

'He told me he never got a penny out of you.'

'Well I gave him fifteen thousand pounds not so long ago.'

'Gave it voluntarily, did you?' Paul said.

'Didn't he tell you that either?'

'No, he didn't.' Frankie's frown morphed into a smile. She put her arms round her dad and gazed into his eyes as she spoke. 'But he gave the money to us for our wedding next year.' She kissed his cheek and he hugged her back.

'Congratulations, I'm really pleased for you both.' Kate thought for a moment. 'Things ended badly with your dad and me.'

'Wow, you don't say.' Paul laughed.

'But I'm glad things are working out for you.'

Frankie nodded and slipped her hand into Matt's.

'There's something I need to check. Could I see your mobile number, please?'

'Yeah, sure.' Frankie switched her phone on and turned the screen round for her to see. The number ended with three twos, not any of the ones that had sent her messages.

'Is this the only mobile you use?'

'Yeah. I've only got one. Don't most people?' She turned to Matt who nodded.

'She thinks you've been sending her cranky messages.' Paul grinned.

'Thanks, Paul. Subtle as always.'

'You thought that?' Frankie wrinkled her nose.

'No, not really, it could be anyone.'

'It's not me.' Frankie tucked her phone in her pocket.

Kate had hoped to take her number so they could keep in touch. She showed her one of the messages: 'I WISH YOU WERE DEAD'.

'Have you been to the police?'

Kate shook her head. 'They're coming from different numbers, so I'm guessing it's a pay-as-you-go phone, so hard to trace. Could we possibly exchange ours? I'd really like to stay in touch with you, if you'll let me?'

'Yeah, why not?' Frankie took her phone back out again.

'How's your mother by the way?' Paul leaned back in his chair, glass in hand.

'She's still very ill, especially after your little visit.' Kate tried to work out what was coming next; the three of them sat in front of her, watching her every move.

'I'm talking about the woman who couldn't wait to see the back of me,' Paul told Frankie. 'Your dear grandmother thought I wasn't good enough for her beloved daughter.'

Kate glowered at him. 'She had her reasons.'

'Now come on, Katie, are you telling me you didn't want to get as far away from her as possible?'

Kate clenched her teeth. 'He turned up at her house unannounced and scared the life out of a seventy-nine-year-old woman.'

'Seriously, Dad?' Frankie seemed genuinely shocked.

'They could barely stand the sight of each other.' Paul crossed his arms.

'That's not true!'

'You told me she was a cold... now what was it?'

Kate scraped back her chair.

'Da-ad.' Frankie pulled at his arm.

'And now all we need to know is why you didn't contact us before now.' He pushed his empty glass onto the table, almost knocking it over.

'Desserts anyone?' asked the waitress in a bold voice as she cleared away the plates.

While everyone answered, Kate eyed up her route to the door and the esplanade beyond. If she could squeeze round the waitress, then two tables, she could be out of there. She didn't appreciate being ambushed.

'So come on, was it convenient not having us around, pretending you didn't have a daughter?' Paul looked to Frankie to join in, but she stayed silent.

'Dad, stop,' Frankie said. Matt laid his hand over hers.

Kate tried to lock eyes with Paul, but he shifted his gaze away from her.

'That looks good,' Paul said as the waitress put his dessert on the table.

'I could eat tiramisu every day,' Frankie said.

'You do, pretty much,' Matt said under his breath.

'I heard that.' Frankie laughed and slapped his arm. Matt grinned at her.

'Try not to eat it all,' Paul said as he went to the bathroom.

Kate smiled apologetically at the couple by the window. She wondered if she could come up with an excuse for leaving.

'Dad's been saving his anger up all these years,' Frankie said.

'I know I should have kept in touch with you, but I honestly thought you'd be better off without me.'

'Why?' Frankie tilted her head, her big blue eyes already knowing the answer.

Flakes of snow were blowing round outside. She willed herself not to cry. 'I'm sorry, I need some air. I'm so sorry.' She scrambled past their astonished faces, tears spilling down her cheeks.

Outside, she took in a deep breath and wiped her face, exhaling into the icy air. All these years she'd managed to lock this part of her life away in a heavy box out of reach, tethered to the bottom of her heart. She pictured Frankie curled up in the plastic cot next to her hospital bed. She'd tried to feel the joy that everyone told her to expect, but instead she'd felt bruised and in pain after almost two days in labour and all she'd wanted was to forget everything and sleep. Days then weeks later she'd still felt nothing for the little mite, no rush of motherly love, only impatience when she cried and cried and wouldn't stop. Then the despicable, unforgivable way she'd lost her temper with an innocent baby. The fear and dread of the damage she might have done.

She ran her fingertips across her bump. Would she be able to bond with her baby this time and feel like a proper mum, or was she going to make the same mistake?

Chapter Thirty-Two

'Blimey, who's left the door open?' Paul stood in the restaurant doorway.

Kate hurried away from him, across the road, and sat on the edge of a bench facing out to the choppy grey sea. Now they'd met, she wanted to stay in touch with Frankie by email and telephone. For now, it would be best all round if she went home.

'So, what are you really here for?' Paul said behind her, taking her by surprise. 'To pay off your debt or see your daughter?'

'How did I know she was going to turn up?'

'Very funny. I told you yesterday she'd be here.'

She ran a finger along the thin layer of snow on the seat. 'Why didn't you tell me about her accident?' She shivered and pulled her coat collar up.

For a few seconds he didn't answer. Without looking at him she knew every muscle in his face was pulled tight.

'You didn't deserve to know.'

Kate caught a glimpse of him rolling up his shirt sleeves as if they were about to slug out their differences.

'How can you say that? How could you keep something like that from me?' She swivelled round to face him.

'I didn't even know if you were alive.' His voice gave the slightest waver.

'You could have gone to my parents' house, told them, demanded they try to find me.'

'Don't you dare tell me what I should have done.'

'You *should* have tried harder,' she shouted.

'And if I could have contacted you, are you saying you would have torn yourself away from your new life?'

'Yes, yes I would.' Even though it would have meant jeopardising her marriage to James. *Wouldn't she?*

Paul didn't reply.

'Yes,' she said again, confirming it to herself, but her voice lacked resonance in their snow-insulated surroundings. She imagined only muffled sounds carrying back to the restaurant. If she'd been a braver person, she would have done the right thing. But she was so used to lying about it, she'd even fooled herself. The truth was she'd thought about Frankie every single day, wondered how she was doing, what she looked like. She'd walked round with this gaping wound that no one could see because she was so good at hiding her shameful secret. She'd made sure she kept busy with the business, even married a man who wouldn't ever talk about children. All the time accepting that whatever she did in life, however successful she appeared to be, she could never ever be completely happy.

'You didn't deserve to know,' he said again, more slowly. And when she didn't respond, he continued, 'I didn't want you turning up just because you felt sorry for us.'

Kate shook her head.

'It was difficult enough...'

She followed his line of vision to a holly bush and the small clots of red that had burst on the ground. 'I can't pretend to know how scared you must have been.'

He rubbed his face in the crook of his arm. 'When it happened, Frankie lay there so still and silent. I knelt next to her and she couldn't speak; she was holding her breath because it was too painful to breathe. It turned out that several of her ribs were broken as well as her spine. I'll never forget when I asked her if she could move and she simply shut her eyes.' Paul wiped his hand across his eyes. 'I thought she'd never walk again.'

'She's a brave and lucky girl.'

He nodded. 'The specialists say she's getting stronger all the time. She hardly needs her stick now.'

> 'Are you two coming in?'

Frankie texted.

Paul showed Kate the message. They looked at each other and a smile ruffled their lips.

> 'Give us a couple of minutes, Frank'

Paul texted back. He took a lighter out of his pocket and flipped open a silver-plated cigarette case, offering her one.

The words, *With love, Kate* were engraved on the inside of the lid. She'd forgotten about that. Her first-anniversary gift to him.

'I gave up years ago,' she said.

He shrugged and lit the cigarette. He still wore the same gold signet ring on his middle finger. The distinctive smell of Marlboro took her back; she could see Paul as he was then, with unruly blond hair and tanned skin, barely shaving when she'd first met him.

'Did you ever think about us after you left?' He drew the smoke in, and it came out of his nostrils.

'Of course I did.' Although she tried not to for a long time. She had pushed it to the back of her mind, out of reach.

'Have you any idea what it was like those first days and weeks after you left?' There was a tremor in his hand when he drew harder on the cigarette until its walls started to collapse. He blew the smoke out and didn't wait for her answer. 'We could have worked things out, you and me, we were great together, special.'

That wasn't how she remembered it towards the end, although she had to admit her attraction to him had never waned. She hadn't been sure she could stay with him long-term because he hadn't been bothered about finding a steady job, which was why it came as such a shock to discover she was pregnant.

'You weren't well after Frankie was born, I can see that now, but you didn't say anything. If you'd have talked to me, I could have helped you; we could have worked it out.'

Kate doubted it. He was too busy drinking and staying up late. He couldn't see the point of her going on any short evening courses at college and university when she already had a *perfectly good job*. He'd wanted her to keep working so he could stay at home and paint portraits.

He gently laid his warm hand on top of hers. 'Can you honestly say you never wondered how it would have been if you'd stayed?'

Kate edged her hand away. He wouldn't like her answer.

'Not even once?'

'Paul, I'm happily married.'

'Someone your mother approves of?' He flicked the remains of the cigarette on the ground. 'Who is he? What's he got that I haven't?'

'I don't want to have this conversation. You still haven't said why you didn't bring Frankie to Mum's house?'

'You wanted me to come begging…?' he mock-laughed. 'You didn't want us.'

'It would have been the natural thing to do, especially as you went to Dad for maintenance.'

'Natural? You make me laugh. Isn't it natural for a mother to *want* her child?'

'Or was that why he paid you, because he thought in doing so he might get to meet his grandchild?'

'He paid up because he was ashamed of what you did.'

Kate leaned over as though he'd winded her. The tiny hope she had that he hadn't told her dad had gone. She started back to the restaurant.

'What kind of woman abandons her child?' Paul shouted after her.

Kate paused and drew in a breath. He caught her up.

'I knew you'd take better care of her,' Kate said quietly. The layer of snow looked deceptively solid.

Paul reached out and touched her shoulder. 'I needed you back. We both did.' His face softened. The glowing warmth in his eyes had drawn her in once. He'd been her hero, standing up for her when he met her parents, especially her mum. He'd helped her find the courage she needed to leave. For a fleeting moment, she longed for the Paul she first knew. The cheeky smile, the way he'd adored everything about her. They'd come to the Isle of Wight for a weekend in his camper and stayed with his friends, dossed on the floor in front of a log fire. Most nights a few of them played guitar, drank tequila slammers, smoked pot and did mad things like glue chairs to the walls. She'd truly believed she was in love with him. But now he was set on destroying her.

'I had to get away,' she said.

Paul shook his head. 'You've never told me why.'

Kate examined the snow delicately balanced on the branch of the holly tree. 'I was so, so tired. Even after I'd finally got Frankie to sleep, I would sit there, knowing if I closed my eyes, she would immediately wake up again, as though she knew and was doing it on purpose. I'm not proud of it.' She imagined herself falling face down in the pillow of snow, letting the ice melt her hot skin. 'And you weren't helping much, sleeping during the day, staying up painting every night—'

'Why didn't you see a doctor?' Paul interrupted. 'Why run away?' He paced up and down, brushing past her.

Kate put her hand out to a branch, disturbing the snow scattering at her feet. She realised how cold she felt. 'I was so scared,' she said not looking at him, 'that I might leave Frankie somewhere or hurt her.' A shiver ran through her body.

'But you did.' His face had turned white.

'I didn't mean to.'

'It's all excuses.' Paul stood too close, swiping her with each word.

'I was scared I might do it again.'

'You never came back; surely a good mother would have?'

Kate felt herself sway. The words reverberated through her head in an aftershock. 'You don't understand...' She touched her tiny bump, '...I didn't *feel* like a mother.'

'I told her what you did.'

Kate stared at him, stunned.

'You should have stayed.' He was shouting now.

'How could I after…?' She knew she sounded pathetic and weak.

Paul lit another cigarette. 'Because you had a daughter – you *have* a daughter!'

Kate turned away.

'I take it you got what you wanted: a big cheque at the end of every month and the important title on your little business card?'

'I've done okay.'

Frankie texted again. Kate waved and started back.

'Didn't you once think of coming back to us?'

She faced him. 'I truly believed I'd done the right thing. I was certain Frankie was better off without me; I thought a clean break was best—'

'It's all down to your bloody mother,' he said.

'You're wrong to blame her.'

He dug his foot in the snow, down to the wilted grass and the mud.

'You're unbelievable.' He kicked mud up, soiling the snow.

'That's it – enough.' Kate swept past him. 'You think you know everything, Paul,' she shouted, 'but you don't.' She marched back to the restaurant and grabbed her handbag.

'I'm sorry, Frankie.'

'What's going on?' Frankie scraped her chair back and stood up.

'Ask your dad.'

'Where are you going?' Frankie asked.

'I'm sorry, I need to go for a walk on my own to calm down…' Kate handed Matt some cash for the meal.

'Leaving again, are we?' Paul stood at the door, arms crossed.

Kate hesitated. 'I hope I see you again soon,' she said to Frankie.

She pushed past Paul and strode back across the grass. It was a mistake coming here. Nothing she did now could ever make up for what she did.

Chapter Thirty-Three

Paul called after her. At first she ignored it, then she broke into a trot, determined to be too far away for him to catch her up. Her footfall was softened by the snow, but after a few yards she slowed her pace, out of breath, the weight of the baby pulling down. As she approached a playground, she saw the light bounce off the top of the slide. Every inch of the climbing frame had been gripped by ice; furlike crystals glistened, and the tarmac shone like a sheet of cracked glass. A graveyard to happy summer days.

A flock of birds, sitting in rows like black socks on a washing line, suddenly rose from the climbing frame, one dropping a hunk of bread from its beak. Kate remembered the wisdom of Aesop's *Fables*, her father reading them to her at night, safe and warm in bed, not knowing that the daddy she loved and adored wasn't really hers at all.

Beyond the playground, a road lined with conifers wound out of sight. Paul called to her again. She glanced over her shoulder. He was catching up. She knew she should walk around the playground, on the grass, but it would take so much longer. If she trod carefully, she wouldn't slip. Each step sounded a crack in the thin ice. A few moments later, he was right behind her. As she glanced round, his arm lashed out and gave her a hefty shove in her shoulder. Her foot slid out and, for a few suspended seconds, she was falling. She let out a squeal as she crashed to the ground, landing on her front with a deadening thud.

Paul stood over her. She pushed onto her side. Her coat fell open.

'Call an ambulance,' she screamed up at him, feeling her hardening bump.

He crouched down, hands hovering above her. 'I didn't mean to, I'm so sorry.'

'Quickly!' Kate stared up at his puzzled face.

'Are you okay? Have you broken anything?' He fumbled in his pocket for his mobile.

'I'm pregnant.'

'You?' His eyes widened.

She said it again, shouting this time.

He blinked at her.

'Please…' She bowed her head.

'How can *you* be pregnant?' He shook his head and wandered away from her as he spoke on the phone.

She dared not move as a fire ripped through her belly.

'They're on their way.' He knelt beside her. 'Let's get you up.'

'I can't,' she wailed.

'Can you at least sit up?'

'No, I daren't, the baby… I'm not sure if it's moving.'

'Tell me what I can do.' He moved to touch her.

'Get away from me!'

'How far gone are you?'

'About fourteen weeks.'

'I thought you'd put on a bit of weight but…' His fingers hovered above her, immediately transporting her back to the time she was pregnant with Frankie, lying in Hyde Park in the warm sunshine, his hand resting on her bare skin, the air fragrant, heavy with pollen. He'd made her feel so safe that she believed everything would slot into place as soon as she was born. She'd thought she'd love Paul more than ever, be content with her life and turn out to be a great mother.

'You're having it then?' he asked, bringing her back to the present.

'Why wouldn't I be?' she snapped.

'I don't understand you,' he said. 'Never have.'

'It'll be your fault if I lose it,' she shouted, pulling away from him.

A dart of sunshine burst through a crack in the clouds. She squinted, trying to see his face. He looked serious as he put a hand on her shoulder and another on her elbow to help her sit up. The pain subsided but her fingers had stiffened in her snow-soaked woollen gloves. Paul took off his jacket and draped it round her shoulders. As they waited, a solitary robin sang its melancholy winter song, echoing around them, bringing their silence into relief. Kate thought over what Paul had told her about Frankie's accident, how she could have died or been paralysed, and how she hadn't known. Her child seriously hurt, and she wasn't there for her.

After what felt like hours, an ambulance siren could be heard faintly in the distance.

Paul put his hands on his head. 'Let me guess – James hasn't got a clue about Frankie?'

She stared at him until her eyes burned from the cold air.

'Why would I keep it from him?'

Paul grinned as if he could read her mind.

The ambulance arrived at high speed and pulled over by the side of the park.

'Don't worry, I'll let him know what's happened,' Paul said as the two paramedics lifted Kate onto a stretcher.

'There's no need,' she said, reaching out her hand.

A paramedic came towards her with an oxygen mask.

'No, please, you don't understand,' Kate said as they lifted the stretcher into the ambulance. The paramedic clamped the mask over Kate's face. Why was this happening to her? She'd come to see her first child and now this had happened. Was it because she had abandoned Frankie and hadn't been there for her after her accident? Because she was a bad mother? What if the baby was hurt? What if she was miscarrying? She wanted this baby more than anything. Tears welled in her eyes. She hoped with every cell in her body that it would be okay. She tried to sit up, to reach out, but the paramedic gently put her hand on Kate's shoulder to keep her down. The other paramedic handed Paul's jacket back to him.

'We'll come and see you later.' Paul stood on the pavement holding his hand up briefly as the doors closed.

Kate's skin and clothes became warm and damp beneath her. The last thing she remembered was her body beginning to shake.

Chapter Thirty-Four

Kate woke up in a hospital bed. It was dark outside, and the ward was reflected in the huge windows. She remembered why she was there. The pain she had experienced at the playground had gone. She touched her belly but could feel no movement. She rubbed the bump gently with both hands. Please, please be all right. She eased herself upright. Where was her phone? She needed to call James, tell him what had happened. Then she remembered that Paul said he would call him. Her heart stopped. Would he tell him everything? He could find James's number on their website. She opened the bedside cupboard and found her handbag inside. She rummaged round and took her phone out.

There was one missed text from James earlier asking her how she was and saying he'd heard what happened from Paul. She texted back, telling him that she and Paul had argued, and he pushed her over. When he replied asking why Paul would do that, she said she couldn't say by text. She needed to tell him in person. A moment later, he called her on FaceTime.

'How are you? You look tired. Tell me what happened with you two.' It looked like he was sitting on the sofa in their hotel room.

'I'm okay. Just worried about this little one.'

'And is the baby all right?'

'I don't know yet.' She tried not to show her anguish.

'So why did Paul push you over?' He pulled a disgusted face. 'He didn't tell me he was the reason you're in hospital.'

'I was trying to get away from him and slipped on ice. I went down with quite a wallop.'

'What were you arguing about?'

Kate blinked at him. There was nowhere to hide. 'He's been sending me messages, threatening and blackmailing me.'

'I don't understand, what for?'

She let out a breath. 'It's complicated.'

'How long has this been carrying on?' He drew back from the screen.

'I bumped into him at Sopwell House.'

'Is there something going on between you?' His voice was uneven.

'No! That's not what it's about.'

'What is it then?'

'I'd rather tell you when you get here.'

'Right. I'm coming over in the morning. And you need to text me if he comes near you again, okay?' He stood up and starting pacing round the room.

'Okay, but don't contact him, will you? You'll only make it worse.'

'Okay, I promise. Now try and get some sleep.'

She ended the call and pressed the phone to her chest. It was going to be hard, but she needed to be honest with him, let him know how sorry she was, and there was a slim chance he might just forgive her.

Her phone buzzed. A notification popped up, saying she'd been tagged on Instagram. Could this be the same person again? She hadn't been on Instagram long and wasn't entirely sure how it all worked apart from the basics. She opened the app and clicked on 'Activity'. Someone called NudeNumberOneGirl had tagged her in a post. She didn't recognise the name and it was obvious she shouldn't touch it, but she needed to see what was being said about her. She clicked on the link and a photo opened of their front door. Neon writing and arrows had been drawn on the picture, pointing to the words:

The Bitch lives here!

Kate covered her mouth. What the fuck? This weirdo knew where they lived. She immediately texted Susie and asked her if she could go round and check everything had been securely locked. Susie replied immediately saying of course she would and asking if there was anything wrong. Kate made up a story about the local Facebook group reporting a rise in burglaries. She took a screenshot of the post and blocked it. Who was doing this? Why were they targeting her?

The beds around her seemed to be full, but the ward was mostly quiet. She wondered how long she'd been asleep. Her hand found her bump again, but still she couldn't detect even the slightest flutter. She cried silently until she felt a hand on her wrist. A young nurse, not much older than Frankie, was reading the watch pinned to her uniform while her cool fingers were pressed firmly on Kate's pulse.

'I'll bring you something to eat before lights out.' She smiled at Kate. 'Hey, are you all right there?'

Kate nodded, unable to hold her tears in.

The nurse folded back the top sheets and tucked them in. 'It's been a nasty shock for you.'

'Is the baby all right?'

'You need plenty of rest. Now then, everyone had sandwiches at tea time, is that okay for you?'

Kate nodded. Had she heard her?

'I'll bring a selection for you.' She picked up a cardboard kidney dish from the bedside table. 'You won't be needing this.'

Kate sat up. 'I so wanted this baby,' she blurted out.

'Hey come on now.' The nurse plucked a couple of tissues from a box on the table. 'The baby's fine. You didn't think…?'

Kate took the tissues and buried her face in them.

The nurse picked up Kate's notes. 'I've only just started my shift, but I believe they spoke to your husband? They said he'll be in tomorrow morning with your daughter.'

'He's not my husband; he's a friend.'

'It says here you did lose some blood, about the time you passed out. They gave you a check over when you came in. Baby's heartbeat was normal, but they want you to have a scan in the morning.'

'But I can't feel it fluttering any more.'

'I'll make a note and come back in an hour. If the baby still hasn't moved, I'll get one of the midwives to come and have a look at you.'

Kate sank back into the pillows.

–

Soon after breakfast the following morning, Paul arrived on the ward with Frankie by his side.

'How are you doing?' Paul stood, ignoring the empty chair. Frankie looked tired.

'Much better, thanks. Hello, Frankie.'

She didn't reply and wouldn't look at her.

'Everything okay with the baby?' Paul asked.

'I've just come back from a scan; the baby is moving, thank goodness.'

'Why didn't you tell me?' Frankie yelled without warning.

Kate winced at the force of Frankie's voice. The ward fell quiet, everyone watching them. A nurse hurried over from an adjacent bed.

'Everything all right here?' The nurse looked at each of their faces. 'You need to keep your voices down or I'll have to ask you to leave.'

Kate nodded and the nurse went back to what she was doing, checking over her shoulder.

'I... I... thought...' Kate cleared her throat. 'I was going to tell you.' She looked to Paul for support but detected the slightest hint of a smile on his lips. 'I wanted to pick the right time.'

'What makes you so sure you want to keep this one?' Frankie's face reddened.

'It's not that I didn't want you...' Kate's words trailed away.

Paul whispered something in Frankie's ear.

'How do you know you won't swan off and leave it after a few months?' Frankie swept her hand out.

Kate had no idea how she was going to feel once this baby was born. What made her think she could be a good mother this time and stick at it? Society had judged her for not being a mother at her age, putting her career above wanting children, so was she trying to fit in or prove that she could do it after failing with Frankie?

She remembered the day she'd left: she'd woken early, barely having slept, thinking over the terrible thing she'd done to her baby. She was startled but comforted by the silence in the flat. Through a wide-open window in the bathroom, she'd listened to the faint buzz of a motorbike driving far off in the distance. As the sun began to show itself at dawn, the tangle of knots in her head had finally started to ease apart. What she needed to do next had finally become clear.

'I'm sorry you're so angry with me. I didn't think you'd want to know about a new baby as soon as we met.' Her voice cracked. Kate shielded her eyes with her hand. 'I don't intend to make the same mistake.'

'But you've not even told James about Frankie, have you?' Paul's lips bloomed into a smirk.

'Not yet, no.'

'Maybe I should have told him when I texted.'

Kate blinked slowly, trying not to look at Paul enjoying her discomfort.

'How could you keep me a secret from your own husband? Why are you so ashamed of me?' Frankie cried.

Her daughter's words sliced through her. Both of them were glaring at her, waiting for a lifetime's worth of explanations. 'I'm not ashamed of you. It's nothing like that.'

'What *is* it like then… Mother?' Frankie's voice grew louder as she emphasised each word.

Silence fell across the ward, everyone listening, watching, holding a collective breath.

'I thought you'd be pleased to meet me. I was prepared to give you a chance, not listen to Dad, but it turns out he was right about you.'

'I am pleased to meet you, Frankie, so pleased…' Kate held out her hand, but Paul stepped aside to let Frankie walk away.

'The truth is my husband didn't want children. I thought if I told him about you…'

'That just about sums you up, doesn't it? You actually married someone who doesn't want kids,' Paul said.

'So what? He doesn't want this one?' Frankie asked.

'He didn't want this baby no, but he does now. We both do.'

'But why would you lie to him? Did you tell him you were coming to see Dad?'

'I was scared of how he would react. I'm still scared.'

'What kind of mother are you?' Frankie's mouth seemed to go up and down in slow motion, carving out each word so she'd never forget it.

'I… I don't know… I'm sorry.'

Frankie shook her head. 'Take me home, Dad.'

'Frankie, please!' Kate climbed out of bed and went after them.

'Don't bother yourself,' Paul said over his shoulder.

They headed towards the exit just as the ward door crashed open and in strolled James.

Chapter Thirty-Five

Before Paul had a chance to speak, James had landed a punch on his jaw sending him into the wall. Frankie screamed and ran towards the nurses' station. Kate cupped her bump as she rushed towards them.

'What was that for?' Paul's words foamed from his lips.

'Kate's told me all about what you've been up to.'

'Has she now.' Paul lifted his fist, but James elbowed him in the side. 'Threatening her, demanding money.'

'Did she tell you why?'

James cocked his head at Kate.

'I'm her daughter's dad, you idiot.' Paul shoved him back with both hands. Two male nurses ran down the corridor shouting at them to stop. James opened his mouth and closed it again. Dazed, he squinted at Kate as though he'd received a blow to the head too. She took in a gulp of breath. There was nothing she could think of to say without making things worse.

'This is Frankie, our daughter,' Paul said, motioning to Frankie to come closer. 'Can't you see that Kate's lied to all of us?' Paul laughed hysterically.

One male nurse held Paul's arm behind his back. The other took James by the elbow. They escorted them out of the ward towards the lift. Kate and Frankie followed.

'Is this true?' James asked.

'I was going to tell you, I promise,' Kate cried.

'When?' He frowned.

'I don't know exactly. I wanted to.'

'You're unbelievable.' Paul jabbed his finger at Kate, trying to break free from the nurse's hold. 'All that time I was bringing up Frankie, you were swanning around with him, pretending she never existed.' Paul spat the words out, his face deepening to a dangerous red. Frankie didn't speak, her eyes squinting with every word.

They all bundled into the lift, and the tallest nurse pressed the button to go down. As the doors closed them in, their sweat and combined breath filled up the small space, mingling together. Kate daren't leave them alone for fear of Paul telling James anything else she'd run away from. She'd tried so hard to stack years and years on top of it all: starting a new life, becoming someone else with a married name, a successful business, all the while pretending nothing had ever happened. But maybe it had always been destined to rise to the surface.

They moved silently down in the lift. Because of the presence of the male nurses, she felt a little safer than she might have done otherwise. They landed with a jolt and a click. James and Paul were escorted out of the building. She trailed behind. Frankie stayed inside, slumped in a seat by a vending machine. She looked like she wanted to be alone. The nurses spoke to Kate on their way back in.

'Will you be okay?' the tall one asked. She gave an uncertain nod and thanked them, then glanced behind at Frankie sitting with her head forward. As she approached, Frankie looked up with forlorn eyes and turned away.

'I'm so sorry,' Kate said. Frankie didn't respond. She'd hoped her future might include her daughter, but what right did she have to even think that?

The sliding doors welcomed her into the cool air.

'I want the truth; how could you abandon your baby?' James asked her the moment she stepped outside. She wished she had a clear-cut answer. In the grey light, she could see shadows of herself and Paul as their younger selves.

'I couldn't cope with a baby. You think I'm not ashamed of that?' A line of smokers standing in the shadows shifted into view, murmuring to one another. Kate noticed one of them was a mum-to-be from her ward, her bump bursting out of her dressing gown.

'What do you mean?' James scratched his head as though he was missing something.

'I didn't know how to calm her down, how to comfort her; she just wouldn't stop crying.' Kate tried to ignore Paul watching her, arms crossed. 'Paul and I were together for four years, and when I fell pregnant, I wasn't ready for it. I was only twenty-two and I admit I struggled.' Her words sounded hollow even to herself. She was no different to all the other mums having children young. But they'd coped, why hadn't she? Why had she been the one to be cruel to her own baby daughter?

'Why haven't you told me about this before?' James asked, taking a step back from her, palms open.

'I didn't think you'd want me if you knew I'd had a child.'

'So you lied to me instead?'

'I'm sorry. I was going to tell you when you told me about you and Susie.'

'So why didn't you?' James shook his head. 'I wish you'd said something. We could have worked it out.'

'Easy to say now, but if I'd told you sooner you wouldn't have wanted me. You didn't want this baby, remember?'

Paul stepped towards them. 'Why would she tell you the truth? Don't you know by now, she's a born liar?'

James fixed his eyes on Kate, ignoring Paul. 'Why not stay in contact with Frankie though? Did he hurt you?'

'Err, no. I never hurt her.'

'I could have helped you stay in touch with your daughter.'

'Frankie was barely six months old. Tell him the *whole* story, Kate.' Paul pointed his finger at her.

She shivered, unable to stop the steamroller coming.

'I wasn't cut out to be a mother and I knew I was leaving Frankie in safe hands.'

'What do you mean? Explain it to me.' James crossed his arms.

'You're such a fucking mug, James.' Paul shook his head. 'She could have seen Frankie any time. She didn't want to. She was too ashamed.'

'You keep out of it,' James said.

Kate half turned away. 'The lack of sleep was driving me crazy. Because the baby cried constantly. I was so exhausted that I had to be taken back into hospital for a few days, but when I got home it started all over again.'

James frowned.

'So I decided to leave because I couldn't be trusted to look after her.'

'I really want to understand, help me out here.' James pulled his collar up against the cold wind.

'Paul was so much better with Frankie than I was. He'd pick her up and she'd stop crying. I thought she hated me going near her, that she knew how much I resented the noise, the lack of sleep. I convinced myself she'd be happier without me.'

'She's full of bullshit. How about telling him the real reason?' Paul's eyes narrowed.

'I'm cold; can we go in?' Kate shivered and bowed her head. Raindrops were speckling the paving slabs. The smokers had gone in.

'Let's get you inside.' James reached round her shoulders, pulling her to him.

'Hang on, what about the rest of it? Like the fifteen grand she's bunged me to keep quiet.'

'You blackmailed me. Don't forget we're here because you pushed me over,' Kate shouted back.

'Leave it, Paul. You're the one who's been harassing her. Haven't you done enough damage for one day?' James turned back to Kate.

'No, honestly, mate, you need to know what you're getting yourself into,' Paul said.

James swung round. 'I'm not your mate, get it?'

Kate hurried towards the sliding doors; the cold breeze had picked up and the sense of a storm looming weighed heavily in the air.

Paul stood still. 'You can't trust her with your baby.'

James stopped dead. 'What are you talking about?'

'Don't listen to him, James.' Kate pulled him through the doorway.

'You don't know what she's capable of, what she did to Frankie.'

'No, no, no, don't listen, he's trying to destroy us.' She touched James's chin, trying to make him look at her, but he was fixed on Paul. A distant clap of thunder flashed a vein of light across the iron sky.

'Tell me what she did.' James stood very still.

'Please, no,' Kate begged and tried to pull him away from the door, but his arms were rigid by his sides.

'She shook our baby, for fuck's sake,' Paul yelled before the doors between them slid shut.

Kate felt for James's hand behind her, but he pulled away and marched past her. Frankie was standing in the middle of the foyer, watching them. Kate needed to go to her, but Paul stepped forward, so the doors opened again like curtains on a stage.

'Did you hear me, James?' he yelled.

Everyone turned in Paul's direction. Kate was powerless to stop him. As if in slow motion, James's then Frankie's faces morphed into shock then disgust as Paul screamed after them, 'I caught her shaking Frankie like she was a fucking rag doll.'

Chapter Thirty-Six

All the next morning Kate waited in her hospital bed, checking each time the doors to the ward opened. Most of the other patients were in the day room watching TV. She'd tried calling Frankie several times, but there was no reply. She texted her to say sorry and asked if they could talk. A few minutes later her phone buzzed. She grabbed her mobile hoping to see her reply, but her face dropped at the words on her screen.

> Why are you even still BREATHING?

It was from yet another number she didn't recognise. If only she could tell James, but there was already so much of her shit that he had to deal with. This could confirm to him what a terrible person she was.

Just before lunch, Kate sat upright. James was stalking towards her, coat collar lifted. For hours she'd gone through a thousand explanations, but now her mind went blank. He glanced up at her as he approached, then his focus fell back to the floor. When he arrived at the end of her bed, his skin was sallow, smudged shadows under his eyes like he'd been crying.

'How are you?' His voice sounded flat.

'Okay. The baby's fine.' She reached out for his hands, but he didn't offer them. Her chest caved in despair. His hair wasn't washed and under his coat she caught a glimpse of an old X-Files T-shirt he normally wore on cold nights in bed.

'I'm still bleeding a bit. They're keeping me in for another night.' *Don't hate me*, she wanted to say.

He drew a finger under his eye.

'I was so scared when I fell; I thought the baby was hurt.'

James didn't move or speak.

'I don't think Frankie wants to see me. She's not answering my calls.' She stole a glance at him to gauge his reaction.

'Frankie and Matt met me for coffee this morning,' he said at last.

'You… you spoke to them. Is she all right?' Had Frankie organised that?

'How d'you think?' He stared at her as though they were strangers. His hands dug into his overcoat pockets dragging them down. 'Frankie's hurt you didn't tell her you're pregnant.'

'How could I tell her straight away? Paul would have called me insensitive.'

'Think about how it makes her feel, knowing you want to keep this one.' He shook his head as if tossing away bad thoughts.

Kate rubbed a hand over her face. 'I thought I had a second chance to try again at being a mother, but maybe I'm kidding myself.' She didn't want to cry, but tears were building behind her eyes. 'What about you? You were ready to walk out on me the moment you found out I was expecting. Have you told her that?'

'That's not the same at all.'

'Isn't it?' She climbed out of the covers, onto her knees. He made a move to go.

'Listen to me, please,' she said grabbing his sleeve, 'as time went on, as she got older, I imagined she wouldn't want to know me anyway.'

'Stop this, will you? Can you hear yourself?' He shook her hand off him. 'You're full of excuses. And what about this fifteen grand hush money?'

'He asked for double that – for my contribution to Frankie's upbringing and her wedding next year. It's out of my own savings.'

'That's not the point though, is it?' he said through clenched teeth, nostrils flaring.

She was losing him, right in front of her eyes.

'Paul was already getting money from my dad every month for years. Mum and I had no idea about it.'

'Was he now?'

'Yes, three hundred and fifty a month. It's eaten up most of her savings. Look, I know I'm not perfect, but tell me how I'm meant to be a better mother than my own? Do you know she left me on a train once when I was five years old? She went to buy a magazine from a kiosk, but the train started to pull out of the station. I couldn't see her anywhere. I thought she'd abandoned me. I thought I'd never see her again. Then I saw her trotting along the platform, waving to the guard and they stopped the train. Do you know what the worst thing was? She didn't realise how petrified I'd been. She didn't think she'd done anything wrong. All I wanted was to be a better mother than that, but I found it so, so hard. I was useless, just like her.'

'You would never have done anything so thoughtless.' His tone softened.

She touched the sheet next to her. 'Please come and sit with me.'

'I'm not staying.'

'How's Mum? She'll be wondering why I've not been to visit.'

'She's improving. I rang and left a message, asked them to tell her you're not well.'

'You didn't say anything about…?'

'No.'

In silence they listening to the squeal of a bed being pushed down the corridor.

Kate braced herself. She'd never seen James so upset. She had to be brave and face what was surely coming, but she wasn't sure if she could. She needed him.

'Frankie doesn't understand why you didn't keep in touch with her.' James's eyes followed the moving bed as it passed through the double doors.

'I thought so many times about contacting Paul, to see how Frankie was, but how could I when I had this thing I did hanging over me? I went to the house once when I'd got back on my feet with a new job and a room to rent in a different town. I didn't knock; I stood in the park next door, watching through the railings. I just wanted to see her, know she was happy and doing well, but another family came out. Paul and Frankie had moved away, and I didn't know where to.'

'When did you plan to tell me?' James cupped his forehead.

'I… I don't know… it's not an easy thing to admit.' She dipped her head. 'I'm sorry.'

'Are you?' He sounded tired, irritated. 'I can just about understand why you wouldn't tell me about Frankie, but the rest of it?' He dug his hands deeper into his pockets. 'So it is true what he said? That you shook her?'

She nodded, looking at the floor.

'Can you try and explain to me what happened? I'm finding it hard to believe you're capable of hurting a baby.'

'I was at my wit's end. She wouldn't stop crying, wouldn't feed from me. I'd been up with her all night every night for weeks. And this one night I picked her up and something in me snapped. I screamed in her face to stop crying and shook her maybe three or four times then Paul was there shouting at me and I bounced her down on the bed.'

'Jesus, Kate. What if he hadn't been there? What if you hadn't stopped?'

'I don't know, I just don't know. I've gone over and over it.' She rubbed her hand over her face. 'But I didn't shake her hard, I swear to you and she wasn't hurt; she was quiet for a moment, but when she cried again it was deafening, high-pitched. I thought I had hurt her, and I was so scared. Paul picked her up and soothed her, said we'd have to take her to the hospital if she didn't calm down, but she did; she was fine. I understand how serious it could have been, how dangerous it is to shake a baby. I honestly didn't realise at the time. I've lived with the shame ever since. The mother who could have given her own child brain damage or worse. That's why I found it so hard to tell you.'

'To Frankie, it's all excuses. You didn't have to abandon her.' He approached the bed and stood over her. Lines gathered on his forehead.

'How could I stay when I wasn't fit to be her mother? I convinced myself she didn't need me.'

'But you are her *mother*. You can't suddenly give that up.'

'I know and I should have told you. I'm so ashamed of what I did.' She bowed her head, tears falling down her face.

'So you should be.' James's stare bore through her. 'Do you know there's something called Shaken Baby Syndrome? Frankie could have suffered with any number of things from a cardiac arrest, a bleed to the brain, a fractured skull... Shall I go on?'

Kate shook her head, wiping her tears away.

'Are you really the same person I've spent the last ten years loving? Because right now, it doesn't feel like it.'

Kate sat back on her heels, head still bowed. 'I'm so, so sorry.' Her voice was nothing more than a whisper.

'There's a long list of injuries according to the internet. She could have died, Kate. It only takes shaking a baby for five seconds to seriously harm them.'

A nurse walked past glancing in their direction. Kate waited for her to be out of earshot.

'I didn't mean to lose control, no matter what Paul says, it was an impulse out of frustration, which I know is no excuse. It was a crazy, crazy moment of blind anger, frustration, exhaustion all rolled into one. And I worried that if I could do that, what else was I capable of? I didn't deserve to have her in my life.'

'You took it out on an innocent baby, Kate.'

'I know, and I hate myself for that. There is nothing I can say to change it, but the truth is I was so bone tired, and Paul wasn't helping. He thought I should be able to manage her on my own, that if I kept handing her to him every time I was struggling, she'd never bond with me. But how could I stay when I might be a danger to her? So, I ended it with him and left. I rented a room on my own for the next six years, dropping in and out of jobs and relationships. I saw a therapist for most of that time. One boyfriend's mother helped me enrol at college and I started to move on. I didn't tell anyone where I was. By the time I met you a few years later, I was in a better place in my head; I had a good job and I'd learned to live with my mistakes.'

'Did you still love him when you left?'

'Yes, I did.' Kate stole a glance at him, his head bowed. She had to be completely honest now if they had any hope of staying together.

'So why swear to me you didn't want children when you already had a grown-up daughter?' His voice rose again in disbelief.

'I didn't want more, that was the truth, because I was too scared to and it suited me that you didn't want kids either. But when I fell pregnant and saw the tiny heartbeat of our baby, I felt such a rush of love. I'd never felt that with Frankie. I believed I'd been given a second chance to nurture a new life. I thought maybe enough time had passed that I could try again at being a mum.'

'And still you didn't tell me,' James said in a weary voice.

'How could I?' She lay down and stared at an old piece of tinsel stuck to the false ceiling. How many patients had been lying there over the past twelve months, staring up, wondering when their pain would end? A new garland had been pinned up earlier that day by a couple of giggling young nurses.

James pushed his fingers through his greasy hair. 'Why did you go ahead and have Frankie if you didn't think you could be a good parent?'

'I thought maybe I would be once she was here. I thought it would come naturally. But people don't tell you how hard it is. All the magazines show photos of perfect mums with their clean, happy, gurgling babies, and tell you how it's the purest form of love. That wasn't my reality. I didn't bond with her like everyone expected me to.'

He turned half circle so she couldn't see his face.

'You and Susie were keeping a secret from me,' she said, 'you still are from Harry. Don't you ever wonder how it would be now if your child had been born?'

'Yes, recently, of course I have. Ever since your scan and now this I've wondered if my child would have been a boy or a girl, what their name would be. Christ, it would be at university now.' He stopped so abruptly that Kate tipped forward to see if he was all right.

'James?'

His fist was pressed to his mouth, eyes wet, rimmed red. He swallowed before he spoke.

'Kate, are you sure you want our baby?'

'Yes, I do. More than anything.'

'And what about Frankie? Would you have told me about her if I hadn't found out?'

Whatever she said would sound inadequate. His forehead was full of lines she was certain hadn't been there before. He was waiting for an answer, but she didn't have the one he wanted.

'I think so. I know I intended to at some point.' She wanted to reach out to him, but he turned away.

'How do I know you're not going to leave us too?'

'I won't, I promise.'

'You can't know that, can you?'

'I'm older now and I understand more about Mum and why she behaved like she did with me, because she didn't have either of her parents and was starved of love. I had my dad. He was kind, caring and patient with me. I didn't suffer the cruelty Mum did. I want to make this work – with you, the baby and Frankie.' She rubbed the heel of her hand in a gentle circle over her bump.

'You can still build a relationship with Frankie, you know that, don't you?'

'Do you think she'll let me?'

'You have to try. She's your daughter. You're lucky to have her.'

'I know, I am.'

At that precise moment there came the lightest flutter of the baby moving, like a butterfly beating its wings for the first time.

'I can feel the baby. Do you want to see if you can?' Kate knelt up on the bed and moved closer. She positioned his hand and pressed gently.

'Oh.' He pulled back an inch.

'You felt it?' She hoped it was strong enough for him to make a connection with their child.

'I think so, there was definitely something.' His eyes were wide, and he was almost smiling.

Kate sat back down.

'And what about you? Are you sure you're still happy that I'm having our baby?'

He nodded.

'You were so against it; you've never explained why.' She held her hand out to him, but he dipped his head, looking at his watch.

'I have to go now.'

She nodded and didn't try to stop him. Hopefully, he'd tell her when he was ready.

After he'd gone, she tried to call Frankie again, but there was still no answer. She wasn't going to give up on her daughter this time, not now she'd come this far.

Chapter Thirty-Seven

The next morning, James collected Kate from hospital. The doctor told her if she started bleeding again, she was to contact her GP straight away. Failing that, she should present herself at A & E.

The trees dripped melted snow leaving the pavements slushy. With her hand to her bump, she trod carefully back to the car while James steamed ahead with her bag in his hand. She stopped at a stretch of ice blocking her path.

'James... please wait,' she called, not sure if he was too far ahead to hear her. He stopped, turned and looked at her as if he'd been called by a whining child.

'Can you help me? I don't want to slip again.'

He stomped back in thick boots, avoiding her eye and offered her his elbow. She clung on to his arm, grateful to feel his strength. He slowed his pace, steering round ice and piles of shovelled snow until they reached the car. He opened the door for her.

'Have you stayed in touch with Frankie? Are we going to visit her before we leave?' she asked.

James didn't answer straight away. 'I have but I don't think visiting her is a good idea. She needs some time.'

His words clunked about in her head like shrapnel. She'd failed her daughter again. Far from being able to start afresh, she'd churned up the past and made it worse. Whatever made her think she could change? She'd run away from her responsibilities and lived a new life. She'd lied to James but also herself.

Once in the car, she was grateful for the noise of the engine bursting in on the silence. Was this the end of their relationship? What about their baby, their business? She wanted to ask him so many questions, but he was fixed on the slippery road ahead.

They caught the afternoon ferry and sat opposite one another drinking plastic-tasting coffee. James pulled his coat collar over his neck and shut his eyes, leaning his head against the salt-stained window. She stared at the seafoam ruffling out of the back of the ferry. She should have told him about Frankie when he told her about the pregnancy with Susie. The truth was there had never been a right time. She should have just said it, but she'd not found the courage to. Now he'd found out the worst way. The baby gave a little flutter as if it understood. She rubbed her bump soothingly. Almost fifteen weeks. The cracked skin on her knuckles had split into tiny red cuts. She licked them like a wounded paw.

James sniffed and checked his watch. 'We'll be landing in fifteen minutes.'

Kate heaved open the salt-corroded door out to the deck and bowed her head into the wind. She breathed in a lungful of clean air. Needle pricks of salty spray bombarded her face. The sea was choppy, and she swayed drunkenly across to the railings. He obviously didn't think she could see the silvery trails of tears on his cheeks. He'd trusted her. From those early days until now. And she'd lied to him in return. What was wrong with her? How did she always manage to destroy her relationships with every single person she was close to? She leaned over the barrier, watching the waves lash the side of the ferry and breathed deeply, trying to keep her balance.

She took out her mobile and clicked it on, hoping to see a missed call or text from Frankie. No new messages. Every cell in her body dragged down. As she put her phone back in her pocket, it pinged. A notification from Twitter. Not again. There was a tiny picture on her screen she could only see properly if she viewed the post. She ought to delete it, but the problem was it was already out there for everyone to see. Pulse racing, she clicked open the app. Yet another profile she'd never heard of, @BabeOnFire101. Click.

AND THE WORLD'S WORST MOTHER AWARD GOES TO... @katemarshall !!!

Below it was a GIF of a woman nodding and saying the words flashing underneath: *Worst of the worst*. As if she didn't feel bad enough already. She blocked and reported the account. Who hated her this much? They seemed to know about Frankie, but Paul was adamant he'd never told anyone. She wracked her brains, but there was no one who sprang to mind that she could have upset enough to be this vicious.

The growling engines slowed to a soft vibrating hum. Kate rejoined James and they shuffled back to his car behind a queue of people and waited for the ferry to dock.

–

On their drive home they passed a church where people were spilling onto the pavement with lanterns on sticks. The throng of voices singing '*Away in a Manger*' followed them as they drove by and seemed to linger in the crisp air right up to when they pulled onto their drive.

'Why don't we go and pick a tree tomorrow?' she asked, determined to stay positive. The snowman air freshener continued to sway after the car had stopped. The spicy cinnamon aroma made her want to rush indoors and bake cakes. She imagined letting their child help her stir in the mixture with James making them laugh with his ho, ho, ho, impression of Father Christmas. She twisted a loose button on her coat.

At last James spoke. 'We'll see.' He got out and took their luggage from the car boot and slammed it shut, shaking the whole car.

She stayed sitting for a moment and pictured a line of suitcases in the hall, guessing his moving out would be permanent this time. The usual wreaths and webs of lights were hanging from neighbours' front doors and hedges. Manufactured promises of joy and goodwill to all men.

Slowly, she eased herself out of her seat. As she stood, James was there to take her hand.

'Be careful, it's icy near the doorstep.' He linked her arm through his and led her to the house.

The light in the hallway was already on and she could see that the only bag there was her own. Perhaps he hadn't finished packing and the cases were still upstairs. Maybe she was the one moving out. She eased open the living room door. He flicked a switch. The glow of coloured fairy lights warmed the darkened room. The decorated tree filled the corner. She turned to him open-mouthed, and his face half lifted in a smile.

'It's beautiful,' she said.

He sloped off to the kitchen. Kate climbed the stairs. Maybe he was being kind before he told her they were over. She could hear him fill the kettle. Was he rehearsing in his head how he would tell her? Perhaps the suitcases were open on the bed half packed, so he didn't need to say anything.

At the top of the stairs she went into their bedroom. The bed was made but there were no suitcases. She opened the wardrobe and drawers. Everything was in its usual place. Yet her heartbeat grew faster. Something had changed. There was a different smell in the air. She carried on along the landing, drawn to what would be the baby's room. Suddenly, all the things she'd need to do and buy before the baby arrived crowded into her head. The thought of coping as a single parent panicked her. She couldn't do this alone.

In the baby's room she took a sharp intake of breath. The walls had been painted with buttercup yellow and white stripes. In the middle of the room stood a white crib. Alongside it was a matching changing table and a chest of drawers.

'Susie and Harry offered to do everything for us,' James said, appearing in the doorway. 'Susie, especially, has been so supportive.'

'It's wonderful.' She hugged him tight. After a second, his body relaxed and he hugged her back, kissing her face all over.

'I've been so worried about you,' he murmured into her hair, 'both of you. I thought we might lose the baby.' He pushed tears from his face and nuzzled into her neck.

'Me too,' she said. 'I'm so sorry for everything.' She pulled back and traced his worry lines. 'I've wanted to tell you about Frankie for so long.'

He drew her to him again.

'I'll understand if you can't forgive me, if you want me to leave,' she whispered.

'Sssh, we're going to learn how to be parents together,' he said.

'But I've already failed miserably.'

'Then I've failed too.'

'What do you mean?' She drew back so she could see his face.

'There's something I need to tell you too.' He hung his head low for a moment, then looked her in the eye. 'My little brother Ben had an accident when he was six, except it was partly my fault. My parents left me to look after him, as usual, while they buggered off down the pub. We were mucking about like brothers do and I pushed him a bit too hard. He lost his balance and put his hands out to stop himself falling, but he fell through a glass panel in the back door. There was blood everywhere. I called an ambulance then ran to the pub to get Mum and Dad. They blamed it all on me. I had this awful pain in my stomach for weeks, like I'd been permanently winded by what I'd done. Ben was badly scarred. I felt so guilty, but I was only ten myself. They've never forgiven me.'

'That's completely unfair. No wonder you don't want anything to do with them. But what about Ben?'

'We lost touch when I left home. They poisoned him against me. Because he was so young, they convinced him I did it on purpose. They failed to mention they were in the pub getting pissed as usual.'

'How could they do that to children in their care?'

'They never really took to me. Maybe because I was that bit older when they adopted me. I wasn't easy to deal with. I used to play them up, go missing in the supermarket, scribble on my bedroom wall, wet the bed.

265

Ben was always the cute younger one. They'd deliberately buy him whatever he wanted pretty much, but if I asked for anything, they either ignored or mocked me.'

'Why didn't you tell me about any of this?' She stroked his arms.

'I suppose I was embarrassed, ashamed. I didn't want you to know how bad I am at looking after children. It was easier not to say anything.'

'But you were just a child yourself. They shouldn't have given you that responsibility. It wasn't your fault, it was theirs.'

'I suppose I've come to accept that now.'

'And you thought it would be easier not to have any of your own?'

'I couldn't face being responsible for someone else again.'

'You told Susie though.' As soon as she said it, she knew she sounded like a jealous teenager.

'I was young then, angry. She helped me to see it wasn't my fault.'

'Is that why you had your baby aborted?'

James tilted his head. 'Partly, but neither of us was mature enough. We both agreed it would be a disaster because we realised we didn't love each other.'

She leaned her head on his chest.

'Have you thought about trying to find Ben, put things right between you?'

'I tried to tell him my side of the story when I was older, but he wouldn't listen.'

'You can try again like I'm going to try with Frankie. It's going to be all right you know. We'll muddle through this together. This baby will be loved, is already loved.' She held his hands to her bump.

'And I love you,' he said and kissed her.
Kate kissed him back.

Chapter Thirty-Eight

At work on Wednesday morning, Kate texted Frankie while waiting for her emails to download. She pleaded with her to call, but there was no reply. She clicked through her emails from the past two days. They'd be playing catch-up all week. There was one from the marketing woman at Shapeshifters, Izzy, saying she could meet her at the Emergency Exit Escape Rooms near Luton anytime next week. The guy who owned the business, Rupert, had also emailed to confirm he could give them a full tour and then a taster of their Haunted House Room at 2.30 p.m., next Monday, the seventeenth of December. It would be her last major appointment before Christmas.

The whole team was gathered together for a meeting. 'Hello, everyone, sorry we've been away. I had a little mishap slipping on ice and ended up in hospital. I hope you're all okay and had a better weekend than we did. I know it's Wednesday, but I thought we'd have our Monday meeting anyway so we all know where we're up to.' She perched on the edge of a desk next to James and gave her usual pep-talk. 'Business is still going strong for this final quarter and the diary is full for the next eleven days up to Christmas. We've already had several new enquiries come in over the weekend via the website for events in the new year.'

A positive murmur circulated the room.

'So it's all looking great. But then we've got the best team in the business, haven't we?' They'd made the short-list in both categories for the Hemel Business Awards and had been invited to the presentation evening in the new year.

James smiled proudly at her.

'Here, here!' Steve shouted and everyone clapped.

'Thanks, everyone. Steve, if you could update us first on the CSI event, then we'll go round clockwise.' She listened closely to all seven members of the team and noted any problems to be actioned. Jane took the minutes. At the end James stood up to speak.

'And there's a little announcement we'd like to make.' He looked round the room then at Kate. She smiled at him.

'I'm delighted to tell you all that, amazingly, we're expecting our first baby.'

Everyone shrieked and clapped then came forward to congratulate them.

'I knew it!' Sally said. 'Well, I didn't, but when you fainted that day, it was the first thing that crossed my mind, but knowing you didn't plan to have children, I thought I must have got it wrong. I'm so happy for you both.'

'Thank you.' Kate hugged her. She was so pleased the news was finally out.

When Kate eventually got back to her office she sat down and James sat on her desk.

'Any luck with Frankie?' he asked.

'No, I must have tried her twenty times.' She checked her phone again, hoping there weren't any other messages. Nothing.

'Maybe leave it a few days.'

'Do you think Paul could be discouraging her from staying in contact with me?'

'Possible, I suppose. But I think it's because she's still upset.'

'This came for you while you were away.' Jane brought in a large package wrapped in black paper. Kate checked the address label. A symbol of hands praying and a cross was in the left-hand corner.

'What's that?' James asked.

'I've not ordered anything.'

'Open it.'

Using a pair of scissors, she carefully scored along the line of Sellotape. She opened the box which was filled with black tissue paper. A crisp white envelope sat on top with a cross in the centre. She took out a thick piece of card with a line drawing of a sleeping baby wrapped in angel wings. She glanced at the writing underneath and dropped the card on the desk, covering her mouth.

'What is it?' James picked the card up and read it out: '"I hope you lose your baby."'

'Who is this from?' he asked Kate as if she could answer. He pulled out the black tissue paper and lifted out a weighty wooden box, like a child's jewellery box but deeper. He turned it in his hands. The top and sides were decorated with white fluffy clouds on a blue background and teddy bears with angel wings, a single tear on each teddy's face.

Kate screamed.

'Fuck, is this what I think it is?' He let it drop back on the desk with a thud, looking at his hands as though they were covered in blood. His face was screwed up in disgust. She shook her head at him in shared disbelief. A child's ashes urn and a memorial card. Who could be so sick? The whole team were crowded at the door, shock on their faces. Could it be from one of them, secretly unhappy or jealous of their success? But they were all so close, almost like family. Did it warrant doing this? What did? This was the action of someone who wasn't in their right mind.

'I'm calling the police.' James picked up the phone and dialled.

Before the officer arrived, Kate showed James all the texts and social media messages she'd received. She told him about finding 'Bitch' daubed in red lipstick on her car. She wished she'd taken a photo of it.

'This is some serious weirdo on the loose,' he said when she showed him the Instagram post of their front door. 'Jesus wept; how does he know where we live?'

'It was when we were away as well. He could have broken in. And there was that flower that arrived that I put in the bin. It came with a nasty message about waiting for me to die, so I assumed it was from Paul, but he denies doing any of it. Whoever it is probably sent me the abortion stuff too.'

'Why haven't you told me about this? This person is dangerous.'

'Because you've had enough to deal with accepting this baby and then finding out about Frankie. And I didn't want you to think any of it was true.'

'Is there anyone you can think of that could have done this, because the police will want to know everything. You can't hold back.'

'I haven't got a clue.'

When the police arrived they took down details of all the evidence and said they would try and trace the phone numbers, but as Kate suspected, they believed they were probably from the same pay-as-you-go mobile using different SIM cards, which would be almost impossible to track down.

Who hated her enough to do this? If it wasn't Paul or Frankie, who else? An old client with a grudge? No, it had to be someone who knew about her pregnancy, but they'd hardly told anyone until today. There was only Susie and Harry, but that just wasn't possible, was it? She'd had her differences with Susie, but would she do this? No, it was far too cruel. Had James told Mac? She guessed he knew they were having problems, but he wasn't the sort of person to interfere let alone do something so vile. Maybe James had confided in someone else, like Jasmine? Did she secretly hate Kate and want to take her place? She hoped not. She was a good worker, a real asset to the team. Whoever it was, it seemed this person would stop at nothing to hurt her. Her life and the life of her unborn baby could be in real danger.

Chapter Thirty-Nine

Kate was pleased to see her mother up and dressed the following morning, a puzzler book in one hand, *The Times* tucked under her arm.

'You're early. I've only just finished breakfast.'

'It's good to see you looking so well, Mum.'

'You look a bit peaky yourself. Are you sure you've not left hospital too soon?'

'They gave me the all clear. I need to take it easy, although I'm back at work already.' Kate moved a chair nearer so her mother could sit down. She was keeping her mobile switched off and only checking it twice a day. So far there had been no new nasty messages for over twenty-four hours. The police had told her to keep a diary of everything that was sent.

Elizabeth picked up her knitting and rearranged the ball of blue speckled wool in her lap. Kate sat on the edge of another chair and scratched a new patch of dry skin on her hand. How was she going to break the news to her mother that she had a grown-up granddaughter?

'Everything all right?' Elizabeth cocked her head to one side.

Kate shook her head.

'What is it?'

'I found out about the money from Dad's account. It was going to Paul.'

'Really? What on earth for?' Her mother looked up from her needles; the blanket of knitting reached over her knees. 'All that money going to *him*? There must be a mistake.'

Kate looked away. She'd made such a mess of her life. Running away as a teenager and then abandoning her baby. How was she going to tell her this? How would her mum ever forgive her for doing the same thing her mother did to her?

'It was for our daughter.'

The needles stopped moving.

'*Your* daughter?' Her mother's eyes searched her face. 'And you didn't tell us?'

'I'm so sorry, I should have told you about her before, but I've only just got in touch with her myself.'

'What do you mean? Where were you?' Her mother's hands gripped the needles so tightly that her fists trembled.

'I… I left her with Paul when she was a baby.'

Her mother unfurled her fingers and laid the needles in her lap. She'd aged ten years in as many seconds.

'When was this?'

'Twenty-three years ago.' Kate wanted to be sick. She couldn't bear the pain she'd caused everyone. Whoever was sending those messages knew full well that she deserved every single malicious word.

Elizabeth slid the needles out of the loops of wool and yanked at the loose end, unravelling row after row of stitches; the length of knitting now a dying bird bobbing about in her lap.

'Mum! What are you doing?' Kate stood up, sending the chair crashing backwards.

'It's all wrong, everything is wrong.' Elizabeth pulled and pulled at the wool until there was a muddled nest at her feet.

'Mum, please stop!'

'Why did you abandon your baby?'

'I'm so sorry, if I'd known what had happened to you…'

'Would it have stopped you?'

'I don't know. I had post-natal depression. I was a terrible mother to her.'

'That doesn't explain why Paul was demanding money from you.'

'He was blackmailing Dad, then when he died, he came after me. He told him I hurt Frankie, but I didn't mean to. She wasn't harmed. I lost control with her for a few seconds. I didn't mean to shake her.' She took a tissue from the bedside table and wiped her tears away.

'Oh Kate, how could you do that?'

'I don't know. I was so ashamed I couldn't tell anyone. She could have been seriously hurt and I felt so bad I had to get away.'

'I wish you could have come to us.'

'I thought about it so much, but I couldn't face either of you, especially after the way I left.'

'And James?'

'He's okay now, I think. I wasn't sure he'd forgive me.'

'But he has?'

'I think so.' Kate pressed her hand to her chest.

'You've both got this baby to look forward to now.'

'I know, and I'm so grateful.' Kate nodded and smiled. She wanted to give her mother a hug but didn't know how.

'So come on, tell me about my granddaughter. What's her name? I bet she's a beautiful young lady.'

'Yes… yes, she is. Her name's Francesca, Frankie.'

'Lovely. I like that.'

Kate stared into space.

'What's the matter?'

'She's upset with me because I hadn't told James about her, and I didn't tell her straight away about the baby.'

'That's understandable. When will you see her again? When can I meet her?'

'I don't know, Mum.'

Elizabeth frowned at what was left of her knitting.

'She says she doesn't want to see me.'

Elizabeth rested her hands in her lap, the needles empty now, crossed over in front of her.

'I've really messed things up.'

'She'll need time to sort it all out in her head. It's a lot to take in.'

A nurse rushed past them to a patient at the end of the ward and zipped the curtains round the bed with such force they blew out like sails.

'Mrs Hubbard,' Elizabeth whispered, straining to hear what was going on. 'They're surprised she's still alive. Had a terrible night. Kept us all awake.'

Kate gazed at the shuffle of feet below the hemmed curtain. The smell of disinfectant hummed in the stagnant air. Every time she visited, she fought the urge to throw open the huge windows.

'When are they going to let you go home?'

'End of the week, they said.'

'That's good news.'

'I honestly didn't think I'd make it this far.'

'Well you have.' Kate sighed. 'Mum, there's something else I need to tell you about Frankie.'

'Oh?'

'She had an accident a few years ago.'

'Oh goodness.'

'She fell off a horse.'

'Is she all right? I mean, you said yourself she's grown into a beautiful young woman.'

Kate nodded. 'But she landed badly and broke her back.'

'Oh no, that's dreadful. How is she?'

'She's okay, she's going to be okay.' Tears welled in Kate's eyes. Saying it aloud made it more real. She was shocked by her delayed reaction. 'She couldn't walk at first, but they've operated on her. She's doing really well.'

Elizabeth reached up and gripped Kate's wrist.

'Write to her, Katie,' she said. 'Don't abandon her again, she needs you.'

'I will.'

'She needs her mum.' Elizabeth gently shook Kate's arm. 'I'd have given anything to see my mother again. You still have that chance.'

'I promise. Thank you.' Kate felt a pang of sadness. Her mother longed for her mum but seemed blind to how cold she'd always been to her.

Elizabeth let go and Kate sank down in the chair.

'Did you never meet your mum?' Kate asked.

'At the start I really believed my mother would visit me. We had something at The Foundling Hospital called "Mum's Day". But it was for the foster mothers. For most of the children, like me, no one turned up. It didn't stop us telling each other stories about how wonderful we imagined our real mums to be. We weren't allowed to be shown any affection. We never had a cuddle or a kiss good night. It hurt that no one cared one jot for me. It toughened me up I suppose, but that longing for your mother never goes away.'

Kate's heart ached thinking of Frankie without a mummy there to tuck her up in bed all those long years she was growing up. How could Kate have been so selfish and not realised the anguish she was causing? She'd pushed it so deep she'd never really faced the loss her daughter would have felt.

'Time for your medicine.' A nurse appeared, rattling a tiny cup of tablets. 'You okay, pet?' She squeezed Elizabeth's hand. 'You're freezing.' She crouched in front of her. 'And you look like you've seen a ghost.'

'I brought a bit of good news and bad news, I'm afraid,' Kate said. She wondered if she should have waited.

'I'll be fine,' Elizabeth said. 'It's this one I'm worried about.' She directed her thumb at Kate. The nurse patted Elizabeth's arm and got up, smiling at Kate as if she knew everything about her.

Kate sat up straight as a new determination seeped through her veins.

—

The first thing she did when she reached home, was to take out a pad of notepaper and pen.

Dear Frankie,
    I'm so deeply sorry I left you. I know what I did is unforgivable, and I understand why you're angry and don't want to speak to me. I didn't want to rush in and tell you as soon as we met that I was expecting a baby because I thought it would

be insensitive. I always intended to tell you about it later.

I understand it is also hard to forgive that I didn't tell James about you and I'm very sorry to have upset you.

Please let me apologise to you in person, on FaceTime or over the phone. James and I would be delighted to see you and Matt again. I would love you to become part of our lives.

Love and regards, Kate.

Kate read the letter back. She was tempted to rip it up, start again from the beginning, but she thought of her mother and knew she would want her to send it as it was. She put the sheet of paper into an envelope and headed straight out to the post box before she could change her mind.

Chapter Forty

Elizabeth sat on the bed packing her suitcase after breakfast the next day, waiting for the all clear to go home that afternoon. Kate was due to arrive after lunch. It was an unusually mild day with bright sunshine. Only a few days until Christmas. Thank goodness they weren't keeping her in any longer.

Kate had brought her papers back in. Every time Elizabeth flicked through them, she hoped to glean a new clue about her mother, or even her father come to that. Maybe it was time to tell Kate more about her real father. But she wasn't convinced the truth about what happened between John and Ray would benefit anyone. If Kate hadn't fixated on Ray's sister dying of cancer at thirty-nine, she might never have told them he wasn't her real dad. But Kate had got it in her head that if she didn't have her breasts removed, she might die young too. Thank goodness she put a stop to that.

What was it about the women on her side that they couldn't bring up their own babies? She hadn't realised being a mother wouldn't come naturally. She remembered how Katherine's little eyes seemed to fix on her from the off, as though waiting for her to make a mistake. Watching her struggle to push pins through fat nappies or pumping at her breast, dry of milk. She couldn't even hold her comfortably; she was so terrified of dropping her like a bag of sugar splitting open and spilling everywhere.

Katherine had been a niggly baby. She wouldn't settle for more than three hours at a time, day or night. But when she smiled, it was pure joy. Ray helped her care for Katherine in those early weeks. She couldn't have managed on her own with all the crying, nappy changing and constant feeding. She reckoned, looking back, she must have been in shock for the first three months at least. Suddenly this tiny person was her priority. Ray was more open than all those men who called child rearing women's work. She was certain he could read her mind at times. Without asking, he'd gently ease Katherine from her arms and straight away she'd stop crying and fix her eyes on him. He'd stroke the tuft of dark downy hair on her head and her eyelids would flutter shut.

Ray often brought home new dresses for her and encouraged her to look after herself again. He was careful what he said and put up with her moods and tantrums, never shouting back, always calm and gentle. He would pop home at lunchtimes and sometimes she'd still be in bed, Katherine wide awake, grizzling in her cot, wet through. Such a kind, thoughtful husband, nothing like John would have been with his waywardness. You can't choose who you fall in love with.

Eventually, she started to look forward to dressing up and taking Katherine out, even if it did take her all morning before she was ready to go anywhere. Everything was such an effort, so exhausting, as though some unseen force was pressing down on her.

People would stop her in the street and peer inside the spanking new Silver Cross pram. She'd proudly tell them

Katherine's name, how much she weighed, and they'd coo and aah and tell her what a beautiful little girl she had.

Although they didn't bond straight away, as time went by they slipped into a routine and became used to one another. But the nights were worst of all; she'd panic at the thought of how she'd manage in the years to come. And, as it turned out, she hadn't managed very well, had she? She'd not been a kind mother. Always snapping at Kate as she grew up, not really listening to her, cutting in when she spoke, telling her off for the slightest thing. She hadn't known *how* to behave with a child let alone how to nurture one. No wonder she'd favoured her dad and then went off as soon as she could with the likes of Paul.

She pushed the papers into the suitcase and zipped it closed. She must tell Kate about Edward, at least. If she'd died, no one would ever have known about him.

Most of the beds in the ward were stripped bare. The sharp smell of fresh disinfectant seeped through to her bones.

'That's me all packed, just waiting for my marching orders now,' Elizabeth said when Kate arrived. 'You look whacked out.' She pushed down on her stick and stood up.

Kate sat on the bed. 'I must admit I am tired, and this baby is starting to feel heavier.'

'Come and sit outside. It's such a mild day, I told them I'd be in the garden drinking my cup of tea.'

Kate followed her out to the expanse of lawn between the hospital buildings. They sat on a bench.

'I can't believe I'm finally coming home. Being here has brought back too many memories of being in the sanatorium.' She gave an involuntary shudder.

'You mean when you had scarlet fever?'

Elizabeth gazed straight ahead, transported back in time. 'It was a serious illness back then. People died from it. It was touch and go with me for a while, so they told me. My best friend Alison died in the bed next to me one night. They carted her out without a word.'

'That's so sad.' Kate examined her mum's face. It was as though she was a different person to the one she'd grown up with.

'The nurses let us have whatever we wanted to eat once we started to get better. I asked for buttered toast. Ooh, I can taste it now.' Elizabeth shut her eyes and put a finger to her lips. 'Nothing has ever tasted better.'

In the distance, the afternoon traffic rumbled by. Kate touched her bump.

'All that matters now is that you and Frankie have found each other – you have a second chance.'

'Except I may well have blown it.' Kate scraped the tops of her shoes on the grass, just like she used to when she was a little girl.

'Did you write to her?'

'Yes, but I've not heard back yet.'

'You mustn't lose touch with her again,' Elizabeth said. 'I hope she'll come and visit.'

'I'd love to meet her.'

'I expect she needs some time to decide if she wants me in her life.'

Elizabeth watched two planes leave contrails across the sky, one path crossing the other. 'I want you to have the silk purse and my disc,' she said, still gazing upwards.

'Mum, you can't do that, not after what I did.'

'You were a child; you didn't know how important it was to me. I understand that now. I'm a silly old woman for getting so upset, as if hanging on to it could change anything.'

'It's not silly at all.' Kate touched her arm.

Elizabeth glanced down as if a butterfly had rested there. 'And I'd like you to pass it on to Frankie when the time comes.'

They sat for a while longer gazing at the pale sun behind the tops of the buildings.

'I had a twin brother once.'

Kate turned towards her.

'I didn't know about him at first because we were kept away from the boys until after the war when they started to relax the strict rules. It was spring 1946, twenty-fourth of March, when they opened the partition doors for the first time ever. It was just after tea. I'll never forget the low hum of excitement as we all watched the doors being folded back like a concertina. The boys were a sea of red waistcoats, all staring at us girls. The name Edward was called out and one dark-haired boy sprang up from his chair. Then my name was called, and I stood up too. The boy stared right at me with big chocolate brown eyes, just like my own. We tipped our heads this way and that as we examined each other. His hair was cut much shorter than mine, but it was so strange, almost like looking at myself in a mirror. When Miss Lea spoke, all the children on both sides of the hall stood to attention, watching the boy and me as we were ushered to the front. I was shaking because I thought we were in for the cane. Instead Miss Lea announced we were twins then she burst into song, singing 'Happy Birthday' at the top of her voice, waving her arms in the air like a conductor until everyone joined in, singing both our names.'

'That's incredible.'

'It truly was. A cake with seven candles was brought in and placed on the table in front of us, but my eyes were on the boy. I couldn't take them off him. I smiled so much my face ached, but I didn't care, I'd never felt such elation. I'd never even known of his existence. I had an overwhelming urge to throw my arms about him. At last I belonged to someone. I touched his arm to see if he was real. Edward grinned at me and squeezed my hand in his chunky little fingers. I could see in his eyes he was equally fascinated with me. For the first time in my life I knew how it felt to be special and belong. That was the only time I've met anyone related to me, who looked like me, until I had you.'

'Oh Mum, that must have been a wonderful day.'

Elizabeth dipped her head for a moment, then carried on. 'The very next day, I was told he'd fallen gravely ill with scarlet fever. No one was allowed to see him in the sanatorium, not even me. I awoke one morning in the sanatorium myself. I didn't know how long I'd been there. Sister Holland told me I had scarlet fever too, but I was over the worst of it. Edward died two days later. There seemed no point to my life after that. I cried for days on end and prayed I would die too. I've never been lonelier in my whole life.' Tears fell from Elizabeth's eyes.

Kate put her hand on her shoulder.

'I think about him every birthday and, as I said, we named your brother after him. It was as though I found part of myself then lost it in a blink.'

Kate patted her mother's hand. 'Oh Mum, I'm so, so sorry.'

Elizabeth nodded. It lightened her a little to tell Kate, but she doubted she really understood the impact on her life. The world was so different then. You had your place and you kept to it without question. The weight of all these secrets dying with her was becoming hard to bear. She had to tell Kate more about her dad.

'When Ray found out your dad was cheating on me, they had a terrible fight, it even made the local paper. I was so upset, I broke up with John and sent him away. It wasn't the first time he'd done that to me you see. I couldn't take the humiliation any more. He emigrated to Australia, as far away from me as possible I imagine. If I'd known I was pregnant with you, I might have tried to forgive him and make it work. But it was too late.'

'Oh Mum, I'm sorry he did that to you. That's really sad.'

'I was ashamed to tell you I sent your dad away, then went off with Ray so quickly afterwards. I knew how Ray felt about me, and I was thirty-four for goodness' sake. An old maid in those days. John guessed we had feelings for each other. I think that's why he didn't argue with me or try to stick around.'

'It's not your fault, Mum. It must have been really difficult for you.'

'I've got the newspaper cutting of him in my Bible at home. I'll show it to you. It's all I have.'

'I'm interested to see it, but Ray was a wonderful dad to me.'

'How are you doing, Elizabeth?' Josie asked as she approached.

'Not bad, thanks. We were just having our little chat.' Sometimes she could swear there was a halo round Josie's head even though she wasn't a religious sort.

'The doctor says you can go home.' Josie dug her hands deep in her uniform pockets and came out with a hanky.

'You don't need me any more.' Her voice faltered. She dabbed her eyes.

'That's great news, Mum.' Kate stood up.

'It's the end of my shift, so I've come to say goodbye.' Josie wiped her nose.

'I don't know how to thank you, for everything.' Elizabeth reached her hands out to her. Josie clasped hers round them.

'Knowing you is thanks enough. It's been my pleasure.' Josie leaned over; her coconut-smelling hair brushed Elizabeth's face as they hugged.

'You look after yourself, you hear me?' Elizabeth said.

'You too, honey, and thank *you*.'

Elizabeth watched Josie go inside.

'I suppose we'd better get a move on. Don't want to outstay my welcome, do I?' Elizabeth smiled at Kate, but her daughter looked puzzled. She was probably wondering how she could have built up such a close friendship so quickly. It had surprised her too. It felt like she had a new chance at life.

She watched for the dimple on Kate's right cheek as she smiled back and, for a moment, she saw her little girl.

'Come to us for Christmas, Mum. Or we can come to you if you don't feel up to travelling.' Kate eased herself out of the seat.

She liked that Kate was eager to mend things between them, which is what Josie said would happen if she could be brave enough to make the first move. *Just open up a little. Small ripples.*

'That's very kind, I will thank you.' Elizabeth tipped her cup upside down and let the last drop of tea fall to the ground in a starburst.

Chapter Forty-One

After their morning meeting and buffet lunch on Monday, Kate arrived at the Emergency Exit Escape Rooms in the back end of Luton. It was only eight days until Christmas, and this was the last major appointment until the new year. If she could get this booking in the bag, she'd be delighted.

Kate parked in front of the imposing building and checked her phone before switching it off and getting out. No new messages. Could that be it?

A tall, elegant-looking woman a bit older than her climbed out of a red Porsche. She held out her hand to Kate.

'I'm Izzy from Shapeshifters; you must be Kate?' Her sculptured blonde curls jiggled as she spoke.

'Nice to meet you, Izzy. Have you been waiting long?' There were only a few other cars in the car park. Monday afternoon was clearly not a peak time.

'Only a few minutes. Ooh, nice car.'

'Thanks, I do like a Merc. Not as stunning as your 911 though. Good thing I didn't bring James, he'd be begging for a ride in it.'

'It is a mean beast.' She threw Kate a smug smile.

'Is this your first time here?' Kate locked her car and started walking towards the building.

'Yes, but I heard how good it was from a friend, so thought I'd give it a whirl for our next corporate event. See what people are made of.' She laughed.

'Let's hope it lives up to your expectations.' Kate headed for the neon sign, 'Emergency Exit Escape Rooms: Entrance', followed closely by Izzy wearing painfully high, green stilettos, a slim DKNY briefcase neatly tucked under her arm.

Rupert invited them in and shook their hands. He looked more like an IT geek with his long straggly hair, black jeans and T-shirt. The building was an old warehouse which had been converted into a warren of escape rooms.

'Let me show you round. As you can see, each door is made of thick oak and bolted with wooden bars and deadlocks, except for the sci-fi room which is industrial thickness steel.'

'So once you've chosen which room you want to try and escape from, then what?' Kate took her pad and pencil out and made notes.

'Then you choose teams of two to eight people. Eight is the limit for most rooms, so you may need more than one. The idea is to work together to escape in sixty minutes or less, so I suggest picking people who don't ordinarily work together, see how they cope in a stressed environment with people who are new to them. There are plenty of puzzles to crack and the goal is to find the key to the exit. Most teams can do it within the sixty minutes, but there's always the odd team that don't, so we have to come and let them out. They usually end up in the rogues' gallery.'

'Do they ever come back?' Izzy asked.

'Yeah definitely, they don't like being beaten.'

'So are we doing the haunted room today?' Izzy followed them into the first room.

'Yeah, we've set up the Haunted Manor House Room for a taster of the experience.'

'How will that work?' Kate scribbled in her notes.

'I lock you in for ten minutes and see how you get on. There will be loads of audio and visual elements to scare the pants off you. Are you both good at problem-solving puzzles?'

'I'm not.' Laughed Izzy. 'I hope you are, Kate.'

'Depends. So what level of scary is it?'

'I'd say it's off the scale. That's what you wanted, wasn't it?' he laughed.

'Yeah, 'course, I want to see what my fellow workmates are made of,' Izzy said.

'So are there emergency exits in case of a fire?' Kate asked.

'Yes, and there's always one of us on hand if you suddenly needed the loo for example. We had one woman here a few months ago whose water's broke.'

'Oh God, don't say that.'

'Why? You're not expecting, are you?' Rupert's eyebrows shot up.

'Wow, I'd never have guessed,' Izzy said.

'I'm not even halfway yet.' She pressed her hand over the curve of her bump, hidden by her coat.

'You'll be fine; I'll dial it back a bit, don't want you having the baby early, do we?'

'Thanks,' Kate said.

'So there's the Horror Room, Zombie Room, adventure, mystery, sci-fi or haunted. Each has a mixture of puzzles and clues, some easy, some more difficult which is why it takes a good team effort. There are padlocks and keys hidden behind clues using magnets and electronic systems. It gives a good variety for all levels of ability. As I said, each room is decked out with audio and visual to give a fully immersive experience. You'll have a dedicated Game Master to look after you all the way through.'

'Sounds good, so can we have a go in the haunted house now?' said Izzy.

'Someone's keen. Yeah, it's all ready for you. There's a spooky baby theme. Is that going to be okay for you?' he asked Kate, looking from her to Izzy and back again.

Kate felt Izzy's gaze pressing into her. She didn't want to lose this client by chickening out. If this was a successful event, Kate had a feeling Izzy would use them again. 'Sure, I'll be fine.'

'Right, come this way.' Rupert took them down a dark corridor to a wooden door with *There's No Escape* daubed on it in fake blood.

'Here we are. Welcome to Morton Manor. You'll be safer taking those off.' He pointed to Izzy's stilettos. 'You're trapped in three-year-old Abigail's bedroom, and you need to find and save her baby brother and escape before the clock strikes midnight.'

He unlocked the door to a dim room. A single candle was burning in a silver candlestick on the mantlepiece. Slow, languorous trumpet music in a 1920s style eerily crackled out of an old-fashioned wireless. Izzy slipped off her shoes, tucked them in her briefcase and strode in. Kate followed in her sensible flats. The door banged shut behind them followed by the rattle of bolts sealing them in. There was a musty smell of dust and damp. The room was larger than she expected, full of dark chunky oak furniture, brown stained walls, wooden floorboards and a threadbare Persian rug. In one corner stood a cot.

Next to it, a child's toy pram and on the mantlepiece a clock ticked loudly.

'Can you see the first clue?' Kate asked, but when she turned round, she couldn't see where Izzy had gone.

You're not afraid of the dark, are you? The angelic voice of a child echoed round the room.

'Izzy, where've you gone?'

Don't hurt us, Mummy, I promise I'll be a good girl. The little voice pleaded.

The curtains at the window started to billow, and the sound of a grizzling baby unnerved Kate. She rubbed her bump.

'Seriously, Izzy, is that you behind the curtain?'

Help me, can you help me? The child's voice had a desperate tone.

Kate's pulse drummed in her head. A bare light bulb hanging from the ceiling began to flicker and swing from side to side.

You won't find me. I'm watching you.

'Izzy?'

The cot gently began rocking.

You can't get out. You're going to die in here.

'Izzy, come on, I can't see you.' Kate pulled back one of the curtains, but there was nothing there. White strobe lighting lit up the room for a few seconds before falling into total darkness. Kate was grabbed from behind and her face pushed against the cold stone wall.

'Did you like your little gift for the baby?' It was Izzy whispering close to her ear, gripping Kate's hands behind her.

'What? That was you? Why?'

'Because you can't have this baby.' Izzy reached round and gripped Kate's bump, pressing her whole body into Kate's back so she couldn't move.

'Why? Was it you sending me nasty messages?'

'And the rose. Did you like it? I thought you'd appreciate my note: "counting down the days until you die".' She shoved Kate harder, her knee digging in the back of her thigh.

'Why are you doing this?' Kate tried to move, but Izzy dug her fingers into her bump like the claws of a digger. Kate screamed, but the grizzling baby became louder. Her mind flipped back to Frankie standing up in her cot, crying for her. 'You're hurting me,' Kate sobbed. Why couldn't Rupert hear her? She tried to think where the emergency exits were when he'd shown them the layout of the room.

'Why should you have everything that was supposed to be mine?'

'I don't understand.'

'James was supposed to marry me, have babies with me.'

'You're Bella?' Kate thought back over the messages, but there hadn't been any clues pointing to her.

'Yes, his ex-fiancée, Isabella. And when you came on the scene, James lost interest in me.'

'What are you talking about? He was single when we started working together, and we didn't get together straight away.'

'Is that what he told you?'

'I'm not the reason why you split up.'

'Yes, you are.' Izzy pushed her hand to Kate's head, banging it on the wall.

'But you're the one who gave him an ultimatum. You left him because he didn't want to have children.'

'He would have changed his mind if he hadn't met you.' She dug her fingers deeper into Kate's bump. 'I hate you,' she shouted in Kate's ear. 'You think you're something special, don't you?'

Kate screamed and tried her hardest to curve backwards, but Izzy's knee pushed into her back keeping her upright. Kate screamed again.

The door suddenly unbolted, and Izzy pulled away. Kate slumped to the floor.

'Come back.' Rupert ran to the opposite corner of the room. Behind a curtain, the emergency door had been pushed open. A gust of wind blew in followed by car exhaust fumes as Izzy drove off.

'Help me, please,' Kate cried, cupping her bump.

Chapter Forty-Two

James arrived as the police were leaving. Kate was sitting with Rupert in the foyer when he rushed in. She stood up and flung her arms round him.

'Are you okay?'

She nodded, clinging on to him.

'Tell me what happened. I could barely understand you on the phone.'

Kate was unable to speak trying to hold in her tears.

'Are you sure it was Bella that did this to you?'

Kate nodded.

'I thought you were meeting someone called Izzy from Shapeshifters?'

'She's your ex. Her name is Isabella, isn't it?'

'God, yes.'

'She told me she was supposed to marry you and have your babies, not me.'

'But we were over years ago. Why is she trying to hurt you?'

'She seemed to think I was on the scene before you two broke up. That it's my fault you split. That's not true, is it?'

'No. You may have started working at New World by then, I don't remember, but we didn't start going out for a while. There was definitely no overlap. I would not do that to either of you.'

'That's not what she thinks. She thinks I've stolen her life and doesn't believe I deserve this baby.'

'That's crazy. I thought she'd moved on, settled down with someone else who wanted kids. Susie said she was happily nesting, although that was a while ago.'

'Susie knows her?'

'Well yes, we used to go out drinking as a foursome.'

Kate bit her bottom lip trying to control her tears. Susie again. How else would she have found out about Kate?

'So Susie is still in touch with her, is she?'

'I don't know. I guess she probably is.'

Was Susie really her friend or had she told this ex about her deliberately?

'So what did the police say?'

Rupert came over and joined them. 'I've given them all the CCTV from that room, although much of it was in darkness or obscured by the curtains. I'm sorry I didn't spot something sooner. I guess I took my eyes off the ball, thinking you two were business associates just checking the place out.'

'It's not your fault. Neither of us realised she was going to turn into a psycho.'

'Fortunately, we've had cameras installed in the car park recently, so they'll be able to track her car down soon enough.'

'I'm taking you to A & E.' James stood up.

'Do I have to? I feel fine now. I just want to go home. I've had enough of hospitals.'

'I know you have, but we need to get you checked out, to make sure the baby's okay and so any injuries are on record.'

Back at home later, she could hear James talking on the phone with Susie. It was the first time she'd ever heard him raise his voice at her. His words were muffled because of the closed door, but Kate guessed Susie had been in touch with his ex.

She'd been given the all clear at the hospital. The baby was growing well, thankfully. The skin on her stomach was tender and the nurse had told her to expect bruising and to take photos of it to use as evidence later.

James brought her in a cup of camomile tea and sat on the bed next to her.

'Susie remembers posting on Facebook about me "finally going to be a dad" to a private group of old work friends, but she clean forgot that Bella was a member as she never posted or commented on anything.'

'Do you think Susie told her things about me?'

'She promises she's not seen or spoken to her for months. Last she heard from Bella was in July after she'd split up with her fiancé. Apparently, they'd been trying for a baby for a few years and after tests they found out he couldn't have kids. She was cut up about it. The boyfriend before that, who she went out with after me, was quite a bit older and already had three kids and didn't want more. Susie says she did ask about me, whether you and I were still together.'

'Did she think you were going to get back together?'

'I haven't got a clue. I just hope the police find her.'

The police told them the next day that Isabella had vanished. Her Shapeshifters company was fake. The homepage was all there was, and the contact details had been removed. She'd rented the Porsche for the day and returned it after leaving the Escape Rooms. According to the taxi driver who picked her up from the car hire place, she had a suitcase in the back and was due to fly out of Heathrow that evening, but she didn't say where to. She'd been staying in a hotel, which she had checked out of that morning, before she met up with Kate. The policeman said that Isabella could be anywhere in the world by now, but it looked very much like this was the end of the harassment.

Kate hoped they were right.

Chapter Forty-Three

February 2019

It was a snowy day at the end of February when the stiff cream envelope arrived through the letterbox. Inside was an evening invitation to Frankie and Matt's wedding that August. It was their first contact in a few days since their last phone call. Just before Christmas, Kate had written telling her about the attack on her by Isabella. Frankie had been horrified and called her straight away. A flurry of conversations followed by letter and phone back and forth and an exchange of cards and a Skype call at Christmas. A note with the invitation read:

> Dear Kate,
>
> Sorry I've been quiet for a few days, I've been so busy painting! We're in London for my new exhibition in May and wondered if we could drop by to see you and James. I'd love to meet my grandmother too and hope she can be there.
>
> Would Saturday 11 May be convenient for everyone?
>
> Best wishes, Frankie

'It's good you're both making such an effort,' James said when Kate showed him the invitation. 'It's not top table but she didn't have to invite us at all, did she?'

'No, she didn't,' Kate agreed. In fact it was a welcome surprise and she couldn't help smiling. She hadn't expected to be invited, although she'd not said so to James. He was still basking in Fearless Events winning Best Innovative Business at the Hemel awards night the week before. She'd scooped Best Businesswoman, which she was delighted with, but strangely it didn't feel as important any more. She was pleased she and Frankie were gradually getting to know each other, but nothing could make up for those lost years.

James had been building bridges of his own. A mutual friend had linked him up with Ben online, so they were talking again on Skype and by email. So much wasted time. Frankie said she wanted to paint her family tree and asked her who Kate's real dad was. She told her as much as she knew – his name was John Stokes and he moved to Australia when he and her mother broke up, but he died in a car crash sometime later. At Christmas, Elizabeth had shown her the newspaper cutting of him and Ray, but it was so tiny and faded, she couldn't make out his face very well.

Frankie also asked Kate about Elizabeth's time at The Foundling Hospital and if she knew anything about the parents who abandoned her, but Kate told her she didn't know anything except that her grandmother's name was Edith Liddle and Elizabeth had a twin called Edward who died when he was seven.

'What's that on the back of the card?' James asked.

Kate turned the invitation over and read:

P.S. Since we last spoke, I've been reading all about Hogarth's involvement in setting up the original Foundling Hospital in Bloomsbury back in 1739

– can you believe it was that long ago? He was helping his friend Captain Thomas Coram. One of Hogarth's most famous paintings, Gin Lane, *shows the horror of babies being slung out on rubbish heaps – I expect you know it. Thomas Coram desperately wanted to save children like this.*

It's taken me a while to get my head round the fact that my own grandmother was brought up in the same institution that was set up all that time ago, but it's inspired me to paint a new collection purely focussing on today's homeless situation and families who have to rely on food banks.

I hope Elizabeth won't mind but I did a bit of research into her time at Berkhamsted, especially since you said she never found out why she and her twin Edward were left there. I've discovered something important about their mother I think she'll want to hear.

Kate passed the note to James. 'What do you make of this?'

He scanned the page. 'Don't you think Elizabeth will want to know?'

'I do, I just wonder if she's ready to find out.'

'Hang on, there's another bit,' James said.

P.P.S I'm trying to find out what happened to your real dad too. No luck yet.

'How would she be able to find out anything? Especially as he moved to Australia so long ago,' Kate said.

'Maybe she'll ask round on social media. Anything's possible once you put a name and a story out there.'

Even the smallest clue about what he was like or what he looked like would fill a missing piece in Kate's life.

Chapter Forty-Four

May 2019

Kate lay on the sunlounger for a few moments' rest to enjoy the May warmth and birdsong. James had gone to pick her mother up and Frankie was due to arrive with Matt in half an hour.

Her hand glided over her tight, solid bump. She'd not been comfortable in the night and had woken up several times. The fold of her linen top fell open. The dappled sunshine through the leaves of the lime tree turned her bump into a speckled egg. The baby started to shift round, and the imprint of a tiny foot pushed out her smooth skin. She touched it gently, hoping for a response, but the baby seemed to tumble right over, leaving her light-headed. Only a month to go now before she became a mother again. They'd both been excited to find out at the last scan that she was having a boy.

She leaned back and rested her head. Fragments of memory of the hours around Frankie's birth floated back to her like falling leaves. Already ten days late by then, she'd tried to work out the pattern of contractions coming every fifteen minutes, occasionally five. Later that night, as she tried to sleep, an intense fire had lashed through her body. She was all alone. Away in Paris on an art project, Paul told her over the phone he wouldn't make it home in time. All their plans for him to cut the cord and take the first photos – gone.

In their dim bedroom, waiting for the ambulance, she'd writhed in tangled sheets as if possessed as the new life made its hasty descent through her body, shrugging her off. All alone and too exhausted to focus, she'd held the pink squawking bundle in her arms. Her head had been in a fug for days and weeks after, but everyone expected her to cope with it all on her own. She resented Paul for not being there when she needed him most, and Frankie for putting her through such trauma. She longed for her mother, at least a mother who could help her and care for her. But no one had even asked her if she was okay.

A car door slammed. Kate snapped out of her daydream.

'We're here,' James called as he and Elizabeth came through the side gate. Kate couldn't remember the last time she'd seen her mother looking so smart.

'You've had your hair done, Mum.'

'It's an important day.' Elizabeth's face flushed down past her neck.

'Come and have some fresh lemonade.' Kate pulled out a chair for her. 'I'll go and fetch some glasses.' She strolled off to the kitchen. As she reached up to the cupboard, her stomach clenched. She gripped the work surface until the wave passed.

'Are you okay?' James said, rushing in. He helped her into a chair.

'It's only the Braxton Hicks. Practising for the big day.' She laughed. 'They're stronger than I remember though.'

'You should come and lie down.'

'I'll be fine. Can you bring the glasses?' She ambled gingerly across the lawn with a box of firelighters.

'How are you?' Elizabeth sat in the shade of the lime tree.

'She's been doing too much, as usual.' James guided Kate into the sunlounger.

'I'm fine, don't fuss.'

Elizabeth sipped her drink, the ice cubes tinkling like finger bells.

James lit the fire as a taxi pulled up outside.

'Here they are now,' Kate said.

Elizabeth craned her neck to see them. Frankie strolled in wearing a floppy hat and a sundress over a T-shirt.

'Goodness me,' Elizabeth whispered and pressed her fingers to her lips.

'It's good to see you,' Kate said, going over. 'How was your journey?' She kissed Frankie and Matt on both cheeks.

'Not bad, thanks. We've been in London for the past two days,' Matt said. 'The exhibition is going really well.'

'These are for you,' Frankie said, handing Kate a bunch of roses.

'They're beautiful, thank you. Come over and have a drink. I'd like you both to meet my mum.'

Elizabeth pressed down on her stick and stood up.

'Lovely to meet you, Granny. Can I call you Granny?' Frankie handed Elizabeth a bunch of flowers.

'Of course. Are these for me? Thank you, dear.' Elizabeth sniffed the petals and laid the bouquet on the table. 'Well I never, just look at you.' She opened her arms wide and folded them round Frankie.

'She's a younger version of you, isn't she, Mum?' Kate said, trying to ignore the pinch of envy in her gut at her mother hugging her granddaughter so easily. She immediately hated herself for feeling that way.

Elizabeth stood back and held Frankie's hands. Had either of them heard her? They were completely lost in each other.

'And this is my fiancé, Matt.'

Elizabeth shook his hand. 'So very pleased to meet you.'

'And you.' Matt bowed his head.

'Look at you both, a beautiful couple about to be married,' Elizabeth said.

Frankie gave a girlish laugh and squeezed Matt's hand. 'You will come, won't you, Granny?'

'Try and keep me away.'

Kate choked up seeing her mother so bubbly and happy. But a wave of guilt crashed down on her, dragging her under. She'd denied Frankie a mother and a granny, and a granddaughter for her mother. If she hadn't left Frankie, maybe she could have mended her relationship with her mother much sooner.

Frankie sat and chatted with Elizabeth while James steered Matt to the kitchen on the promise of a cold beer. It was lovely how easily her mother and daughter had bonded as though they'd always known each other. She was enjoying this calmer, softer Elizabeth, if only it hadn't been hidden from her all these years.

'How I wish your granddad Ray could see you,' Elizabeth said, sandwiching Frankie's hand between hers.

'Come on, Mum, don't go upsetting yourself.' Kate turned away holding herself round her middle as the crushing enormity of her actions sank in. The relationships that were never forged because of her. The impulsive teenager so keen to hurt her parents, too proud to admit to her mistakes, had done untold damage.

'Wouldn't he have been proud of her though?' her mother continued, still holding Frankie's hands.

Kate nodded. There were no words because it could never be put right.

James marched out of the kitchen with a beer can in each hand followed by Matt carrying a tray of tall glasses. James poured a beer for Frankie and more lemonade for Elizabeth.

'Tell us about your exhibition, Frankie,' Kate said, trying to restore some semblance of normality in herself.

'It's in a new gallery in Shoreditch, with six other up and coming artists. I've sold two paintings already.' Frankie leaned into Matt, standing behind her.

'Well done. Isn't that great, Mum?'

'Wonderful. I'd love to see your work,' Elizabeth said.

'I can show you a few on my phone. It's an exhibition exploring the homeless community and the wide range of people who need to rely on food banks. I was inspired by some of Hogarth's paintings. It's very exciting. I'll try and get some VIP tickets for you.'

'She was interviewed by a couple of newspapers.' Matt rubbed his hand across Frankie's shoulders.

'They were talking to all the artists,' Frankie added.

'But yours are the ones that have hit a nerve, highlighting food poverty in today's society, as it actually is.' He poured a beer into his glass and turned to Elizabeth. 'Sometimes both parents are working, but they still can't afford to feed their children because their rents are high and the cost of childcare and travelling to work is extortionate.'

'Sometimes I think society is moving backwards,' Elizabeth said.

'The situation seems to be getting worse every year. There are more children than ever going without breakfast because their parents can't afford it. Schools are trying to help by running breakfast clubs, but it's often not enough.'

James tossed sausages and kebabs onto the hot grill. Kate brought out various salads, breads and sauces. She caught snippets of Frankie and Matt's conversation with Elizabeth.

'I was very sad to hear about your accident,' Elizabeth was saying.

'It was a while ago now. Happened at the local trials. My horse refused a jump. Pulled up sharply and I went down hard.'

Elizabeth shut her eyes and touched her forehead. 'Why on earth didn't your dad contact your mum about it?'

'He had his reasons. It wasn't easy for him.'

'I dare say, but he knew where we were.'

'Dad wanted to manage on his own, not rely on anyone.'

Elizabeth nodded, but Kate imagined she was fighting an inferno inside now she knew that Ray had been subsidising him.

'It's not like he had a choice, at the beginning anyway.'

'You know your mum wasn't well after she had you?'

'Yeah he told me. I know what she did, and I understand it was a desperate moment losing control, but she didn't have to go and leave. Dad didn't want her to.'

'It's not quite as straightforward as that,' Elizabeth told her. 'There are always two sides to a story.'

Kate moved away. She didn't want to go over it all again.

'Maybe, but she could have hurt me badly, couldn't she?'

Kate squinted as though she'd been physically struck. She pretended she was listening to James chatting to Matt about cars while he cooked.

'She didn't though, and you mustn't blame her. Caring for a baby is not easy.'

'She could have contacted me though, couldn't she?' Frankie sounded like a child.

'She didn't know where you'd moved to. Anyway, she has got in touch now and the time is right. Like I said, your dad knew where we were, but there's not always a simple solution, is there? In the end you have to believe she made the right decision for you at the time.'

Kate blinked back tears and pressed her lips together tightly. She'd never heard her mother defending her before.

'I suppose so. Anyway, I know I was lucky to have Dad.'

Elizabeth patted her arm. 'So what's he doing with himself these days?'

'He runs a small gardening business on the Isle of Wight.'

Elizabeth smiled with a knowing nod. She was probably wondering how long the money Kate had given him would last before he tried to come back for more.

'Kate told me about you being a foundling,' Frankie said.

Elizabeth folded her napkin.

'Did she tell you I've been doing some research?'

Elizabeth nodded.

'It sounds so regimented for such young children.'

'It wasn't all bad. We got up to a few larks.'

'I'd love to hear about it.' Frankie shifted closer.

Kate came and sat with them.

'My best friend was a girl called Alison. She had glorious red curly hair and freckles. We used to sneak round the back of the school to the allotments, scrumping for carrots, which we'd rub up and down our pinafores to clean.'

'You've not told me this, Mum.' Kate laughed.

'No, well,' she gave a deep sigh, 'Alison and I did everything together. We put the rest down our stockings to stick under our pillows for a midnight feast. The whole ward would talk of nothing else for weeks. This one night there was a full moon, so the room was well lit because we didn't have curtains. All the girls were gathered round my bed telling each other ghost stories when Miss Rudling stormed in. She was so mad at us she made us march up and down the courtyard fifty times right then in our nightgowns!'

'Oh Mum, that's awful.'

'It was, looking back, but we found it amusing at the time.'

'I visited The Foundling Museum in London yesterday,' Frankie said. 'I saw lots of the tokens that were left with the babies. There's an early letter on display from one mother who was about to be hanged, begging The Foundling Hospital to look after her newborn.'

'Goodness, that's heartbreaking,' Kate said.

'The tokens were left so the mothers could identify their babies when they went back for them. Few were ever able to though,' Frankie said.

Elizabeth knitted her fingers together.

'Did you know that when the site in Berkhamsted closed, The Foundling Hospital continued fostering children under the Coram name?'

Elizabeth shook her head.

'The site at Berkhamsted is Ashlyns School now and Coram is still going today as a children's charity. I've been allowed to search through the archives and see your records, Granny.'

Elizabeth's body stiffened. Her face appeared to freeze.

'I found out something about my great-grandmother, your mum, Edith Liddle. I don't know if you were told anything about it.'

'Are you okay with this, Mum?' Kate leaned forward. Maybe she ought to have given her a bit more warning.

Elizabeth nodded, her eyes roving over Frankie's face.

'Granny, did you know your mum came back for you?' Frankie held her hands.

'What?' Elizabeth took in a sharp breath.

'She came back for you and Edward.'

As Elizabeth exhaled, her body seemed to turn to water.

'Are you all right, Mum?' Kate sprang up as Frankie slipped her arm round her grandmother's shoulders. Kate wished she could reach out to her mother as easily.

'Do you need a glass of water?' Kate asked.

Elizabeth nodded. James poured it for her.

'Are you okay for Frankie to continue?'

'I'm fine, it's such a shock.' Elizabeth took a tiny sip.

'Oh Mum, isn't that wonderful to know? Thank you, Frankie,' Kate said.

'It was at the time you both had scarlet fever, so she wasn't allowed to see you, let alone take you home. But she didn't come back again because sadly she died a few weeks later of tuberculosis, at the age of twenty-five.'

Elizabeth took her hanky from her sleeve and dabbed the tears rolling from her eyes.

'That's so desperately sad,' Kate said.

Frankie poured her another glass of water.

'Look at me, silly old woman,' Elizabeth whispered.

'No, you're not.' Kate touched her mum's hand with her fingertips.

'Sorry, Granny, I didn't mean to upset you.' Frankie put her arms round her. Kate admired Frankie's openness and warmth. She longed to reach out and hug her mother too.

'Don't be sorry, dear, I'm overjoyed to hear she came back for us. I hoped for it all my life.'

Kate hadn't seen this tender, vulnerable side to her mum until a few weeks ago. She was like a different person now she'd let this secret out.

Kate waved to James to start bringing the food over. Back in the kitchen, she was about to collect the cutlery when there was a light tap, tap on the front door. It was probably the postman, late again.

She couldn't see anyone through the crackled glass round the door. Maybe it had been something else tapping. Next door had a broken slat in their fence, but would she have heard it in the kitchen? She checked the spyhole. There didn't seem to be anyone there, so she opened the door to check.

In the next split second she registered Isabella's grinning face and her arm swinging a bucket of liquid towards her. Kate screamed as it drenched her and immediately started burning her skin. James came hurtling round from the garden and grabbed Izzy's arm as she tried to run away.

'What have you done to Kate?'

'Acid,' she shouted, 'so you can never look at her again.'

'Are you fucking crazy?' He reached out to Kate, but Izzy pulled on his arm, not letting him go. Frankie ran down the hallway, Matt behind on the phone to the ambulance.

'You lied to me, James,' Isabella screamed. 'I loved you, but you didn't want my babies.' She collapsed onto her knees, sobbing.

'Oh my god, what is that stuff?' Frankie cried.

'It… it's burning.' Kate could barely speak as her face, neck and shoulders swelled, the pain bone deep. Frankie led her to the downstairs wet room and switched on the cool shower, guiding her under the water. Kate stood there shivering.

Moments later a police car and ambulance arrived. Kate heard Isabella screaming and crying as she was taken away.

Kate staggered out of the shower towards the paramedic, but an iron girdle gripped round her middle. Frankie took her hand. Kate doubled over, her body ripping apart, splitting in two. As she was guided out of the wet room, her mother was standing by the kitchen door, hands covering her mouth. Seconds later James clasped his arms round her as she felt herself falling.

Chapter Forty-Five

Stunned by what had happened, Elizabeth said a silent prayer for Kate and the baby. 'They say second ones are quicker.' It seemed a useless thing to say. She feared for Kate. Could she recover from this? And if so, what if she was left blind?

'I hope they get to the hospital in time. Do you think Kate is going to be okay?' Frankie said.

'I'm sure they wouldn't want us to sit here and worry, although it's hard not to.' Elizabeth's eyes were glued to Frankie. It was like looking at her younger self. All those years they'd lost. Why hadn't she been braver? Told Kate about her childhood as a foundling sooner? It might have prevented her from leaving Frankie. She could imagine the moment Kate walked out, Frankie crying in her cot. And then her own mother, leaving twins, surely desperate to have to do such a thing. What had she been thinking when she handed them over? Did she kiss them goodbye? Avoid looking back? She would never know the agony of it.

'Are you all right, Granny?' Frankie was frowning, a piece of tomato and cucumber threaded on her fork. When Elizabeth didn't answer, she put the fork down and took a mouthful of beer.

'I just hope... Kate's face...' she shook her head. 'I was thinking that when a woman has a baby of her own, it's when she needs her mother most of all. In those first years of Kate's life, I felt the emptiness of not having a mum to call upon. Thoughts of what my mother might have been like plagued me daily. From the moment I fell, truth be told. I wondered how she felt when she found out *she* was pregnant, if we were an unfortunate mistake. I tried so hard to picture her, to remember something of her, any tiny thing, but there was nothing. There's a silly saying that you don't miss what you don't have, but I can tell you it isn't true.'

'I felt like that to start with too, Granny. Well for years after to be honest. But I never told Dad. He couldn't bear to think of me missing out on anything,' Frankie said. Matt sat next to her and gently squeezed her hand.

'I'm sorry we share so much in this regard, I really do. I recall seeing girls out pushing prams with their mothers, parading around all showy. I longed to enjoy the simple pleasure of shopping for baby clothes with my mother, her holding up a dear little bonnet.' Elizabeth finished her drink.

'I secretly asked Santa to bring me my mother every year.' Frankie looked down at her lap. Matt put his arm round her. 'I've never told anyone that.' Frankie sniffed.

'Are you okay?' He kissed her hair and they exchanged a brief smile.

'Do you want another drink, Elizabeth?' Matt asked, pouring Frankie another beer.

'I think I'll have a stiff port if they've got some.'

'Did Ray's mother help you out though?' Frankie asked.

'Not likely. Told me once she didn't understand what Ray saw in a girl with no family and no means. Made Katherine plenty of clothes out of old skirts and patterned curtains, I'll give her that. One time, I was helping her prepare tea and I didn't know how to slice the bread. "Give it here," she said, "didn't your mother…" She stopped dead. I didn't say a word, but she wrestled the loaf from me.'

'She sounds awful! I was lucky; one of my friends' mums took me under her wing. But there was no one else, no family nearby. I dreaded Mother's Day and the mum's race at sport's day. I wish I'd had you round too, Granny. Dad was brilliant and everything, but he'd do things like cut my hair too short. I'm sure it was so he didn't have to do plaits or bunches every morning. The children at school, especially the girls with fancy hairstyles, said I looked like a boy.'

'I'm so sorry I didn't know about you. I can't get over that Ray kept it from me. He could be terribly old-fashioned. I know he would have been trying to protect me; given what happened to me he wouldn't have wanted me to know that my own daughter abandoned her baby. But I'd rather have known. We've missed out on so much of each other, haven't we?'

Frankie nodded and held Elizabeth's hand.

'I can't say I was the easiest person to live with. His damn mother was determined to make a housewife of me. Died young, at fifty-one. No age now, is it? Dropped dead on her kitchen floor while her best mutton stew was still bubbling on the stove. We ate it anyway, after they carted her away. She couldn't abide waste.'

'Granny!' Frankie laughed.

'Ray was cut up, of course. He had a brother, Stan, who never married. I often wonder what became of him. Three years older than Ray, owned a fishmonger. Lord, the smell would linger for hours when he came over straight from work. I could never tell if he was really looking at me with that glass eye of his. And I wonder now if he was gay. We never saw him with a lady. Shame he had to hide it. Lovely, cheerful man. Seems I was never destined to be an aunty.'

'Cup of tea?' Matt asked.

He'd been waiting to speak. Probably thought she was a crazy old goat for rambling on. Bless him. Kind sparkling eyes. So young and bursting with love and life the pair of them.

'That would be grand, thank you, Matthew. I didn't mean to go on.'

'Don't be silly, Granny, we love hearing your stories.'

'Never told anyone half these things. You being here has set something off inside me, and now there's no stopping me.'

'Oh no, Granny, don't cry.' Frankie clasped her hands round Elizabeth's.

'It's just so lovely that you're here,' Elizabeth dabbed her eyes with her hankie, 'and now with the baby coming, the family feels complete. But what's happened to Kate today is a dreadful, evil thing.'

'I didn't really know what to do. I just thought, whatever it is needs washing off.'

'I'm sure it was the best thing to do.'

There was a moment's silence before any of them spoke. Frankie kept checking her phone for word from James. Elizabeth dared not think what the outcome could be. It was too awful to contemplate.

'There's a little bit more I found out about your mum, Granny.'

'Really?' Elizabeth blinked at her.

'She was eighteen when she became pregnant, and your dad was a seventeen-year-old farm hand called Bert. She was sent away to an unmarried mothers' home in Salisbury. There was no other choice because her mother, your grandmother, had died so there wasn't anyone to look after her. Her dad was busy running the farm with her older brothers. It was someone at the mothers' home that suggested The Foundling Hospital.'

Elizabeth couldn't find any words. She was having the most extraordinary day. It was all so astonishing. And this young girl, this beautiful granddaughter of hers who until recently she hadn't known existed, here she was finding out so much about her. Things she'd agonised over all her life.

'It was still frowned upon to be single and pregnant even when I had Kate.'

'Is that why you married Ray, if you don't mind me asking?' Frankie fixed her eyes on her.

'I loved Ray, still do. I didn't know I was pregnant when we started courting. He and John were friends once, but they fell out.'

'Oh, were they? And Kate told me her real father died in a car crash.'

'That's right.' Elizabeth brushed imaginary crumbs from her lap.

'Are you absolutely certain about that?'

'Well I didn't see the body if that's what you mean. It's only what I heard.' Elizabeth pursed her lips.

'What was his surname?'

'Stokes, why? Are you trying to find out where he was buried?' She drew her eyes away from Frankie's penetrating stare. John would have made a dreadful father.

Might as well have stabbed her in the heart, running off with that floozy. Good thing Ray sorted him out.

Frankie's phone beeped. She scrambled to pick it up and almost knocked it onto the grass.

Matt brought tea and cake on a tray. 'No news yet?'

Frankie checked her phone. 'Nothing. I hope everything's all right. Do you think I should call?'

'They may not be able to answer anyway if your mum is still in labour or being treated. And they'll need a bit of time on their own once the baby's born.'

Elizabeth scooped two sugars into her tea and stirred, eyeing up Frankie, wondering if she was going to complain about her calling Kate her mum. Well she was, and that was that. A blackbird landed on a branch of the blossom tree, scattering a flurry of petals on the ground.

Frankie cut three pieces of honey cake. 'We bought this in London. Will you try some?'

'Just a small slice, thank you.'

Frankie passed them each a piece and moved her chair a bit closer to Elizabeth, dabbing up the crumbs with her finger.

'Didn't you ever want to come looking for Kate?' Elizabeth asked.

Frankie sat back. 'I thought about it a few times, but Dad wasn't all that kind about her, and he said that if you turn over stones you have to take responsibility for what you find underneath. So I always thought it was probably better not knowing. I'd managed without her. Why should I make the effort when it was her that left me and never came back? Why put myself through rejection again? Dad said it was up to her to get in touch.'

'But he did make the first move, blackmailing Ray, then going after Kate for money.'

'I didn't know about that at the time. I guess he was more desperate financially than he let on, but he did want to help us pay for our wedding too.'

Elizabeth raised an eyebrow. 'I wish Paul had told me about you. But at least we're all together now.'

Frankie's mobile beeped. She picked it up. 'It's James.' Her face dropped as she read the screen.

'Kate's fine; it wasn't acid, thank God, it was hot water, so the cold-water shower really helped.' She swallowed, pressing her fingers under her nose. 'He says, "Our baby boy was born at 6.28 p.m. Both are well. Will call as soon as I can, J.x." Oh my goodness,' Frankie cried and gave Elizabeth a warm hug.

'That's wonderful.' Elizabeth fanned her face, the relief palpable from all of them. They clinked their glasses. She'd never felt so relieved and elated.

Chapter Forty-Six

Kate had been determined to try breastfeeding. The nursery nurse was so kind and patient showing her how to help the baby latch on. After all her worrying and doubts about whether she could do it, it wasn't so bad.

'Because he's a month early, they want to keep you in for a couple of days to make sure he's feeding well,' the nurse said. 'He's looking a bit jaundiced, so I'll come and do a blood test for you in a little while.' She tucked Kate's notes into the folder at the end of the bed. 'Isn't he a sweetheart? Does he have a name yet?'

'We're calling him Edward, after his great uncle.' Kate held him closer and smelled his fresh skin. His eyes were shut, and his miniature hands were curled together under his chin. She'd forgotten how delicate a newborn's fingers and nails were. He couldn't have been more perfect.

'Lovely name. I have a brother called Teddy.'

James strolled up with a cup of tea, beaming at the nurse.

'I'll be back later to change your dressings.' She smiled as she left.

'Is your face feeling any better?' he asked.

'A little bit; the cream they put on has helped. Did you call everyone?'

'Yes, but I had a missed call from the police, so I called them back. Bella has been charged with ABH and harassment. They found a box of empty thermos flasks in the boot of her car. All eight had been used to carry the hot water.'

'Can you imagine if it had been acid?' Kate shuddered.

'I don't even want to think about it. I'm so glad she can't hurt you any more.'

'So am I. Do they know why she waited so long before attacking me again?'

'They think she was waiting until you were almost due to give birth.'

They held hands and gazed at Edward.

'I spoke to Harry. They're coming up tomorrow afternoon. He says he's taking me out to wet the baby's head.'

'I bet he's still in shock that you're a daddy at last.' Kate laughed, wondering what Susie would have to say to her about Isabella.

'So am I! Now he'll have to put up with me droning on about the colour of nappies.'

'Did you call Mum?'

'I spoke to all of them together. They're going to visit tomorrow morning, if you're up to early visitors? Your mum wanted to know what we're calling him.' He took his son in his arms. James looked the most contented she'd ever seen him.

'You didn't say?'

'Of course not,' he kissed the baby's nose, 'it's your surprise.'

Kate pictured her mum's face when she told her. For once in her life she was confident she'd made a good decision, something her mum might approve of. She reached for his hand. 'I want this to be a new start for all of us.'

'It will be. It is.' He laughed and kissed her forehead.

'I've been thinking about everything and I've decided I want to spend more time with Mum.'

'Hey, stop fretting.'

'We're all she has now.'

'It will be fine. She has two grandchildren.'

'We must keep in touch with Frankie and Matt too. They're part of the family now. And it would be lovely to meet Ben. He's little Edward's uncle.'

'We've got the wedding to look forward to and we can have Edward's christening before that, to get everyone together.' He kissed the baby's downy head and laid him in Kate's arms.

'No more secrets, no more lies.'

James smoothed her frown away with his fingertips, then wrapped his arms round her and the baby.

Kate settled Edward at her breast. The nursery nurse recommended skin to skin contact whenever possible. His inquisitive dark eyes resembled her mum's and she could see James's nose and chin in the tiny features. She felt an enormous sense of achievement at being able to feed her own baby. Such a different experience to when she'd had Frankie and was too exhausted to even try. She felt so much calmer and in control. How amazing to think that her two children would come to know one another. Just a year ago none of this would have seemed possible. She couldn't wait for her family to meet him in the morning. And most of all, she couldn't wait to tell her mother his name.

A letter from Ruby

Dear Reader,

Thank you for reading *A Mother Like You*. If you've enjoyed it, I'd be delighted if you could leave a short review on Amazon, Kobo or Goodreads. It really makes a huge difference!

I've always been interested in cycles of behaviour, in particular how trauma is carried across generations. I wanted to explore this in a novel about abandonment. I was fascinated to learn about The Foundling Hospital, a safe place for women to leave their babies if they weren't able to bring them up themselves. As you may know from my first novel, giving away a baby for whatever reason is something I'm a little obsessed with, because for me it would be the hardest decision to have to make. Watching programmes like *Long Lost Family* with stories of modern-day foundlings is utterly heartbreaking. I always want to write about subjects that terrify me and having no choice but to give up a child is one of them.

I visited The Foundling Museum in London with my dad to find out more. It is the original Foundling Hospital site and is packed full of history – I highly recommend a visit. I was shocked to discover that the last foundling hospital in Berkhamsted, Hertfordshire was still in operation until the 1950s. I listened over and over to many personal accounts at the Museum and on the website: men and women who were brought up not knowing who their mum or dad were, where they'd come from or why they'd been abandoned. Mothers would leave a small token so that if they were able to come back and reclaim their child, they could identify them. But that rarely happened. I've taken the liberty of bringing this historical tradition forward to my modern-day story.

Although without doubt The Foundling Hospital was well meaning and saved the lives of many babies, the lack of love and affection shown to these children struck me hard. After I wrote my first draft, I felt brave enough to enquire about interviewing one of the last foundlings. It was a privilege to meet Guy Chesham and listen to his experiences of life as a little foundling boy. He was similar in some ways to my character Elizabeth – how she found it impossible to show affection to her own daughter but easier once she had a granddaughter. Other details about my characters' experiences are fictionalised and not directly Guy's experiences. Meeting a real foundling gave me a sense of how such a harsh upbringing affected him, and how that impacted the rest of his life.

To find out more about the history of The Foundling Hospital, do take a look at The Foundling Museum website: foundlingmuseum.org.uk

Warmest regards,

Ruby x

Website: Rubyspeechley.com
Twitter: @rubyspeechley
Facebook: Ruby Speechley Author
Instagram: @rubyjtspeechley

Acknowledgments

It takes many skilled people behind the scenes to bring a book together for readers to enjoy.

Heartfelt thanks to my incredible agent, Jo Bell, and the whole team at Bell Lomax Moreton. I am incredibly indebted to the wonderful Keshini Naidoo and Lindsey Mooney at Hera Books for publishing this novel and to Keshini for her forensic editing skills, gently bringing out the best in me and my manuscript. Thank you to my excellent copy editor, proof-reader, and cover designer. Any errors in this novel are wholly my own.

There are many friends online and in real life who have supported me through my writing ups and downs, including Olimpia Silvestre, Aileen Davis, Glenys Escott, Kerri Speechley, Rose McGinty, Lucille Grant, Isabel Costello, Jeanet McKenzie, Charlotte Anderson, Debra Brown, Debi Alper, Alva Holland, Jane Elms, Susan Elliot Wright, Jude Brown, Dave Sivers, Anne Coates, Caroline Priestly and Philippa Ronan, to name just a few. Thank you all. Special thanks to Jill Dawson, who guided me through the first draft of this novel via the Gold Dust mentoring scheme.

Thanks too for your early editorial feedback: Margaret James and Cathie Hartigan at the Exeter Novel prize, Sara Sarre at Blue Pencil Agency, Sheila McIlwraith at The Literary Consultancy and Amanda Saint at Retreat

West. My writing group at Faber Academy gave me their support and wise comments over our many months together, thank you – Emma Goode, Kate Poll, Emma Cook, Laura Church, Phil Cavanagh, Nicola Bye, Mia Roberts, Clare Cowburn Baker, Cleo Harrington, Isaac Jay, Louise Macqueron, and of course our incredible tutor, Richard Skinner.

None of this would have been possible without the kind help of Alison Duke at The Foundling Museum in London. The museum website foundlingmuseum.org.uk has been an invaluable resource, in particular the moving personal memories of former foundlings told through the 'Foundling Voices' oral history project: foundling-voices.foundlingmuseum.org.uk

I found the following books useful for research and would recommend them: A memoir – *The Last Foundling* by Tom H. MacKenzie and *London's Forgotten Children – Thomas Coram and The Foundling Hospital* by Gillian Pugh.

Thank you as always to my husband and children and to my dear parents for igniting a life-long curiosity in me, which means I am never bored! Thanks to my dad for taking me to The Foundling Museum with his usual gusto and thanks to my mum for being my biggest fan.

Finally, thank you to former foundling John Caldicott for putting me in touch with fellow foundling, Guy Chesham, who generously shared with me his personal story of growing up in The Foundling Hospital. I am full of admiration for him – the original child number 23.